D0009875

ACCLAIM FOR DEAN KOONTZ

"Perhaps more than any other author, Koontz writes fiction perfectly suited to the mood of America: novels that acknowledge the reality and tenacity of evil but also the power of good; that celebrate the common man and woman; that at their best entertain vastly as they uplift."

—*Publishers Weekly* (starred review)

"A modern Swift . . . a master satirist."—*Entertainment Weekly*

"Koontz is a superb plotter and wordsmith. He chronicles the hopes and fears of our time in broad strokes and fine detail, using popular fiction to explore the human condition [and] demonstrating that the real horror of life is found not in monsters, but within the human psyche." —*USA Today*

"Koontz has a knack for making the bizarre and uncanny seem as commonplace as a sunrise. BOTTOM LINE: the Dean of Suspense." —*People*

"If Stephen King is the Rolling Stones of novels, Koontz is the Beatles." —*Playboy*

"[Koontz is] far more than a genre writer. Characters and the search for meaning, exquisitely crafted, are the soul of his work. This is why his novels will be read long after the ghosts and monsters of most genre writers have been consigned to the attic. One of the master storytellers of this or any age."

—*The Tampa Tribune*

"Dean Koontz is not just a master of our darkest dreams, but also a literary juggler." —*The Times* (London)

"Dean Koontz writes page-turners, middle-of-the-night-sneak-up-behind-you suspense thrillers. He touches our hearts and tingles our spines."

—*The Washington Post Book World*

"Dean Koontz almost occupies a genre of his own. He is a master at building suspense and holding the reader spellbound."

—*Richmond Times-Dispatch*

"Demanding much of itself, Koontz's style bleaches out clichés while showing a genius for details. He leaves his competitors buried in the dust." —*Kirkus Reviews*

"One author . . . redefining mainstream fiction . . . is Dean Koontz. [He] continues to explore the larger issues of life—friendship, faith, courage and salvation . . . an astounding mix of suspense, humor, wonder and fear."   —*South End*

"His style is a model of clarity, his prose so smooth that it goes down like apple juice . . . with the delayed punch of hard cider."   —Cleveland *Plain Dealer*

"Koontz has one of the most incredible gifts for the art of language—a master of images and descriptions. His characters are timeless and beautifully constructed. He proves you can be on the bestseller lists and don't have to be dead or named Hemingway to have the depth and feeling of the classics."
     —*Michigan State News*

"Koontz is a literary phenomenon."   —*Kirkus Reviews*

"Dean Koontz's books dwell in the heavy macabre, but . . . point to that glow of hope that may rise with the sun."
     —*San Jose Mercury News*

"Koontz's skill at edge-of-the-seat writing has improved with each book. He can scare your socks off."   —*Boston Herald*

"Powerful emotion tinged with spiritual wonder."
     —*Publishers Weekly*

"Koontz tries to create serious literature. He largely succeeds."   —*USA Today*

"Classic Koontz features a distinctive narrative that verges on the wise-crackingly facetious. . . . He is also a dab hand at tying in a wacky love story . . . an acquired taste, but one acquired by millions."   —*The Times* (London)

"Dean Koontz . . . is at the top of his field. [He] delivers all we have come to expect from him, including suspense, action, violence and general weirdness . . . wonderfully understated . . . being raised above [his] contemporaries by excellent, deceptively detailed characterization."   —*January Magazine*

"While dazzling the reader with magnificent turns of phrase that will evoke simultaneous admiration and envy, [Koontz] alternates the mood between tenderness and suspense."
     —Bookreporter.com

Novels by DEAN KOONTZ

DEAN KOONTZ'S FRANKENSTEIN

DEAN KOONTZ'S

FRANKE

BOOK ONE

BANTAM BOOKS

NSTEIN

PRODIGAL SON

A NOVEL

DEAN KOONTZ

2009 Bantam Books Mass Market Edition

Published in the United States by Bantam Books,
an imprint of The Random House Publishing Group,
a division of Random House, Inc., New York.

BANTAM BOOKS and the rooster colophon are registered trademarks
of Random House, Inc.

Originally published in paperback in the United States by Bantam
Books in 2005, and published here with a brief explanatory comment
from the author.

ISBN: 978-0-553-59332-7
Cover design by Scott Biel

Printed in the United States of America
Published simultaneously in the United States and Canada

www.bantamdell.com

2 4 6 8 9 7 5 3 1

FIRST . . .

Although I'm a chatty kind of guy, never before have I found it necessary to explain up front how a book came to be written. In the case of the series to be known as *Dean Koontz's Frankenstein*, a few words of explanation seem necessary.

I wrote a script for a sixty-minute television-series pilot with this title. A producer and I made a deal for the pilot plus episodes to be broadcast on USA Network. Because he liked my script, Martin Scorsese—the legendary director—signed on as executive producer. A hot young director, also enamored of the script, signed on as well. At the request of USA Network, I wrote a two-hour version. On the basis of this script, a wonderful cast was assembled.

Then USA Network and the producer decided that major changes must be made. I had no interest in the show in its new form, and I withdrew from association with it. I wished them well—and turned to the task of realizing the original concept in book form. I hoped *both* versions would succeed in their different media.

Subsequently, Marty Scorsese also expressed the desire to exit the series. I am grateful to Marty for being so enthusiastic and insightful about the show we wanted to make. For a man of his accomplishments, he is refreshingly humble, the very definition of grace, and anchored to real-world values in a business where many are not.

I would also like to thank the late Philip K. Dick, great writer and nice man, who twenty-three years ago shared with me the story of asking for "something too exotic for the menu" in his favorite Chinese restaurant. I've finally found a novel in which the anecdote fits. The entrée that sent Phil fleeing makes Victor Frankenstein lick his lips.

The first two volumes of this trilogy were originally published with the bylines of co-writers. Each gentleman did his job well, but I discovered another character flaw in myself (it's a long list): I am not able to collaborate. I have sat alone at the keyboard for so many years that alone is the only way I know how to do this. Given a good first draft from a co-author, I nevertheless strike out in my own direction. I should have known. As a kid in school, I never got a positive mark in the plays-well-with-others column.

For the power of man to make himself what he pleases means, as we have seen, the power of some men to make other men what they *please.*

— C. S. LEWIS, *The Abolition of Man*

DEAN KOONTZ'S
FRANKENSTEIN
PRODIGAL SON

ROMBUK MONASTERY
TIBET

CHAPTER 1

DEUCALION SELDOM SLEPT, but when he did, he dreamed. Every dream was a nightmare. None frightened him. He was the spawn of nightmares, after all; and he had been toughened by a life of terror.

During the afternoon, napping in his simple cell, he dreamed that a surgeon opened his abdomen to insert a mysterious, squirming mass. Awake but manacled to the surgical table, Deucalion could only endure the procedure.

After he had been sewn shut, he felt something crawling inside his body cavity, as though curious, exploring.

From behind his mask, the surgeon said, "A messenger approaches. Life changes with a letter."

He woke from the dream and knew that it had been prophetic. He possessed no psychic power of a classic nature, but sometimes omens came in his sleep.

IN THESE MOUNTAINS OF TIBET, a fiery sunset conjured a mirage of molten gold from the glaciers and the snowfields. A serrated blade of Himalayan peaks, with Everest at its hilt, cut the sky.

Far from civilization, this vast panorama soothed Deucalion. For several years, he had preferred to avoid people, except for Buddhist monks in this windswept rooftop of the world.

Although he had not killed for a long time, he still harbored the capacity for homicidal fury. Here he strove always to suppress his darker urges, sought calm, and hoped to find true peace.

From an open stone balcony of the whitewashed monastery, as he gazed at the sun-splashed ice pack, he considered, not for the first time, that these two elements, fire and ice, defined his life.

At his side, an elderly monk, Nebo, asked, "Are you looking at the mountains—or beyond them, to what you left behind?"

Although Deucalion had learned to speak several Tibetan dialects during his lengthy sojourn here, he and the old monk often spoke English, for it afforded them privacy.

"I don't miss much of that world. The sea. The sound of shore birds. A few friends. Cheez-Its."

"Cheeses? We have cheese here."

Deucalion smiled and pronounced the word more clearly than he'd done previously. "Cheez-Its are cheddar-flavored crackers. Here in this monastery we seek enlightenment, meaning, purpose... God. Yet often the humblest things of daily life, the small pleasures, seem to define existence for me. I'm afraid I'm a shallow student, Nebo."

Pulling his wool robe closer about himself as wintry breezes bit, Nebo said, "To the contrary. Never have I had one less shallow than you. Just hearing about Cheez-Its, I myself am intrigued."

A voluminous wool robe covered Deucalion's scarred patchwork body, though even the harshest cold rarely bothered him.

The mandala-shaped Rombuk monastery—an architectural wonder of brick walls, soaring towers, and graceful roofs—clung precariously to a barren mountainside: imposing, majestic, hidden from the world. Waterfalls of steps spilled down the sides of the square towers, to the base of the main levels, granting access to interior courtyards.

Brilliant yellow, white, red, green, and blue prayer flags, representing the elements, flapped in the breeze. Carefully written sutras adorned the flags, so that each time the fabric waved in the wind, a prayer was symbolically sent in the direction of Heaven.

Despite Deucalion's size and strange appearance, the monks had accepted him. He absorbed their teaching and filtered it through his singular experience. In time, they had come to him with philosophical questions, seeking his unique perspective.

They didn't know who he was, but they understood intuitively that he was no normal man.

Deucalion stood for a long time without speaking. Nebo waited beside him. Time had little meaning in the clockless world of the monks, and after two hundred years of life, with perhaps more than that ahead of him, Deucalion often lived with no awareness of time.

Prayer wheels clicked, stirred by breezes. In a call to sunset prayer, one monk stood in the window of a high tower, blowing on a shell trumpet. Deep inside the monastery, chants began to resonate through the cold stone.

Deucalion stared down into the canyons full of purple twilight, east of the monastery. From some of Rombuk's windows, one might fall more than a thousand feet to the rocks.

Out of that gloaming, a distant figure approached.

"A messenger," he said. "The surgeon in the dream spoke truth."

The old monk could not at first see the visitor.

His eyes, the color of vinegar, seemed to have been faded by the unfiltered sun of extreme altitude. Then they widened. "We must meet him at the gates."

SALAMANDERS OF TORCHLIGHT crawled the iron-bound beams of the main gate and the surrounding brick walls.

Just inside the gates, standing in the open-air outer ward, the messenger regarded Deucalion with awe. "Yeti," he whispered, which was the name that the Sherpas had coined for the abominable snow-man.

Words escaping him on plumes of frosted breath, Nebo said, "Is it custom now to precede a message with a rude remark?"

Having once been pursued like a beast, having lived two hundred years as the ultimate outsider, Deucalion was inoculated against all meanness. He was incapable of taking offense.

"Were I a yeti," he said, speaking in the messenger's language, "I might be as tall as this." He stood six feet six. "I might be muscled this solidly. But I would be much hairier, don't you think?"

"I . . . I suppose so."

"A yeti never shaves." Leaning close, as if imparting a secret, Deucalion said, "Under all that hair, a yeti has *very* sensitive skin. Pink, soft . . . quick to take a rash from a razor blade."

Summoning courage, the messenger asked, "Then what are you?"

"Big Foot," Deucalion said in English, and Nebo laughed, but the messenger did not understand.

Made nervous by the monk's laughter, shivering not only because of the icy air, the young man held out a scuffed goatskin packet knotted tightly with a leather thong. "Here. Inside. For you."

Deucalion curled one powerful finger around the leather thong, snapped it, and unfolded the goatskin wrapping to reveal an envelope inside, a wrinkled and stained letter long in transit.

The return address was in New Orleans. The name was that of an old and trusted friend, Ben Jonas.

Still glancing surreptitiously and nervously at the ravaged half of Deucalion's face, the messenger evidently decided that the company of a yeti would be preferable to a return trip in darkness through the bitter-cold mountain pass. "May I have shelter for the night?"

"Anyone who comes to these gates," Nebo assured him, "may have whatever he needs. If we had them, I would even give you Cheez-Its."

From the outer ward, they ascended the stone ramp through the inner gate. Two young monks with lanterns arrived as if in answer to a telepathic summons to escort the messenger to guest quarters.

In the candlelit reception hall, in an alcove that smelled of sandalwood and incense, Deucalion read the letter. Ben's handwritten words conveyed a momentous message in neatly penned blue ink.

With the letter came a clipping from a newspaper, the *New Orleans Times-Picayune*. The headline and the text mattered less to Deucalion than the photograph that accompanied them.

Although nightmares could not frighten him, though he had long ago ceased to fear any man, his hand shook. The brittle clipping made a crisp, scurrying-insect sound in his trembling fingers.

"Bad news?" asked Nebo. "Has someone died?"

"Worse. Someone is still *alive*." Deucalion stared in disbelief at the photograph, which felt colder than ice. "I must leave Rombuk."

This statement clearly saddened Nebo. "I had taken comfort for some time that you would be the one to say the prayers at my death."

"You're too full of piss to die anytime soon," Deucalion said. "As preserved as a pickle in vinegar. Besides, I am perhaps the last one on Earth to whom God would listen."

"Or perhaps the first," said Nebo with an enigmatic but knowing smile. "All right. If you intend to walk again in the world beyond these mountains, first allow me to give you a gift."

LIKE WAXY STALAGMITES, yellow candles rose from golden holders, softly brightening the room. Gracing the walls were painted mandalas, geometric designs enclosed in a circle, representing the cosmos.

Reclining in a chair padded with thin red silk cushions, Deucalion stared at a ceiling of carved and painted lotus blossoms.

Nebo sat at an angle to him, leaning over him, studying his face with the attention of a scholar deciphering intricate sutra scrolls.

During his decades in carnivals, Deucalion had been accepted by carnies as though nothing about him was remarkable. They, too, were all outsiders by choice or by necessity.

He'd made a good living working the freak shows, which were called ten-in-ones because they offered ten exhibits under one tent.

On his small stage, he had sat in profile, the handsome side of his face turned to the sawdust aisle along which the marks traveled from act to act, from fat lady to rubber man. When they gathered before him, puzzling over why he was included in such a show, he turned to reveal the ruined side of his face.

Grown men gasped and shuddered. Women fainted, though fewer as the decades passed. Only adults eighteen and older were admitted, because children, seeing him, might be traumatized for life.

Face fully revealed, he had stood and removed his shirt to show them his body to the waist. The keloid scars, the enduring welts from primitive metal sutures, the strange excrescences . . .

Now beside Nebo stood a tray that held an array of thin steel needles and tiny vials of inks in many colors. With nimble skill, the monk tattooed Deucalion's face.

"This is my gift to you, a pattern of protection." Nebo leaned over to inspect his work, then began an even more intricate tracing in dark blues, blacks, greens.

Deucalion did not wince, nor would he have cried out at the stings of a thousand wasps. "Are you creating a puzzle on my face?"

"The puzzle *is* your face." The monk smiled down at his work and at the uneven canvas on which he imprinted his rich designs.

Dripping color, dripping blood, needles pricked, gleamed, and clicked together when, at times, Nebo used two at once.

"With this much pattern, I should offer something for the pain. The monastery has opium, though we do not often condone its use."

"I don't fear pain," Deucalion said. "Life is an ocean of pain."

"Life outside of here, perhaps."

"Even here we bring our memories with us."

The old monk selected a vial of crimson ink, adding to the pattern, disguising grotesque concavities and broken planes, creating an illusion of normalcy under the decorative motifs.

The work continued in heavy silence until Nebo said, "This will serve as a diversion for the curious eye. Of course, not even such a detailed pattern will conceal everything."

Deucalion reached up to touch the stinging tattoo that covered the surface of the cracked-mirror scar tissue. "I'll live by night and by distraction, as so often I have before."

After inserting stoppers in the ink vials, wiping his needles on a cloth, the monk said, "Once more before you leave . . . the coin?"

Sitting up straighter in his chair, Deucalion plucked a silver coin from midair with his right hand.

Nebo watched as Deucalion turned the coin across his knuckles—*walked* it, as magicians say— exhibiting remarkable dexterity considering the great size and brutal appearance of his hands.

That much, any good magician could have done.

With thumb and forefinger, Deucalion snapped the coin into the air. Candlelight winked off the piece as it flipped high.

Deucalion snatched it from the air, clutching it in his fist . . . opened his hand to show it empty.

Any good magician could have done this, too, and could have then produced the coin from behind Nebo's ear, which Deucalion also did.

The monk was mystified, however, by what came next.

Deucalion snapped the coin into the air again. Candlelight winked off it. Then before Nebo's eyes, the coin just . . . vanished.

At the apex of its arc, turning head to tail to

head, it turned out of existence. The coin didn't fall to the floor. Deucalion's hands were not near it when it disappeared.

Nebo had seen this illusion many times. He had watched it from a distance of inches, yet he couldn't say what happened to the coin.

He had often meditated on this illusion. To no avail.

Now Nebo shook his head. "Is it truly magic, or just a trick?"

Smiling, Deucalion said, "And what is the sound of one hand clapping?"

"Even after all these years, you're still a mystery."

"As is life itself."

Nebo scanned the ceiling, as if expecting to see the coin stuck to one of the carved and painted lotus blossoms. Lowering his stare to Deucalion once more, he said, "Your friend in America addressed your letter to seven different names."

"I've used many more than that."

"Police trouble?"

"Not for a long time. Just . . . always seeking a new beginning."

"Deucalion . . . ," the monk said.

"A name from old mythology—not known to many people anymore." He rose from the chair, ignoring the throbbing pain of countless pin-pricks.

The old man turned his face upward. "In America, will you return to the carnival life?"

"Carnivals have no place for me. There aren't freak shows anymore, not like in the old days. They're politically incorrect."

"Back when there were freak shows, what was your act?"

Deucalion turned from the candlelit mandalas on the wall, his newly tattooed face hidden in shadows. When he spoke, a subtle pulse of luminosity passed through his eyes, like the throb of lightning hidden behind thick clouds.

"They called me . . . the Monster."

NEW ORLEANS

CHAPTER 2

MORNING RUSH-HOUR TRAFFIC on the I-10 Express-way flowed as languidly as the Mississippi River that wound through New Orleans.

When Detective Carson O'Connor got off the expressway in the suburb of Metairie, intending to use surface streets to make better time, the morning took a turn for the worse.

Stopped interminably at an intersection, she impatiently kneaded the steering wheel of her plainwrap sedan. To dispel a growing sense of suffo-cation, she rolled down the window.

Already the morning streets were griddles. None of the airheads on the TV news, however, would try to cook an egg on the pavement. Even journalism school left them with enough brain cells to realize that on these streets you could flash-fry even ice cream.

Carson liked the heat but not the humidity. Maybe one day she'd move somewhere nicer, hot but dry, like Arizona. Or Nevada. Or Hell.

Without advancing a foot, she watched the minute change on the dashboard clock display—then spotted the reason for the jam-up.

Two young hoods in gang colors lingered in the crosswalk to block traffic each time the light turned green. Three others worked the line, car to car, tapping on windows, extorting payoffs.

"Clean your windshield. Two bucks."

Like a patter of semiautomatic gunfire, car doors locked one after another as the young entrepreneurs made their sales pitch, but no car could move forward until the driver paid the tariff.

The apparent leader appeared at Carson's window, smug and full of false good humor. "Clean your windshield, lady."

He held a filthy rag that looked as if it had been fished out of one of the city's many weedy canals.

A thin white scar on one darkly tanned cheek was puckered at several suture points, suggesting that he'd gotten into a knife fight on a day when the ER physician had been Dr. Frankenstein. His wispy beard implied testosterone deficiency.

Getting a second, closer look at Carson, Scarface grinned. "Hey, pretty lady. What you doin' in these shabby wheels? You was made for Mercedes." He lifted one of the wipers and let it slap back onto the windshield. "Hello, where's your mind? Not that a long-legged fresh like you *needs* a mind."

An unmarked sedan had advantages in low-profile detective work; however, back when she'd driven a black-and-white patrol car, Carson had never been bothered by crap like this.

"You're breaking the law," she told him.

"Somebody in a *mood* this mornin'."

"The windshield's clean. This is extortion."

"I charge two bucks to clean it."

"I advise you to step back from the car."

The kid lifted his rag, prepared to smear the windshield. "Two bucks to clean it, three bucks *not* to clean it. Most ladies, whether they're male or female ladies, take option two."

Carson unbuckled her seatbelt. "I asked you to step back from the car."

Instead of retreating, Scarface leaned into the window, inches from her. Breath sweetened by a morning joint, soured by gum disease. "Gimme three bucks, your phone number, a nice apology— and maybe I don't mess with your fine face."

Carson grabbed the gink's left ear, twisted it hard enough to crack cartilage, and slammed his head sideways against the door post. His howl sounded less like that of a wolf than like that of an infant.

She let go of his ear and, exiting the sedan,

opened the door into him with enough force to knock him off his feet.

As he sprawled backward, rapping his head on the pavement hard enough to summon constellations to an inner planetarium, she planted one foot on his crotch, grinding down just enough to make him squirm and to pin him in place for fear that she'd make paste of his jewels.

Shoving her police ID toward his face, she said, "My phone number is nine-one-one."

Among the hostage cars, heads up and alert, Scarface's four ace kools were looking at him, at her, stunned and angry but also amused. The guy under her foot was a homey, and a humiliation to one home boy was a humiliation to all, even if maybe he was a little bit of what they called *hook homey,* a phony.

To the nearest of Scarface's friends, Carson said, "Stall it out, shithead, unless you want a hole in your doo-rag."

The gink under her foot tried to crab-walk away, but she stepped down harder. Tears sprang to his eyes, and he chose submission over the prospect of three days with an ice pack between his legs.

In spite of her warning, two of the other four gangbangers began to edge toward her.

Almost with the nimbleness of prestidigitation, Carson put away her ID and produced the pistol from her holster.

"Check it out, this lady under my foot, he's been

scratched"—which meant embarrassed—"but none of you has. Nothin' here for you but two years in stir, maybe lit up and crippled for life."

They didn't split, but they stopped moving closer.

Carson knew they were less concerned about her pistol than about the fact that she talked the talk. Since she knew the lingo, they assumed—correctly—that she had been in situations like this before, lots of them, and still looked prime, and wasn't afraid.

Even the dumbest gangbanger—and few would win a dime on *Wheel of Fortune*—could read her credentials and calculate the odds.

"Best to break, best to book," she said, advising them to leave. "You insist on bumping titties, you're gonna lose."

Ahead of her plainwrap sedan, closer to the intersection, cars began to move. Whether or not they could see what was happening in their rearview mirrors, the drivers sensed the shakedown had ended.

As the cars around them began to roll, the young entrepreneurs decided there was no point to lingering when their customer base had moved on. They whidded away like walleyed horses stampeded by the crack of thunder.

Under her foot, the windshield-washer couldn't quite bring himself to admit defeat. "Hey, bitch, your badge, it said *homicide*. You can't touch me! I ain't killed nobody."

"What a moron," she said, holstering the pistol.

"You can't call me a moron. I graduated high school."

"You did not."

"I *almost* did."

Before the creep—predictably—took offense at her impolite characterization of his mental acuity and threatened to sue for insensitivity, Carson's cell phone rang.

"Detective O'Connor," she answered.

When she heard who was calling and why, she took her foot off the gangbanger.

"Beat it," she told him. "Get your sorry ass out of the street."

"You ain't lockin' me?"

"You're not worth the paperwork." She returned to her phone call.

Groaning, he got to his feet, one hand clutching the crotch of his low-rider pants as if he were a two-year-old overwhelmed by the need to pee.

He was one of those who didn't learn from experience. Instead of hobbling away to find his friends, telling them a wild story about how he'd gotten the best of the cop bitch after all and had punched out her teeth, he stood there holding himself, ragging her about abusive treatment, as though his whining and threats would wring from her a sudden sweat of remorse.

As Carson concluded the call, pressed END, and

pocketed the phone, the offended extortionist said, "Thing is, I know your name now, so I can find out where you live."

"We're obstructing traffic here," she said.

"Come jack you up real good one night, break your legs, your arms, break every finger. You got gas in your kitchen? I'll cook your face on a burner."

"Sounds like fun. I'll open a bottle of wine, make tapas. Only thing is, the face gets cooked on the burner—I'm lookin' at it."

Intimidation was his best tool, but she had a screwhead that it couldn't turn.

"You like tapas?" she asked.

"Bitch, you're crazy as a red-eyed rat on meth."

"Probably," she agreed.

He backed away from her.

With a wink, she said, "I can find out where *you* live."

"You stay away from me."

"You got gas in *your* kitchen?" she asked.

"I mean it, you psycho twat."

"Ah, now you're just draggin' me," Carson said, *draggin'* meaning *sweet-talking*.

The gangbanger dared to turn his back on her and hobble away fast, dodging cars.

Feeling better about the morning, Carson got behind the wheel of the unmarked sedan, pulled her door shut, and drove off to pick up her partner, Michael Maddison.

They had been facing a day of routine investigation, but the phone call changed all that. A dead woman had been found in the City Park lagoon, and by the look of the body, she hadn't accidentally drowned while taking a moonlight swim.

CHAPTER 3

WITHOUT USING HER SIREN and portable flasher, Carson made good time on Veterans Boulevard, through a kaleidoscope of strip malls, lube shops, car dealerships, bank branches, and fast-food franchises.

Farther along, subdivisions of tract homes alternated with corridors of apartment buildings and condos. Here Michael Maddison, thirty and still single, had found a bland apartment that could have been in any city in America.

Bland didn't bother him. Working to the jazz beat and the hoodoo hum of New Orleans, especially as a homicide dick, he claimed that he ended every day in local-color overload. The ordinary apartment was his anchor in reality.

Dressed for work in a Hawaiian shirt, tan sports

jacket that covered his shoulder holster, and jeans, Michael had been waiting for her to drive up. He looked wry and easy, but like certain deceptive cocktails, he had a kick.

Carrying a white paper bag in one hand, holding an unbitten doughnut in his mouth with the delicacy of a retriever returning to a hunter with a duck, Michael got into the passenger's seat and pulled the door shut.

Carson said, "What's that growth on your lip?"

Taking the doughnut from between his teeth, intact and barely marked, he said, "Maple-glazed buttermilk."

"Gimme."

Michael offered her the white bag. "One regular glazed, two chocolate. Take your pick."

Ignoring the bag, snatching the doughnut from his hand, Carson said, "I'm crazy for maple."

Tearing off a huge bite, chewing vigorously, she swung the car away from the curb and rocketed into the street.

"I'm crazy for maple, too," Michael said with a sigh.

The yearning in his voice told Carson that he longed not only for the maple-glazed doughnut. For more reasons than merely the maintenance of a professional relationship, she pretended not to notice. "You'll enjoy the regular glazed."

As Carson took Veterans Avenue out of Jefferson Parish into Orleans Parish, intending to catch

Pontchartrain Boulevard to Harrison and then head to City Park, Michael rummaged in the doughnut bag, making it clear that he was selecting one of the other treats only from cruel necessity.

As she knew he would, he settled on chocolate—not the glazed that she had imperiously recommended—took a bite, and scrunched the top of the paper bag closed.

Glancing up as Carson cruised through a yellow light an instant before it changed to red, he said, "Ease off the gas and help save the planet. In my church, we start every workday with an hour of sugar and meditation."

"*I* don't belong to the Church of Fat-Assed Detectives. Besides, just got a call—they found number six this morning."

"Six?" Around another bite of chocolate doughnut, he said, "How do they know it's the same perp?"

"More surgery—like the others."

"Liver? Kidney? Feet?"

"She must've had nice hands. They found her in the City Park lagoon, her hands cut off."

CHAPTER 4

PEOPLE CAME TO THE fifteen-hundred-acre City Park to feed the ducks or to relax under the spreading live oaks draped with gray-green curtains of Spanish moss. They enjoyed the well-manicured botanical gardens, the Art Deco fountains and sculptures. Children loved the fairy-tale theme park and the famous wooden flying horses on the antique merry-go-round.

Now spectators gathered to watch a homicide investigation in progress at the lagoon.

As always, Carson was creeped out by these morbidly curious onlookers. They included grandmothers and teenagers, businessmen in suits and grizzled winos sucking cheap blends out of bagged bottles, but she got a *Night of the Living Dead* vibe from every one of them.

Centuries-old oaks loomed over a pool of green water fringed with weeds. Paved paths wound along the edge of the lagoon, connected by gracefully arched stone bridges.

Some rubberneckers had climbed the trees to get a better view past the police tape.

"Doesn't look like the same crowd you see at the opera," Michael said as he and Carson shouldered through the gawkers on the sidewalk and the jogging path. "Or at monster-truck rallies, for that matter."

In the eighteenth and nineteenth centuries, this area had been a popular place for hot-blooded Creoles to engage in duels. They met after sunset, by moonlight, and clashed with thin swords until blood was drawn.

These days, the park remained open at night, but the combatants were not equally armed and matched, as in the old days. Predators stalked prey and felt confident of escaping punishment in this age when civilization seemed to be unraveling.

Now uniformed cops held back the ghouls, any one of whom might have been the killer returned to revel in the aftermath of murder. Behind them, yellow crime-scene tape had been strung like Mardi Gras streamers from oak tree to oak tree, blocking off a section of the running path beside the lagoon.

Michael and Carson were known to many of the

attending officers and CSI techs: liked by some, envied by others, loathed by a few.

She had been the youngest ever to make detective, Michael the second youngest. You paid a price for taking a fast track.

You paid a price for your style, too, if it wasn't traditional. And with some of the cynical marking-time-till-pension types, you paid a price if you worked as if you believed that the job was important and that justice mattered.

Just past the yellow tape, Carson stopped and surveyed the scene.

A female corpse floated facedown in the scummy water. Her blond hair fanned out like a nimbus, radiant where tree-filtered Louisiana sunlight dappled it.

Because the sleeves of her dress trapped air, the dead woman's arms floated in full sight, too. They ended in stumps.

"New Orleans," Michael said, quoting a current tourist bureau come-on, "the romance of the bayou."

Waiting for instruction, the CSI techs had not yet entered the scene. They had followed Carson and stood now just the other side of the marked perimeter.

As the investigating detectives, Carson and Michael had to formulate a systematic plan: determine the proper geometry of the search, the subjects and angles of photographs, possible sources of clues. . . .

In this matter, Michael usually deferred to Carson because she had an intuition that, just to annoy her, he called witchy vision.

To the nearest uniform on the crime line, Carson said, "Who was the responding officer?"

"Ned Lohman."

"Where is he?"

"Over there behind those trees."

"Why the hell's he tramping the scene?" she demanded.

As if in answer, Lohman appeared from behind the oaks with two homicide detectives, older models, Jonathan Harker and Dwight Frye.

"Dork and Dink," Michael groaned.

Although too far away to have heard, Harker glowered at them. Frye waved.

"This blows," Carson said.

"Big time," Michael agreed.

She didn't bluster into the scene but waited for the detectives to come to her.

How nice it would have been to shoot the bastards in the knees to spare the site from their blundering. So much more satisfying than a shout or a warning shot.

By the time Harker and Frye reached her, both were smiling and smug.

Ned Lohman, the uniformed officer, had the good sense to avoid her eyes.

Carson held her temper. "This is our baby, let us burp it."

"We were in the area," Frye said, "caught the call."

"Chased the call," Carson suggested.

Frye was a beefy man with an oily look, as if his surname came not from family lineage but from his preferred method of preparing every food he ate.

"O'Connor," he said, "you're the first Irish person I've ever known who wasn't fun to be around."

In a situation like this, which had grown from one bizarre homicide to six killings in a matter of weeks, Carson and her partner would not be the only ones in the department assigned to research particular aspects of the case.

They had caught the first murder, however, and therefore had proprietary interest in associated homicides if and until the killer piled up enough victims to force the establishment of an emergency task force. And at that point, she and Michael would most likely be designated to head that undertaking.

Harker tended to burn easily—from sunshine, from envy, from imagined slights to his competence, from just about anything. The Southern sun had bleached his blond hair nearly white; it lent his face a perpetually parboiled look.

His eyes, as blue as a gas flame, as hard as gemstones, revealed the truth of him that he attempted to disguise with a soft smile. "We needed to move fast, before evidence was lost. In this climate, bodies decompose quickly."

"Oh, don't be so hard on yourself," Michael said. "With a gym membership and a little determination, you'll be looking good again."

Carson drew Ned Lohman aside. Michael joined them as she took out her notebook and said, "Gimme the TPO from your involvement."

"Listen, Detectives, I know you're the whips on this. I told Frye and Harker as much, but they have rank."

"Not your fault," she assured him. "I should know by now that vultures always get to dead meat first. Let's start with the time."

He checked his watch. "Call came in at seven forty-two, which makes it thirty-eight minutes ago. Jogger saw the body, called it in. When I showed up, the guy was standing here running in place to keep his heart rate up."

In recent years, runners with cell phones had found more bodies than any other class of citizens.

"As for place," Officer Lohman continued, "the body's just where the jogger found it. He made no rescue attempt."

"The severed hands," Michael suggested, "were probably a clue that CPR wouldn't be effective."

"The vic is blond, maybe not natural, probably Caucasian. You have any other observations about her?" Carson asked Lohman.

"No. I didn't go near her either, didn't contaminate anything, if that's what you're trying to find out. Haven't seen the face yet, so I can't guess the age."

"Time, place—what about occurrence?" she asked Lohman. "Your first impression was . . . ?"

"Murder. She didn't cut her hands off herself."

"Maybe one," Michael agreed, "but not both."

CHAPTER 5

THE STREETS OF NEW ORLEANS teemed with possibilities: women of every description. A few were beautiful, but even the most alluring were lacking in one way or another.

During his years of searching, Roy Pribeaux had yet to encounter one woman who met his standards in every regard.

He was proud of being a perfectionist. If he had been God, the world would have been a more ordered, less messy place.

Under Roy Almighty, there would have been no ugly or plain people. No mold. No cockroaches or even mosquitoes. Nothing that smelled bad.

Under a blue sky that he could not have improved upon, but in cloying humidity he would not have allowed, Roy strolled along the Riverwalk, the

site of the 1984 Louisiana World's Fair, which had
been refurbished as a public gathering place and
shopping pavilion. He was hunting.

Three young women in tank tops and short
shorts sashayed past, laughing together. Two of
them checked Roy out.

He met their eyes, boldly ogled their bodies,
then dismissed each of them with a glance.

Even after years of searching, he remained an
optimist. *She* was out there somewhere, his ideal,
and he would find her—even if it had to be one
piece at a time.

In this promiscuous society, Roy remained a virgin at thirty-eight, a fact of which he was proud.
He was saving himself. For the perfect woman. For
love.

Meanwhile, he polished his own perfection. He
undertook two hours of physical training every day.
Regarding himself as a Renaissance man, he read literature for exactly one hour, studied a new subject
for exactly one hour, meditated on the great mysteries and the major issues of his time for another
hour every day.

He ate only organic produce. He bought no meat
from factory farms. No pollutants tainted him, no
pesticides, no radiological residue, and certainly no
strange lingering genetic material from bioengi-
neered foods.

Eventually, when he had refined his diet to perfection and when his body was as tuned as an

atomic clock, he expected that he would cease to eliminate waste. He would process every morsel so completely that it would be converted entirely to energy, and he would produce no urine, no feces.

Perhaps he would *then* encounter the perfect woman. He often dreamed about the intensity of the sex they would have. As profound as *nuclear fusion*.

Locals loved the Riverwalk, but Roy suspected that most people here today were tourists, considering how they paused to gawk at the caricature artists and street musicians. Locals would not be drawn in such numbers to the stands piled with New Orleans T-shirts.

At a bright red wagon where cotton candy was sold, Roy suddenly halted. The fragrance of hot sugar cast a sweet haze around the cart.

The cotton-candy vendor sat on a stool under a red umbrella. In her twenties, less than plain, with unruly hair. She looked as baggy and as simply made as a Muppet, though without as much personality.

But her eyes. *Her eyes.*

Roy was captivated. Her eyes were priceless gems displayed in a cluttered and dusty case, a striking greenish blue.

The skin around her eyes crinkled alluringly as she caught his attention and smiled. "Can I help you?"

Roy stepped forward. "I'd like something sweet."

"All I've got is cotton candy."

"Not all," he said, marveling at how suave he could be.

She looked puzzled.

Poor thing. He was too smooth for her.

He said, "Yes, cotton candy, please."

She picked up a paper cone and began to twirl it through the spun sugar, wrapping it with a cloud of sugary confection.

"What's your name?" he asked.

She hesitated, seemed embarrassed, averted her eyes. "Candace."

"A girl named Candy is a candy vendor? Is that destiny or just a good sense of humor?"

She blushed. "I prefer Candace. Too many negative connotations for a ... a heavy woman to be called Candy."

"So you're not an anorexic model, so what? Beauty comes in lots of different packages."

Candace obviously had seldom if ever heard such kind words from an attractive and desirable man like Roy Pribeaux.

If she herself ever thought about a day when she would excrete no wastes, she must know that he was far closer to that goal than she was.

"You have beautiful eyes," he told her. "Strikingly beautiful eyes. The kind a person could look into for years and years."

Her blush intensified, but her shyness was overwhelmed by astonishment to such a degree that she made eye contact with him.

Roy knew he dared not come on to her too strong. After a life of rejection, she'd suspect that he was setting her up for humiliation.

"As a Christian man," he explained, though he had no religious convictions, "I believe God made everyone beautiful in at least one respect, and we need to recognize that beauty. Your eyes are just . . . perfect. They're the windows to your soul."

Putting the cloud of cotton candy on a counter-top holder, she averted her eyes again as though it might be a sin to let him enjoy them too much. "I haven't gone to church since my mother died six years ago."

"I'm sorry to hear that. She must have died so young."

"Cancer," Candace revealed. "I got so angry about it. But now . . . I miss church."

"We could go together sometime, and have cof-fee after."

She dared his stare again. "Why?"

"Why not?"

"It's just . . . You're so . . ."

Pretending a shyness of his own, he looked away from her. "So not your type? I know to some people I might appear to be shallow—"

"No, please, that's not what I meant." But she couldn't bring herself to explain what she *had* meant.

Roy withdrew a small notepad from his pocket, scribbled with a pen, and tore off a sheet of paper.

"Here's my name—Ray Darnell—and my cell-phone number. Maybe you'll change your mind."

Staring at the number and the phony name, Candace said, "I've always been pretty much a... private person."

The dear, shy creature.

"I understand," he said. "I've dated very little. I'm too old-fashioned for women these days. They're so... bold. I'm embarrassed for them."

When he tried to pay for his cotton candy, she didn't want to take his money. He insisted.

He walked away, nibbling at the confection, feeling her gaze on him. Once out of sight, he threw the cotton candy in a trash can.

Sitting on a bench in the sun, he consulted the notepad. On the last page at the back of it, he kept his checklist. After so much effort here in New Orleans and, previously, elsewhere, he had just yesterday checked off the next-to-last item: *hands*.

Now he put a question mark next to the final item on the list, hoping that he could cross it off soon.

EYES?

CHAPTER 6

HE IS A CHILD of Mercy, Mercy-born and Mercy-raised.

In his windowless room he sits at a table, working with a thick book of crossword puzzles. He never hesitates to consider an answer. Answers come to him instantly, and he rapidly inks letters in the squares, never making an error.

His name is Randal Six because five males have been named Randal and have gone into the world before him. If ever he, too, went into the world, he would be given a last name.

In the tank, before consciousness, he'd been educated by direct-to-brain data downloading. Once brought to life, he had continued to learn during sessions of drug-induced sleep.

He knows nature and civilization in their intricacies, knows the look and smell and sound of places he has never been. Yet his world is largely limited to a single room.

The agents of Mercy call this space his billet, which is a term to describe lodging for a soldier.

In the war against humanity—a secret war now but not destined to remain secret forever—he is an eighteen-year-old who came to life four months ago.

To all outward appearances, he is eighteen, but his knowledge is greater than that of most elderly scholars.

Physically, he is sound. Intellectually, he is advanced.

Emotionally, something is wrong with him.

He does not think of his room as his billet. He thinks of it as his cell.

He himself, however, is his own prison. He lives mostly within himself. He speaks little. He yearns for the world beyond his cell, beyond himself, and yet it frightens him.

Most of the day he spends with crossword puzzles, immersed in the vertical and horizontal patterns of words. The world beyond his quarters is alluring but it is also . . . disorderly, chaotic. He can feel it pressing against the walls, pressing, pressing, and only by focusing on crosswords, only by bringing *order* to the empty boxes by filling them with the *absolutely right* letters can he keep the outer disorder from invading his space.

Recently, he has begun to think that the world frightens him because Father has *programmed* him to be afraid of it. From Father, he has received his education, after all, and his life.

This possibility confuses him. He cannot understand why Father would create him to be ... dysfunctional. Father seeks perfection in all things.

One thing gives him hope. Out in the world, and not far away, right here in New Orleans, is another like him. Not one of Father's creations, but likewise afflicted.

Randal Six is not alone. If only he could meet his equal, he would better understand himself ... and be free.

CHAPTER 7

AN OSCILLATING FAN riffled the documents and case notes—held down by makeshift paperweights—on Carson's desk. Beyond the windows, an orange sunset had deepened to crimson, to purple.

Michael was at his desk in the Homicide Division, adjacent to Carson's, occupied by much of the same paperwork. She knew that he was ready to go home, but he usually let her define the workday.

"You checked our doc box lately?" she asked.

"Ten minutes ago," Michael reminded her. "You send me out there one more time, I'm going to eat a get-small mushroom and just *stay* in the doc box until the report shows up."

"We should've had the prelim autopsy on that floater hours ago," she complained.

"And I shoulda been born rich. Go figure."

She consulted photos of cadavers in situ while Michael watched.

The first victim, a young nurse named Shelley Justine, had been murdered elsewhere and dumped beside the London Street Canal. Tests revealed the chemical signature of chloroform in her blood.

After the killer rendered her unconscious, he killed her with a knife to the heart. With exquisite precision he removed her ears. A peptide profile found no elevated endorphin levels in the blood, indicating that the surgery occurred after she was dead. Had she been alive, the pain and terror would have left telltale chemistry.

The second victim, Meg Saville, a tourist from Idaho, had also been chloroformed and knifed while unconscious. The Surgeon—the press's name for him—had neatly sawed off Saville's feet.

"If he'd just *always* take feet," Michael said, "we'd know he was a podiatrist, and we'd have found him by now."

Carson shuffled the next photo to the top of the stack.

The first two victims had been women; however, neither Shelley Justine nor Meg Saville had been molested.

When the third victim was a man, the killer established his bona fides as an equal-opportunity maniac. The body of Bradford Walden—a young bartender from a hole-in-the-wall across the river in

Algiers—had been found with the right kidney surgically removed.

The switch to souvenirs of internal origin wasn't troubling—an urge to collect feet and ears was no less disturbing than a fancy for kidneys—but it *was* curious.

Chemical traces of chloroform were found, but this time peptide profiles showed that Walden had been alive and awake for the surgery. Had the chloroform worn off too soon? Or had the killer intentionally let the man wake up? In either case, Walden died in agony, his mouth stuffed with rags and sealed with duct tape to muffle his screams.

The fourth victim, Caroline Beaufort, Loyola University student, had been discovered with both legs missing, her torso propped on an ornate bench at a trolley-car stop in the upscale Garden District. She had been chloroformed and unconscious when murdered.

For his fifth kill, the Surgeon dispensed with the anesthetic. He murdered another man, Alphonse Chaterie, a dry cleaner. He collected Chaterie's liver while the victim was alive and fully awake: not a trace of chloroform.

Most recently, this morning's body in the City Park lagoon was missing both hands.

Four women, two men. Four with chloroform, one without, one set of results pending. Each victim missing one or more body parts. The first three women were killed before the trophies were removed, while the men were alive and conscious for the surgery.

Apparently none of the victims had known any of the others. Thus far no mutual acquaintances had come to light, either.

"He doesn't like to see women suffer, but men in agony are okay with him," Carson said, and not for the first time.

Michael had a new thought. "Maybe the killer's a woman, has more sympathy for her own gender."

"Yeah, right. How many serial killers have ever been women?"

"There've been a few," he said. "But, I am proud to say, men have been a *lot* more successful at it."

Carson wondered, "Is there a fundamental difference between lopping off female body parts and digging out male internal organs?"

"We've been down this road. *Two* serial killers collecting body parts in the same city in the same three-week period? 'Is such a coincidence logical, Mr. Spock?' 'Coincidence, Jim, is just a word superstitious people use to describe complex events that in truth are the mathematically inevitable consequences of a primary cause.'"

Michael made this work a lot less gruesome and more tolerable, but sometimes she wanted to thump him. Hard.

"And what does that mean?" she asked.

He shrugged. "I never did understand Spock."

Appearing as if conjured into a pentagram,

Harker dropped an envelope on Carson's desk. "ME's report on the floater. Delivered to my doc box by mistake."

Carson didn't want a push-and-shove with Harker, but she could not let obvious interference pass unremarked. "One more time your foot's on mine, I'll file a complaint with the chief of detectives."

"I'm so afraid," Harker dead-panned. His reddened face glistened with a sheen of sweat. "No ID on the floater yet, but it looks pretty much like she was chloroformed, taken someplace private, and killed with a stiletto to the heart before her hands were taken."

When Harker continued to stand there, the day's sun bottled in his glassy face, Michael said, "And?"

"You've checked out everyone with easy access to chloroform. Researchers doing animal experimentation, employees at medical supply companies . . . But two sites on the Internet offer formulas for making it in the kitchen sink, out of stuff you can buy at the supermarket. I'm just saying this case doesn't fit in any standard box. You're looking for something you've never seen before. To stop this guy, you've got to go to a weirder place—one level below Hell."

Harker turned from them and walked away across the squad room.

Carson and Michael watched him leave. Then

Michael said, "What was *that*? It almost seemed like genuine concern for the public."

"He was once a good cop. Maybe a part of him still is."

Michael shook his head. "I liked him better as an asshole."

CHAPTER 8

OUT OF THE LAST of the twilight came Deucalion with a suitcase, in clothes too heavy for the sultry night.

This neighborhood offered markedly less glamour than the French Quarter. Seedy bars, pawn shops, liquor stores, head shops.

Once a grand movie house, the Luxe Theater had become a shabby relic specializing in revivals. On the marquee, unevenly spaced loose plastic letters spelled out the current double feature:

THURS THRU SUNDAY
DON SIEGEL REVIVAL
INVASION OF THE BODY SNATCHERS
HELL IS FOR HEROES

The marquee was dark, the theater closed either for the night or permanently.

Not all of the streetlamps were functioning. Approaching the Luxe, Deucalion found a route of shadows.

He passed a few pedestrians, averting his face without seeming to, and drew attention only for his height.

He slipped into a service walk beside the movie palace. For more than two centuries, he had used back doors or even more arcane entrances.

Behind the theater, a bare bulb in a wire cage above the back door shed light as drab and gray as this litter-strewn alleyway.

Sporting multiple layers of cracked and chipped paint, the door was a scab in the brick wall. Deucalion studied the latch, the lock . . . and decided to use the bell.

He pushed the button, and a loud buzz vibrated through the door. Inside the quiet theater, it must have echoed like a fire alarm.

Moments later, he heard heavy movement inside. He sensed that he was being studied through the fish-eye security lens.

The lock rattled, and the door opened to reveal a sweet face and merry eyes peering out of a prison of flesh. At five feet seven and perhaps three hundred pounds, this guy was twice the man he should have been.

"Are you Jelly Biggs?" Deucalion asked.

"Do I look like I'm not?"

"You're not fat enough."

"When I was a star in the ten-in-one, I weighed almost three hundred more. I'm half the man I used to be."

"Ben sent for me. I'm Deucalion."

"Yeah, I figured. In the old days, a face like yours was gold in the carnival."

"We're both blessed, aren't we?"

Stepping back, motioning Deucalion to enter, Biggs said, "Ben told me a lot about you. He didn't mention the tattoo."

"It's new."

"They're fashionable these days," said Jelly Biggs.

Deucalion stepped across the threshold into a wide but shabby hallway. "And me," he said drily, "I've always been a fashion plate."

BEHIND THE BIG theater screen, the Luxe featured a labyrinth of passages, storage closets, and rooms that no patron had ever visited. With a rolling gait and heavy respiration, Jelly led the way past crates, mildewed cardboard boxes, and moisture-curled posters and stand-ups that promoted old films.

"Ben put seven names on the letter he sent me," Deucalion said.

"You once mentioned Rombuk monastery, so he

figured you might still be there, but he didn't know what name you'd be using."

"He shouldn't have shared my names."

"Just knowin' your aliases doesn't mean I can mojo you."

They arrived at a door that wore an armor-thick coat of green paint. Biggs opened it, switched on a light, gestured for Deucalion to enter ahead of him.

A windowless but cozy apartment lay beyond. A kitchenette was adjacent to the combination bedroom and living room. Ben loved books, and two walls were lined with them.

Jelly Biggs said, "It's a sweet place you inherited."

The key word whipped through Deucalion's mind before lashing back with a sharp sting. "Inherited. What do you mean? Where's Ben?"

Jelly looked surprised. "You didn't get my letter?"

"Only his."

Jelly sat on one of the chrome and red-vinyl chairs at the dinette table. It creaked. "Ben was mugged."

The world is an ocean of pain. Deucalion felt the old familiar tide wash through him.

"This isn't the best part of town, and getting worse," Biggs said. "Ben bought the Luxe when he retired from the carnival. The neighborhood was supposed to be turning around. It didn't. The place would be hard to sell these days, so Ben wanted to hold on."

"How did it happen?" Deucalion asked.

"Stabbed. More than twenty times."

Anger, like a long-repressed hunger, rose in Deucalion. Once anger had been his meat, and feasting on it, he had starved.

If he let this anger grow, it would quickly become fury—and devour him. For decades he had kept this lightning in a bottle, securely stoppered, but now he longed to pull the cork.

And then . . . what? Become the monster again? Pursued by mobs with torches, with pitchforks and guns, running, running, running with hounds baying for his blood?

"He was everybody's second father," said Jelly Biggs. "Best damn carnie boss I ever knew."

During the past two centuries, Ben Jonas had been one of a precious handful of people with whom Deucalion had shared his true origins, one of the few he had ever trusted completely.

He said, "He was murdered after he contacted me."

Biggs frowned. "You say that like there's a connection."

"Did they ever find the killer?"

"No. That's not unusual. The letter to you, the mugging—just a coincidence."

At last putting down his suitcase, Deucalion said, "There are no coincidences."

Jelly Biggs looked up from the dinette chair and met Deucalion's eyes. Without a word they understood that in addition to years in the carnival, they shared a view of the world that was as rich with meaning as with mysteries.

Pointing toward the kitchenette, the fat man said, "Besides the theater, Ben left you sixty thousand cash. It's in the freezer."

Deucalion considered this revelation for a moment, then said, "He didn't trust many people."

Jelly shrugged. "What do I need with money when I've got such good looks?"

CHAPTER 9

SHE WAS YOUNG, poor, inexperienced. She'd never had a manicure before, and Roy Pribeaux proposed that he give her one.

"I give myself manicures," he said. "A manicure can be erotic, you know. Just give me a chance. You'll see."

Roy lived in a large loft apartment, the top half of a remodeled old building in the Warehouse District. Many rundown structures in this part of the city had been transformed into expansive apartments for artists.

A printing company and a computer-assembly business shared the main floor below. They existed in another universe, as far as Roy Pribeaux was concerned; he didn't bother them, and they reciprocated.

He needed his privacy, especially when he took a

new and special woman to his loft. This time, her name was Elizabeth Lavenza.

As odd as it might seem on a first date—or a tenth, for that matter—to suggest a manicure, he had charmed Elizabeth into it. He knew well that the modern woman responded to sensitivity in men.

First, at the kitchen table, he placed her fingers in a shallow bowl of warm oil to soften both the nails and the cuticles.

Most women also liked men who enjoyed pampering them, and young Elizabeth was no different in this regard.

In addition to sensitivity and a desire to pamper, Roy had a trove of amusing stories and could keep a girl laughing. Elizabeth had a lovely laugh. Poor thing, she had no chance of resisting him.

When her fingertips had soaked long enough, he wiped them with a soft towel.

Using a natural, nonacetone polish remover, he stripped the red color from her nails. Then with gentle strokes of an emery board, he sculpted the tip of each nail into a perfect curve.

He had only begun to trim the cuticles when an embarrassing thing happened: His special cell phone rang, and he knew that the caller had to be Candace. Here he was romancing Elizabeth, and the *other* woman in his life was calling.

He excused himself and hurried into the dining area, where he had left the phone on a table. "Hello?"

"Mr. Darnell?"

"I know that lovely voice," he said softly, moving into the living room, away from Elizabeth. "Is this Candace?"

The cotton-candy vendor laughed nervously. "We talked so little, how could you recognize my voice?"

Standing at one of the tall windows, his back to the kitchen, he said, "Don't you recognize mine?"

He could almost feel the heat of her blush coming down the line when she admitted, "Yes, I do."

"I'm so glad you called," he said in a discreet murmur.

Shyly, she said, "Well, I thought . . . maybe coffee?"

"A get-acquainted coffee. Just say where and when."

He hoped she didn't mean *right now*. Elizabeth was waiting, and he was enjoying giving her the manicure.

"Tomorrow evening?" Candace suggested. "Usually business on the boardwalk dies down after eight o'clock."

"Meet you at the red wagon. I'll be the guy with the big smile."

Unskilled at romance, she said awkwardly, "And . . . I guess I'll be the one with the eyes."

"You sure will," he said. "Such *eyes*."

Roy pressed END. The disposable phone wasn't registered to him. Out of habit, he wiped it clean of prints, tossed it on the sofa.

His modern, austere apartment didn't contain much furniture. His exercise machines were his pride. On the walls were reproductions of Leonardo da Vinci's anatomical sketches, the great man's studies of the perfect human form.

Returning to Elizabeth at the kitchen table, Roy said, "My sister. We talk all the time. We're very close."

When the manicure was complete, he exfoliated the skin of her perfect hands with an aromatic mixture of almond oil, sea salt, and essence of lavender (his own concoction), which he massaged onto her palms, the backs of the hands, the knuckles, the fingers.

Finally, he rinsed each hand, wrapped it in clean white butcher paper, and sealed it in a plastic bag. As he placed the hands in the freezer, he said, "I'm so happy you've come to stay, Elizabeth."

He didn't find it peculiar to be talking to her severed hands. Her hands had been the essence of her. Nothing else of Elizabeth Lavenza had been worth talking about or to. The hands were *her*.

CHAPTER 10

THE LUXE WAS an ornate Deco palace, glamorous in its day, a fit showcase for the movies of William Powell and Myrna Loy, Humphrey Bogart, Ingrid Bergman. Like many a Hollywood face, this glamour had peeled and sagged.

Deucalion accompanied Jelly Biggs down the center aisle, past rows of musty, patched seats.

"Damn DVDs screwed the revival business," Jelly said. "Ben's retirement didn't turn out like he expected."

"Marquee says you're still open Thursday through Sunday."

"Not since Ben died. There's *almost* enough thirty-five-millimeter fanatics to make it worthwhile. But some weekends we run up more expenses than receipts. I didn't want to take responsibility for that since it's become your property."

Deucalion looked up at the screen. The gold and crimson velvet curtains drooped, heavy with dust and creeping mildew. "So . . . you left the carnival when Ben did?"

"When freak shows took a fade, Ben made me theater manager. I got my own apartment here. I hope that won't change . . . assuming you want to keep the place running."

Deucalion pointed to a quarter on the floor. "Finding money is always a sign."

"A sign of what?"

Stooping to pick up the quarter, Deucalion said, "Heads, you're out of a job. Tails, you're out of a job."

"Don't like them odds."

Deucalion snapped the coin into the air, snatched it in midflight. When he opened his fist, the coin had disappeared.

"Neither heads nor tails. A sign for sure, don't you think?"

Instead of relief at having kept his job and home, Jelly's expression was troubled. "I been having a dream about a magician. He's strangely gifted."

"Just a simple trick."

Jelly said, "I'm maybe a little psychic. My dreams sometimes come sorta true."

Deucalion had much he could have said to that, but he remained silent, waiting.

Jelly looked at the moldering drapes, at the threadbare carpet, at the elaborate ceiling, everywhere but at Deucalion. At last he said, "Ben told me some about you, things that don't seem they could be real." He finally met Deucalion's eyes. "Do you have two hearts?"

Deucalion chose not to reply.

"In the dream," Jelly said, "the magician had two hearts . . . and he was stabbed in both."

A flutter of wings overhead drew Deucalion's attention.

"Bird got in yesterday," Jelly said. "A dove, by the look of it. Haven't been able to chase it out."

Deucalion tracked the trapped bird's flight. He knew how it felt.

CHAPTER 11

CARSON LIVED ON A tree-lined street in a house nondescript except for a gingerbread veranda that wrapped three sides.

She parked at the curb because the garage was packed with her parents' belongings, which she never found time to sort through.

On her way to the kitchen door, she paused under an oak draped with Spanish moss. Her work hardened her, wound her tight. Arnie, her brother, needed a *gentle* sister. Sometimes she couldn't decompress during the walk from car to house; she required a moment to herself.

Here in the humid night and the fragrance of jasmine, she found that she couldn't shift into domestic gear. Her nerves were twisted as tight as dreadlocks, and her mind raced. As never before, the scent of jasmine reminded her of the smell of blood.

The recent killings had been so gruesome and had occurred in such rapid succession that she could not put them aside during her personal time. Under normal circumstances, she was seventy percent cop, thirty percent woman and sister; these days, she was all cop, twenty-four/seven.

When Carson entered the kitchen, Vicky Chou had just loaded the dishwasher and switched it on. "Well, I screwed up."

"Don't tell me you put laundry in the dishwasher."

"Worse. With his brisket of beef, I gave him carrots and peas."

"Oh, never orange and green on the same plate, Vicky."

Vicky sighed. "He's got more rules about food than kosher and vegan combined."

On a cop's salary, Carson could not have afforded a live-in caregiver to look after her autistic brother. Vicky took the job in return for room and board—and out of gratitude.

When Vicky's sister, Liane, had been indicted with her boyfriend and two others for conspiracy to commit murder, she seemed helplessly snared in a web of evidence. She'd been innocent. In the process of sending the other three to prison, Carson had cleared Liane.

As a successful medical transcriptionist, Vicky worked flexible hours at home, transcribing microcassettes for physicians. If Arnie had been a more demanding autistic, Vicky might not have been able to keep up with her work, but the boy was mostly quiescent.

Widowed at forty, now forty-five, Vicky was an Asian beauty, smart and sweet and lonely. She wouldn't grieve forever. Someday when she least expected it, a man would come into her life, and the current arrangement would end.

Carson dealt with that possibility the only way that her busy life allowed: She ignored it.

"Other than green and orange together, how was he today?" Carson asked.

"Fixated on the castle. Sometimes it seems to calm him, but at other times . . ." Vicky frowned. "What is he so afraid of?"

"I don't know. I guess . . . life."

BY REMOVING A WALL and combining two of the upstairs bedrooms, Carson had given Arnie the largest room in the house. This seemed only fair because his condition stole from him the rest of the world.

His bed and nightstand were shoved into a corner. A TV occupied a wheeled metal stand. Sometimes he watched cartoons on DVD, the same ones over and over.

The remainder of the room had been devoted to the castle.

Four low sturdy tables formed a twelve-by-eight-foot platform. Upon the tables stood an architectural wonder in Lego blocks.

Few boys of twelve would have been able to create a model castle without a plan, but Arnie had put together a masterpiece: walls and wards, barbican and bastions, ramparts and parapets, turreted towers, the barracks, the chapel, the armory, the castle keep with elaborate bulwark and battlements.

He'd been obsessed with the model for weeks, constructing it in an intense silence. Repeatedly he tore down finished sections only to remodel and improve them.

Most of the time he was on his feet while adding to the castle—an access hole in the table arrangement allowed him to build from within the project as well as from every side—but sometimes, like now, he worked while sitting on a wheeled stool. Carson rolled a second stool to the table and sat to watch.

He was a dark-haired, blue-eyed boy whose looks alone would have ensured him a favored place in the world if he'd not been autistic.

At times like this, when his concentration on a task was total, Arnie would not tolerate anyone being too near to him. If Carson drew closer than four or five feet, he would grow agitated.

When enthralled by a project, he might pass days in silence except for wordless reactions to any attempt to interrupt his work or to invade his personal space.

More than eighteen years separated Carson from Arnie. He'd been born the year that she moved out of her parents' house. Even if he'd been spared from autism, they would not have been as close as many brothers and sisters, for they would have shared so few experiences.

Following the death of their parents four years ago, Carson gained custody of her brother. He had been with her ever since.

For reasons that she could not fully articulate, Carson had come to love this gentle, withdrawn child. She didn't think she could have loved him more if he had been her son rather than her brother.

She hoped that someday there would be a breakthrough either in the treatment of autism in general or in Arnie's particular case. But she knew her hope had little chance of being fulfilled.

Now she pondered the most recent changes he had made to the outer curtain wall of the castle compound. He had fortified it with regularly spaced buttresses that doubled as steep flights of stairs by which defenders could reach the walkways behind the battlements.

Recently Arnie had seemed to be more fearful

than usual. Carson could not shake the feeling that he sensed some trouble coming and that he was urgently determined to prepare for it. He could not build a real castle, so he took refuge in this fantasy of a fortress home.

CHAPTER 12

RANDAL SIX CROSSES SPHINX with XENOPHOBE, finishing the last crossword puzzle in the book.

Other collections of puzzles await him. But with the completion of this current book, he is armored against the fearsome disorder of the world. He has earned protection.

He will be safe for a while, although not forever. Disorder builds. Chaos presses at the walls. Eventually he will have to fill more patterns of empty boxes with more judiciously chosen letters for the purpose of denying chaos entrance to his private space.

Temporarily safe, he gets up from the worktable, sits on the edge of his bed, and presses a call button on his nightstand. This will summon lunch.

He is not served meals on a regular schedule because he cannot eat when obsessed with crossword puzzles. He will let food grow cold rather than interrupt the important work of fending off chaos.

A man in white brings his tray and places it on the worktable. While this attendant is present, Randal Six keeps his head bowed to discourage conversation and to prevent eye contact.

Every word he speaks to another person diminishes the protection that he has earned.

Alone again, Randal Six eats his lunch. Very neatly.

The food is white and green, as he likes it. Sliced turkey breast in cream sauce, mashed potatoes, white bread, peas, beans. For dessert, vanilla ice cream with crème de menthe.

When he finishes, he dares to open his door and slide the tray into the corridor. He quickly closes the door again, and feels as safe now as he ever does.

He sits on the edge of his bed and opens his nightstand drawer. The drawer contains a few magazines.

Having been educated by direct-to-brain data downloading, Randal Six is encouraged by Father to open himself to the world, to stay abreast of current events by the more ordinary means of reading various periodicals and newspapers.

He cannot tolerate newspapers. They are unwieldy. The sections become confused; the pages fall out of order.

Worse, the ink. The ink comes off on his hands, as if it is the dirty disorder of the world.

He can wash the ink away with enough soap and hot water in the bathroom that adjoins this chamber, but surely some of it seeps into his pores and thence into his bloodstream. By this means, a newspaper is an agent of contagion, infecting him with the world's disorder.

Among the magazines in the drawer, however, is a story that he tore from a local newspaper three months ago. This is his beacon of hope.

The story concerns a local organization raising research funds to find a cure for autism.

By the strictest definition of the affliction, Randal Six might not have autism. But he suffers from something very much like that sad condition.

Because Father has strongly encouraged him to better understand himself as a first step toward a cure, Randal reads books on the subject. They don't give him the peace he finds in crossword puzzles.

During the first month of his life, when it wasn't yet clear what might be wrong with him, when he had still been able to tolerate newspapers, he read about the local charity for autism research and at once recognized himself in descriptions of the condition. He then realized that he was not alone.

More important, he has seen a photo of another like himself: a boy of twelve, photographed with his sister, a New Orleans police officer.

In the photo, the boy isn't looking at the camera

but to one side of it. Randal Six recognizes the evasion.

Incredibly, however, the boy is smiling. He looks happy.

Randal Six has never been happy, not in the four months since he has come out of the creation tank as an eighteen-year-old. Not once. Not for a moment. Occasionally he feels sort of safe...but never happy.

Sometimes he sits and stares at the newspaper clipping for hours.

The boy in the photo is Arnie O'Connor. He smiles.

Maybe Arnie is not happy all the time, but he must be happy sometimes.

Arnie has knowledge that Randal needs. Arnie has a secret to happiness. Randal *needs* it so bad he lies awake at night desperately trying to think of some way to get it.

Arnie is in this city, so near. Yet for all practical purposes, he is beyond reach.

In his four months of life, Randal Six has never been outside the walls of Mercy. Just being taken to another floor in this very building for treatment is traumatic.

Another neighborhood of New Orleans is as unaccessible to him as a crater on the moon. Arnie lives with his secret, untouchable.

If only Randal can get to the boy, he will learn the secret of happiness. Perhaps Arnie will not want to share it. That won't matter. Randal will get it from him. Randal will *get* it.

Unlike the vast majority of autistics, Randal Six is capable of extreme violence. His inner rage is almost equal to his fear of the disordered world.

He has hidden this capacity for violence from everyone, even from Father, for he fears that if it is known, something bad will happen to him. He has seen in Father a certain . . . coldness.

He puts the newspaper photo in the drawer once more, under the magazines. In his mind's eye, he stills sees Arnie, smiling Arnie.

Arnie is out there on the moon in New Orleans, and Randal Six is drawn to him like the sea to lunar tides.

CHAPTER 13

IN THE SMALL dimly lighted projection booth, a sprung sofa slumped against one wall, and stacks of paperbacks stood on every flat surface. Evidently Jelly liked to read while the movie ran.

Pointing to a door different from the one by which they had entered, the fat man said, "My apartment's through there. Ben left a special box for you."

While Jelly went to fetch the box, Deucalion was drawn to the old projector, no doubt original to the building. This monstrous piece of machinery featured enormous supply and take-up reels. The 35mm film had to be threaded through a labyrinth of sprockets and guides, into the gap between the high-intensity bulb and the lens.

He studied the adjustment knobs and worked

forward until he could peer into the cyclopean eye of the projector. He removed a cover plate to examine the internal gears, wheels, and motors.

Across the balcony, the mezzanine, and the lower seats, this device could cast a bright illusion of life upon the big screen.

Deucalion's own life, in its first decade, had often seemed like a *dark* illusion. With time, however, life had become too real, requiring him to retreat into carnivals, into monasteries.

Returning with an old shoebox full of papers, Jelly halted when he saw Deucalion tinkering with the projector. "Makes me nervous, you messing with that. It's an antique. Hard to get parts or a repairman. That thing is the life's blood of this place."

"It's hemorrhaging." Deucalion replaced the cover to protect the delicate parts. "Logic reveals the secrets of any machine—whether it's a projector, a jet engine, or the universe itself."

"Ben warned me you think too much." Jelly set the shoebox on a stack of entertainment-gossip magazines. "He sent you one newspaper clipping with his letter, right?"

"And it brought me halfway around the world."

Jelly took the lid off the box. "Ben collected lots of this."

Deucalion picked up the top clipping, scanned the photo, then the headline: VICTOR HELIOS GIVES ONE MILLION TO SYMPHONY.

The sight of the man in the photo, virtually unchanged after so much time, jolted Deucalion as before, in the monastery.

SCIMITARS OF LIGHTNING gut a black-bellied night, and then crashes of thunder shake darkness across the tall casement windows once more. From flickering gas lamps, light capers over the stone walls of a cavernous laboratory. An electric arc crackles between the copper wire-wrapped poles of eldritch equipment. Sparks spray from dangerously overloaded transformers and piston-driven machinery.

The storm grows more violent, hurling bolt after bolt into the collector rods that stud the tallest towers. The incredible energy is channeled down into—

—him.

He opens his heavy eyelids and sees another's eye magnified by an ocular device resembling a jeweler's loupe. The loupe flips up, and he sees the face of Victor. Young, earnest, hopeful.

In white cap and blood-spattered gown, this creator, this would-be god . . .

HANDS TREMBLING, Deucalion dropped the clipping, which fluttered to the floor of the projection room.

Ben had prepared him for this, but he was shocked anew. Victor alive. *Alive.*

For a century or more, Deucalion had explained

his own longevity to himself by the simple fact that he was unique, brought to life by singular means. He might therefore exist beyond the reach of death. He never had a cold, the flu, no ailment or physical complaint.

Victor, however, had been born of man and woman. He should be heir to all the ills of the flesh.

From an inner jacket pocket, Deucalion withdrew a rolled sheet of heavy paper, which he usually kept in his carryall. He slipped the knot of the securing ribbon, unrolled the paper, and stared at it for a moment before showing it to Jelly.

Scrutinizing the pencil portrait, Jelly said, "That's Helios."

"A self-portrait," Deucalion said. "He's . . . talented. I took this from a frame in his study . . . more than two hundred years ago."

Jelly evidently knew enough to receive that statement without surprise.

"I showed this to Ben," Deucalion said. "More than once. That's how he recognized Victor Helios and knew him for who he really is."

Setting aside Victor's self-portrait, Deucalion selected a second clipping from the box and saw a photo of Helios receiving an award from the mayor of New Orleans.

A third clipping: Victor with the district attorney during his election campaign.

A fourth: Victor and his lovely wife, Erika, at a benefit auction.

Victor purchasing a mansion in the Garden District.

Victor endowing a scholarship at Tulane University.

Victor, Victor, *Victor.*

Deucalion did not recall casting aside the clippings or crossing the small room, but he must have done so, for the next thing he knew, he had driven his right fist and then his left into the wall, through the old plaster. As he withdrew his hands, clutching broken lengths of lath, a section of the wall crumbled and collapsed at his feet.

He heard himself roar with anger and anguish, and managed to choke off the cry before he lost control of it.

As he turned to Jelly, Deucalion's vision brightened, dimmed, brightened, and he knew that a subtle pulse of luminosity, like heat lightning behind clouds on a summer night, passed through his eyes. He had seen the phenomenon himself in mirrors.

Wide-eyed, Jelly seemed ready to bolt from the room, but then let out his pent-up breath. "Ben said you'd be upset."

Deucalion almost laughed at the fat man's understatement and aplomb, but he feared that a laugh would morph into a scream of rage. For the first time in many years, he had almost lost control of himself, almost indulged the criminal impulses that had been a part of him from the moment of his creation.

He said, "Do you know what I am?"

Jelly met his eyes, studied the tattoo and the ruin that it only half concealed, considered his hulking size. "Ben . . . he explained. I guess it could be true."

"Believe it," Deucalion advised him. "My origins are a prison graveyard, the cadavers of criminals—combined, revitalized, *reborn*."

CHAPTER 14

OUTSIDE, THE NIGHT was hot and humid. In Victor Helios's library, the air-conditioning chilled to the extent that a cheerful blaze in the fireplace was necessary.

Fire featured in some of his less pleasant memories. The great windmill. The bombing of Dresden. The Israeli Mossad attack on the secret Venezuelan research complex that he had shared with Mengele in the years after World War II. Nevertheless he liked to read to the accompaniment of a cozy crackling fire.

When, as now, he was perusing medical journals like *The Lancet, JAMA,* and *Emerging Infectious Diseases,* the fire served not merely as ambience but as an expression of his informed scientific opinion. He frequently tore articles from the magazines and tossed them into the flames. Occasionally, he burned entire issues.

As ever, the scientific establishment could teach him nothing. He was far ahead of them. Yet he felt the need to remain aware of advancements in genetics, molecular biology, and associated fields.

He felt the need, as well, for a wine that better complemented the fried walnuts than did the Cabernet that Erika had served with them. Too tannic. A fine Merlot would have been preferable.

She sat in the armchair opposite his, reading poetry. She had become enthralled with Emily Dickinson, which annoyed Victor.

Dickinson had been a fine poet, of course, but she had been God-besotted. Her verses could mislead the naive. Intellectual poison.

Whatever need Erika might have for a god could be satisfied here in this room. Her maker, after all, was her husband.

Physically, he had done a fine job. She was beautiful, graceful, elegant. She looked twenty-five but had been alive only six weeks.

Victor himself, though two hundred and forty, could have passed for forty-five. His youthful appearance had been harder to maintain than hers had been to achieve.

Beauty and grace were not his only criteria for an ideal wife. He also wished her to be socially and intellectually sophisticated.

In this regard, in many small ways, Erika had

failed him and had proved slow to learn in spite of direct-to-brain downloads of data that included virtual encyclopedias of etiquette, culinary history, wine appreciation, witticisms, and much else.

Knowledge of a subject did not mean that one could apply that knowledge, of course, but Erika didn't seem to be trying hard enough. The Cabernet instead of the Merlot, Dickinson . . .

Victor had to admit, however, that she was a more appealing and acceptable creature than Erika Three, her immediate predecessor. She might not be the final version—only time would tell—but whatever her faults, Erika Four was not a complete embarrassment.

The drivel in the medical journals and Erika reading Dickinson at last drove him up from his armchair. "I'm in a creative mood. I think I'll spend some time in my studio."

"Do you need my help, darling?"

"No. You stay here, enjoy yourself."

"Listen to this." Her delight was childlike. Before Victor could stop her, she read from Dickinson: "The pedigree of honey / Does not concern the bee / A clover, any time, to him / Is aristocracy."

"Charming," he said. "But for variety, you might read some Thom Gunn and Frederick Seidel."

He could have told her what to read, and she would have obeyed. But he did not desire an automaton for a wife. He wanted her to be free-spirited. Only in sexual matters did he demand utter obedience.

In the immense restaurant-quality kitchen from which staff could serve a sit-down dinner for a hundred without problem, Victor entered the walk-in pantry. The shelves at the back, laden with canned goods, slid aside when he touched a hidden switch.

Beyond the pantry, secreted in the center of the house, lay his windowless studio.

His public labs were at Helios Biovision, the company through which he was known to the world and by which he had earned another fortune atop those he had already accrued in earlier ages.

And in the Hands of Mercy, an abandoned hospital converted to serve his primary work and staffed with men of his making, he pursued the creation of the new race that would replace flawed humanity.

Here, behind the pantry, measuring twenty by fifteen feet, this retreat provided a place for him to work on small experiments, often those on the leading edge of his historic enterprise.

Victor supposed that he was to arcane laboratory equipment what Santa Claus was to gizmo-filled toy workshops.

When Mary Shelley took a local legend based on truth and crafted fiction from it, she'd made Victor a tragic figure and killed him off. He understood her dramatic purpose for giving him a death scene, but he loathed her for portraying him as tragic and as a failure.

Her judgment of his work was arrogant. What else of consequence did *she* ever write? And of the two, who was dead—and who was not?

Although her novel suggested his workplace was a phantasmagoria of gizmos as ominous in appearance as in purpose, she had been vague on details. Not until the first film adaptation of her book did the name Frankenstein become synonymous with the term "mad scientist" and with laboratories buzzing-crackling-humming with frightening widgets, thingums, and doohickeys.

Amusingly, Hollywood had the set design more than half right, not as to the actual machines and objects, but as to ambience. Even the studio behind the pantry had a flavor of Hell with machines.

On the center worktable stood a Lucite tank filled with a milky antibiotic solution. In the tank rested a man's severed head.

Actually, the head wasn't severed. It had never been attached to a body in the first place.

Victor had created it only to serve as a braincase. The head had no hair, and the features were rough, not fully formed.

Support systems serviced it with nutrient-rich, enzyme-balanced, oxygenated blood and drained away metabolic waste through numerous plastic tubes that entered through the neck.

With no need to breathe, the head was almost

dead still. But the eyes twitched behind the lids, which suggested that it was dreaming.

The brain within the skull was self-aware but had only the most rudimentary personality, sufficient to the experiment.

Approaching the table, Victor addressed the resident of the open Lucite tank: "Time to work, Karloff."

No one could say that Victor Helios, alias Frankenstein, was a humorless man.

In the head, the eyes opened. They were blue and bloodshot.

Karloff had been selectively educated by direct-to-brain data downloading; therefore, he spoke English. "Ready," he said, his voice thick and hoarse.

"Where is your hand?" Victor asked.

The bloodshot eyes shifted at once to regard a smaller table in a far corner of the room.

There, a living hand lay in a shallow bowl of milky antibiotic solution. As in the case of the head, this five-fingered wonder was served by numerous tubes and by a low-voltage electrical pump that could empower its nerves and, thereby, its musculature.

The systems sustaining the head and those sustaining the hand were independent of each other, sharing no common tubing or wiring.

After reading the status displays on the equipment and making a few adjustments, Victor said, "Karloff, move your thumb."

In the dish, the hand lay motionless. Motionless. And then . . . the thumb twitched, bent at the knuckle, straightened again.

Victor had long sought those genes that might carry the elusive psychic powers that humankind had sometimes experienced but had never been able to control. Recently he had achieved this small success.

This ultimate amputee, Karloff, had just exhibited psychomotor telekenesis, the control of his entirely detached hand strictly by means of mental exertion.

"Give me an arpeggio," Victor said.

In the shallow bowl, the hand raised on the heel of its palm and strummed the air with all fingers, as if plucking at the strings of an invisible harp.

Pleased by this display, Victor said, "Karloff, make a fist."

The hand slowly clenched, tighter, tighter, until the knuckles were sharp and white.

No emotion showed in Karloff's face, yet the hand seemed to be an exquisite expression of anger and the will to violence.

CHAPTER 15

NEW DAY, NEW DEATH. For the second morning in a row, Carson chased breakfast with the discovery of a mutilated corpse.

A TV crew was at the library, hauling gear out of a satellite van, when Carson jammed the brakes, twisted the wheel, and slotted her plainwrap between two black-and-whites that were angled to the curb.

"I break land-speed records getting here," she grumbled, "and the media's already on the scene."

"Bribe the right people," Michael suggested, "and next time you might get the call before Channel 4."

As she and Michael crossed the sidewalk toward the library, a reporter shouted to her, "Detective

O'Connor! Is it true the Surgeon cut out a heart this time?"

"Maybe they're so interested," she told Michael, "because none of those bastards *has* a heart."

They hurried up stone steps to the ornate redstone building with gray granite arches and columns.

Admitting them, the police guard at the door said, "It fits the pattern, guys. It's one of his."

"Seven murders in a little over three weeks isn't a pattern anymore," Carson replied. "It's a rampage."

As they entered the reading foyer with the elevated main desk, Michael said, "I should've brought my overdue book."

"You checked out a book? Mr. DVD with a *book*?"

"It was a DVD guide."

Crime-scene techs, police photographers, criminalists, jakes, and personnel from the medical examiner's office served as Indian guides without saying a word. Carson and Michael followed their nods and gestures through a labyrinth of books.

Three quarters of the way along an aisle of stacks, they found Harker and Frye, who were cordoning off the scene with yellow tape.

Establishing that the territory belonged to him and Carson, Michael said, "Yesterday's hand bandit is this morning's thief of hearts."

Frye managed to look greasy *and* blanched. His face had no color. He kept one hand on his expansive gut as if he had eaten some bad pepper shrimp for breakfast.

He said, "Far as I'm concerned, you take the lead on this one. I've lost my taste for the case."

If Harker, too, had a change of heart, his reasons were not identical to Frye's. His face was as boiled red as ever, his eyes as challenging.

Running one hand through his sun-bleached hair, Harker said, "Looks to me like whoever has point position on this is walking a high wire. One mistake on a case this high profile, the media will flush your career down the toilet."

"If that means cooperation instead of competition," Michael said, "we accept."

Carson wasn't as ready as Michael to forgive the toe-tramping they had received from these two, but she said, "Who's the vic?"

"Night security man," Harker said.

While Frye remained behind, Harker ducked under the yellow tape and led them to the end of the aisle, around the corner to another long row of stacks.

The end-stack sign declared ABERRANT PSY-CHOLOGY. Thirty feet away, the dead man lay on his back on the floor. The victim looked like a hog halfway through a slaughterhouse.

Carson entered the new aisle but did not proceed into the blood spatter, leaving the wet zone unspoiled for CSI.

As she quietly sized the scene and tried to fit herself to it, planning the approach strategy, Harker said from behind her, "Looks like he cracked the breastbone neat as a surgeon. Went in there with complete professionalism. The guy travels with tools."

Moving to Carson's side, Michael said, "At least we can rule out suicide."

"Almost *looks* like suicide," Carson murmured thoughtfully.

Michael said, "Now, let's remember the fundamentals of this relationship. *You* are the straight man."

"There was a struggle," Harker said. "The books were pulled off the shelves."

About twenty books were scattered on the floor this side of the dead man. None was open. Some were in stacks of two and three.

"Too neat," she said. "This looks more like someone was *reading* them, then set them aside."

"Maybe Dr. Jekyll was sitting on the floor, researching his own insanity," Michael conjectured, "when the guard discovered him."

"Look at the wet zone," Carson said. "Tightly contained around the body. Not much spatter on the books. No signs of struggle."

"No struggle?" Harker mocked. "Tell that to the guy without a heart."

"His piece is still in his holster," Carson said. "He didn't even draw, let alone get off a shot."

"Chloroform from behind," Michael suggested.

Carson didn't respond at once. During the night,

madness had entered the library, carrying a bag of surgical tools. She could hear the soft footsteps of madness, hear its slow soft breathing.

The stench of the victim's blood stirred in Carson's blood a quivering current of fear. Something about this scene, something she could not quite identify, was extraordinary, unprecedented in her experience, and so unnatural as to be almost *super*natural. It spoke first to her emotions rather than to her intellect; it teased her to see it, to know it.

Beside her, Michael whispered, "Here comes that old witchy vision."

Her mouth went dry with fear, her hands suddenly icy. She was no stranger to fear. She could be simultaneously afraid but professional, alert and quick. Sometimes fear sharpened her wits, clarified her thinking.

"Looks more," she said at last, "as if the vic just laid down there and waited to be butchered. Look at his face."

The eyes were open. The features were relaxed, not contorted by terror, by pain.

"Chloroform," Michael suggested again.

Carson shook her head. "He was awake. Look at the eyes. The cast of the mouth. He didn't die unconscious. Look at the hands."

The security guard's left hand lay open at his side, palm up, fingers spread. That position suggested sedation before the murder.

The right hand, however, was clenched tight. Chloroformed, he would have relaxed the fist.

She jotted down these observations in her notebook and then said, "So who found the body?"

"A morning-shift librarian," Harker said. "Nancy Whistler. She's in the women's lav. She won't come out."

CHAPTER 16

THE WOMEN'S REST ROOM smelled of pine-scented disinfectant and White Diamonds perfume. Regular janitorial service was the source of the former, Nancy Whistler of the latter.

A young, pretty woman who put the lie to the stereotypical image of librarians, she wore a clingy summer dress as yellow as daffodils.

She bent to one of the sinks and splashed cold water in her face from a running faucet. She drank from cupped hands, swished the water around her mouth, and spat it out.

"I'm sorry I'm such a mess," she said.

"No problem," Carson assured her.

"I'm afraid to leave here. Every time I think I just *can't* puke again, I do."

"I love this job," Michael told Carson.

"The officers who did a perimeter check tell me there are no signs of forced entry. So you're sure the front door was locked when you arrived for work?" Carson pressed.

"Absolutely. Two deadbolts, both engaged."

"Who else has keys?"

"Ten people. Maybe twelve," said Nancy Whistler. "I can't think names right now."

You could only push a witness so far in the aftermath of her encounter with a bloody corpse. This wasn't a time to be hard-assed.

Carson said, "E-mail a list of keyholders to me. Soon."

"All right, sure. I understand." The librarian grimaced as if she might hurl again. Instead she said, "God, he was such a toad, but he didn't deserve *that*." Michael's raised eyebrows drew an explanation from her: "Bobby Allwine. The guard."

"Define *toad*," Michael requested.

"He was always . . . looking at me, saying inappropriate things. He had a way of coming on to me that was . . . just weird."

"Harassment?"

"No. Nothing forceful. Just weird. As if he didn't *get* a lot of things, the way to act." She shook her head. "And he went to funeral homes for fun."

Carson and Michael exchanged a look, and he said, "Well, who doesn't?"

"Viewings at funeral homes," Whistler clarified.

"Memorial services. For people he didn't even know. He went two, three times a week."

"Why?"

"He said he liked to look at dead people in their caskets. Said it . . . relaxed him." She cranked off the water faucet. "Bobby was sort of a geek. But . . . why would someone cut out his heart?"

Michael shrugged. "Souvenir. Sexual gratification. Dinner."

Appalled, repelled, Nancy Whistler bolted for a toilet stall.

To Michael, Carson said, "Oh, nice. Real nice."

CHAPTER 17

PEELING PAINT, crumbling stucco, rusting wrought iron, sagging trumpet vines yellowing in the heat, and a pustulant-looking fungus flourishing in the many cracks in the concrete walkway established a design motif carried out in every aspect of the apartment building.

On the patchy lawn, which looked as if someone had salted it, a sign announced APARTMENT AVAILABLE / ONLY LOSERS NEED APPLY.

Actually, only the first two words were on the sign. The other four didn't have to be spelled out; Carson inferred them from the condition of the place as she parked at the curb.

In addition to the sign, the front lawn actually contained a flock of seven pink flamingos.

"Bet my ass there's a couple plastic gnomes somewhere around here," Michael said.

Someone had painted four of the flamingos other tropical hues—mango green, pineapple yellow—perhaps hoping that a color change would render these lawn ornaments less absurd if not less tacky. The new paint had worn off in places; the pink shone through.

Not because of the implication of borderline poverty but because of the weirdness of the place, it was an ideal building for odd ducks and geeks like Bobby Allwine, he of the stolen heart. They would be drawn here, and in the company of their own kind, no one among them would receive particular attention.

A grizzled old man knelt on the front steps, fixing a railing brace.

"Excuse me. You work here?" Michael asked, flashing his ID.

"No more than I have to." The old man looked Carson up and down appreciatively, but still spoke to Michael. "Who's she?"

"It's bring-your-sister-to-work day at the department. Are you the super here?"

"'Super' don't seem to be a word that fits anyone or anything about this dump. I'm just sort of the jack-of-all around here. You come to see Bobby Allwine's place?"

"News travels fast."

Putting down his screwdriver, getting to his feet, the jack-of-all said, "Good news does. Follow me."

Inside, the public stairwell was narrow, dark, peeling, humid, and malodorous.

The old guy didn't smell so good, either, and as they followed him up to the second floor, Michael said, "I'll never complain about my apartment again."

At the door to 2-D, as he fumbled in his pockets for a passkey, the jack-of-all said, "Heard on the news his liver was cut out."

"It was his heart," Carson said.

"Even better."

"You didn't like Bobby Allwine?"

Unlocking the door, he said, "Hardly knew him. But this makes the apartment worth fifty bucks more." He read their disbelief and assured them, "There's people that'll pay extra."

"Who," Michael asked, "the Addams family?"

"Just people who like some history about a place."

Carson pushed inside the apartment, and when the old man would have followed her, Michael eased him aside and said, "We'll call you when we're done."

The blinds were drawn. The room was uncommonly dark for a bright afternoon.

Carson found the switch for the ceiling fixture and said, "Michael, look at this."

In the living room, the ceiling and walls were painted black. The wood floors, the baseboards, the door and window casings were black, as well. The blinds were black.

The sole piece of furniture was a black vinyl armchair in the center of the room.

Closing the front door behind him, Michael said, "Does Martha Stewart have an emergency design hotline?"

The windows were closed. No air conditioning. The moist heat and the blackness and a tauntingly familiar sweet fragrance made Carson feel slow, stupid.

"What's that smell?" she asked.

"Licorice."

Thick, sweet, pervasive, the aroma was indeed licorice. Though it should have been pleasant, the smell half nauseated Carson.

The black floor had a glossy sheen, unmarred by dust or lint. She wiped a hand along a windowsill, down a door casing, and found no grime.

As it had in the library with Allwine's corpse, fear found Carson, a creeping disquiet that climbed her spine and pressed a cold kiss to the back of her neck.

In the meticulously clean kitchen, Michael hesitated to open the black door of the refrigerator. "This feels like a Jeffrey Dahmer moment, severed heads among the bottles of pickles and mayonnaise, a heart in a OneZip bag."

Even the interior of the refrigerator had been spray-painted black, but it held no heads. Just a coffee cake and a quart of milk.

Most of the cupboards were empty, too. A drawer contained three spoons, two forks, two knives.

According to his employee file, Allwine had lived

here for two years. An inventory of his possessions would give the impression that he'd been prepared to leave on a moment's notice and to travel light.

The third room was the bedroom. The ceiling, the walls, and the floor were black. Even the bed and sheets: black. A black nightstand, black lamp, and black radio with glowing green numbers.

"What *is* this place?" Carson wondered.

"Maybe he's a satanist? Or just an over-the-top metal fan."

"No music system. No TV."

Michael found the source of the licorice odor. On the unpadded windowseat sat a tray holding several fat black candles, none burning at the moment. Bending down to sniff, he said, "Scented."

Carson considered the time and effort required to create this unrelieved blackness, and suddenly she thought of Arnie and his Lego castle. Bobby Allwine held a job and interacted with the world, but on some level he was as dysfunctional as her brother.

Arnie was benign, however, whereas judging by the available evidence, Allwine's psychology must be, at the core, malignant.

"This place is worth an extra *hundred* bucks a month," Michael declared.

When Carson switched on the light in the adjacent bathroom, the startling contrast stung her eyes. Paint, floor tile, sink, toilet—everything was a dazzling *white,* assiduously polished. The pungent smell of ammonia allowed no intrusion of the scent of licorice.

Opposite the vanity mirror, hundreds of single-edged razor blades bristled from the wall. Each had been pressed at the same angle into the sheetrock, leaving half of the blade exposed, like a wicked silver fang. Row after row after row of clean, sparkling, unused razor blades.

"Seems like," she said, "the victim was even crazier than his killer."

CHAPTER 18

IN NEW ORLEANS uptown society, formal dinner parties were a political necessity, and Victor took his responsibilities seriously.

Inside the sprawling Garden District mansion, his housekeepers—Christine and Sandra—and his butler, William, had spent the day preparing for the evening's event. They cleaned every room, added flowers and candles, swept the covered porches. Gardeners tended to the lawn, trees, flower beds, and shrubs.

These people were all his creations, made at the Hands of Mercy, and were therefore tireless and efficient.

In the formal dining room, the table was set for twelve with Pratesi linens, Buccelatti silverware, Limoges china, historic Paul Storr silver chargers, and a monumental Storr candelabrum featuring Bacchus and attendants. The sparkle factor was greater—and embodied greater value—than any display case of diamonds at Tiffany's.

The housekeepers and butler awaited their master's inspection. He entered the dining room, already dressed for dinner, and considered the preparations.

"Sandra, you've selected the right china for tonight's guests."

His approval drew a smile from her, though it was uneasy.

"But, William, there are fingerprints on a couple of these glasses."

At once the butler took the indicated glasses away.

Two centerpieces of cream-colored roses flanked the candelabrum, and Victor said of them, "Christine, too much greenery. Strip some of it out to emphasize the blooms."

"I didn't arrange the roses, sir," she said, and seemed to be dismayed to have to reveal that his wife had taken charge of the roses. "Mrs. Helios preferred to do it herself. She read a book on flower arranging."

Victor knew that the staff liked Erika and worried that she should do well.

He sighed. "Redo the arrangements anyway, but don't say anything to my wife." Wistfully, he removed one of the white roses and slowly turned it between thumb and forefinger. He sniffed it, noting that a few of the petals already showed early signs of wilt. "She's so . . . young. She'll learn."

AS THE HOUR drew near, Victor went to the master bedroom suite to determine what had delayed Erika.

He found her in the dressing room, at her vanity. Her shoulder-length bronze hair was as lustrous as silk. The exquisite form and buttery smoothness of her bare shoulders stirred him.

Unfortunately, she had too much enthusiasm for the effects of makeup.

"Erika, you can't improve on perfection."

"I so much want to look nice for you, Victor."

"Then wash most of that stuff off. Let your natural beauty shine through. I've given you everything you need to dazzle."

"How sweet," she said, but she seemed uncertain whether she had been complimented or criticized.

"The city councilman's wife, the university president's wife—none of them will be painted like pop-music divas."

Her smile faltered. Victor believed that directness with a subordinate—or a wife—was always preferable to criticism couched to spare feelings.

Standing close behind her, he slid his hands along her bare shoulders, bent close to smell her hair. He pulled that glorious mane aside, kissed the nape of her neck—and felt her shiver.

He fingered her emerald necklace. "Diamonds would be a better choice. Please change it. For me."

In the vanity mirror, she met his eyes, then lowered her gaze to the array of makeup brushes and bottles before her. She spoke in a whisper: "Your standards for everything are . . . so high."

He kissed her neck again and matched her whisper: "That's why I made you. My wife."

CHAPTER 19

IN THE CAR, on the way to the Quarter for a grab-it dinner in Jackson Square, Carson and Michael ping-ponged the case.

She said, "Allwine wasn't chloroformed."

"We don't have blood results yet."

"Remember his face. He wasn't chloroformed. That makes him and the dry cleaner, Chaterie, the exceptions."

"The other male, Bradford Walden, *was* chloroformed," Michael said. "Otherwise, those three make a set."

"The Surgeon took their internal organs as souvenirs."

"But from the women he only takes ears, feet, hands. . . . Did Nancy Whistler e-mail you that list of people with library keys?"

"Yeah. But after seeing Allwine's apartment, I think he opened the door for the killer, the guy didn't need a key."

"How do you get to that?"

"I don't know. It's just a feeling."

"Let's do some victimology analysis," Michael suggested. "First... I've given up on the idea the victims are connected to one another somehow. They're random prey."

"How did you analyze your way to that?"

"Now and then," he said, "I have a feeling of my own."

"Any significance to which body part he takes from any particular victim?"

"Elizabeth Lavenza, swimming without her hands. Are hands of special importance in her life, her work? Is she a pianist? Maybe an artist? Maybe a massage therapist?"

"As you know, she was a clerk in a bookstore."

"Meg Saville, the tourist from Idaho."

"Took her feet."

"She wasn't a ballet dancer. Just a receptionist."

"He takes a nurse's ears, a university student's legs," Carson said. "If there's significance, it's inscrutable."

"He takes the dry cleaner's liver, the bartender's kidney. If he'd carved the bartender's liver, we might build a theory on that."

"Pathetic," she said.

"Totally," he agreed. "The bartender had a Goth

lifestyle, and Allwine lived in black. Is that a connection?"

"I didn't get *Goth* from his apartment, just *crazy*."

She parked illegally in Jackson Square, near a
Cajun restaurant favored by cops.

Just as they reached the entrance, Harker exited
the place with a large bag of takeout, bringing with
him the mouthwatering aroma of blackened cat-
fish, reminding Carson that she'd skipped lunch.

As if not in the least surprised to see them, as if
picking up in midconversation, Harker said,
"Word is the mayor might push for a task force as
early as the weekend. If we'll be teaming this later,
we might as well start swapping thoughts now."

To Harker, Carson said, "Surely you gotta know
your reputation. Everyone in the department pegs
you and Frye for glory hogs."

"Envy," Harker said dismissively. "We close more
cases than anyone."

"Sometimes by popping the suspect," Michael
said, referring to a recent officer-involved shooting
for which Harker had narrowly avoided being
brought up on charges.

Harker's smile was contemptuous. "You want my
theory about the library security guard?"

Michael said, "Do I want pancreatic cancer?"

"The black rooms are a death wish," Harker conjectured.

"Damn," Carson said.

"He tried to slash his wrists with each of those

razor blades in the bathroom wall," Harker continued. "But he just couldn't find the courage."

"You and Frye went to Allwine's apartment?"

"Yeah. You two," Harker said, "you're *our* babies, and we sometimes feel the need to burp you."

He pushed between them, walked away, glanced back after a few steps. "When you *have* a theory, I'll be happy to listen to it."

To Carson, Michael said, "I've got a short list of hearts *I'd* like to cut out."

CHAPTER 20

AFTER VICTOR LEFT the master suite, Erika slipped into a St. John dress that managed to be sensational yet respectable, subtly sexy but classy.

Standing in front of a full-length mirror in her enormous walk-in closet, which was as big as most master bedrooms, she knew that she looked enchanting, that she would leave an indelible impression on every man at the dinner. Nevertheless, she felt inadequate.

She would have tried other dresses if the first guests had not been scheduled to arrive in mere minutes. Victor expected her to be at his side to greet each arrival, and she dared not fail him.

All of her clothes were behind doors or in drawers along three aisles. She owned literally hundreds of outfits.

She hadn't shopped for any of them. Having created her to his ideal measurements, Victor had purchased everything while she had still been in the tank.

Perhaps he'd bought some of these things for the previous Erika. She didn't like to think about that.

She hoped that someday she would be allowed to shop for herself. When Victor allowed that, she would know she had at last met his standards and earned his trust.

Briefly, she wondered what it would be like not to care what Victor—or anyone—thought of her. To be herself. Independent.

Those were dangerous thoughts. She must repress them.

At the back of the closet, perhaps two hundred pairs of shoes were stored on canted shelves. Although she knew that time was of the essence, she dithered between Gucci and Kate Spade.

Behind her in the closet, something rustled, something thumped.

She turned to look back at the center aisle but saw only closed cherrywood doors behind which hung some of her seasonal wardrobe, and pale yellow carpet. She peeked into the right-hand aisle, then into the left, but they were also deserted.

Refocusing on her dilemma, she finally resolved it by choosing the Kate Spades. Carrying them in one hand, she hurried out of the closet into her dressing room.

Entering, she thought she saw movement from the corner of her eye, on the floor at the open doorway to the bedroom. When she turned her head, nothing was there.

Curious, she went into the bedroom nevertheless—just in time to see the silk spread flutter behind something that had just slipped under the king-size bed.

They had no house pets, no dog, no cat.

Victor would be furious if it turned out that a rat had gotten into the house. He had zero tolerance for vermin.

Erika had been made to be cautious of danger but to fear nothing in the extreme—although her programmed respect for her maker came close to fear at times.

If a rat had gotten into the house and if now it hid under the bed, she would not hesitate to snare it and dispose of it.

She set aside the Kate Spades and dropped to her knees beside the bed. She had no doubt that her reflexes were quick enough to snatch a scurrying rat.

When she lifted the spread and looked under the bed, her superb vision required no flashlight. But nothing lurked beneath the boxed springs.

She got to her feet and turned, surveying the room. She sensed that something was here, but she didn't have time to search behind every piece of furniture.

Conscious of time racing rat-fast, she sat on the edge of an armchair, near the fireplace, and pulled on her shoes. They were beautiful, but she would have liked them more if she had bought them herself.

She sat for a moment, listening. Silence. But this was the kind of silence that suggested something might be listening to her as she listened for it.

When she left the master suite for the upstairs hall, she closed the door behind her. It fit tight. Nothing could get under it. If a rat was loose in the bedroom, it couldn't get downstairs to spoil the dinner party.

She descended the grand staircase, and as she reached the foyer, the doorbell rang. The first guests had arrived.

CHAPTER 21

AS ROY PRIBEAUX dressed in black slacks, a pale-blue silk sport jacket, and a white linen shirt for his date with Candace—those *eyes!*—an all-news channel on TV did a segment about the Surgeon.

What an absurd name they had given him. He was a romantic. He was an idealist from a family of idealists. He was a purist. He was many things, but he was not a surgeon.

He knew they were talking about him, though he did not closely follow the media response to his harvests. He hadn't begun his collection of female perfection with the hope that he would become a celebrity. Fame had no appeal for him.

Of course his quest generated public interest for all the wrong reasons. They saw violence, not art. They saw blood, not the work of a dreamer who sought perfection in all things.

He had only contempt for the media and for the audience to which they pandered. Knaves speaking to fools.

Having come from a prominent family of politicians—his father and grandfather had served the city of New Orleans and the state of Louisiana—he had seen with what ease the public could be manipulated by the clever use of envy and fear. His family had been expert at it.

In the process, the Pribeauxs had greatly enriched themselves. His grandfather and father had done so well in public service that Roy himself had never needed to work and never would.

Like great artists during the Renaissance, he had patrons: generations of taxpayers. His inheritance allowed him to devote his life to the pursuit of ideal beauty.

When the TV reporter mentioned the most recent two victims, Roy's attention was suddenly focused by the coupling of an unknown name—Bobby Allwine—with that of Elizabeth Lavenza. He had harvested Elizabeth's lovely hands before consigning the depressingly imperfect remainder of her to the City Park lagoon.

The *heart* had been removed from this Allwine person.

Roy had no interest in hearts. He wasn't about internals. He was about externals. The kind of beauty that moved Roy *was* skin deep.

Furthermore, this Allwine person was a *man*. Roy

had no interest in the ideal beauty of men—except in the constant refinement and perfection of his own physique.

Now, standing before the TV, he was further surprised to hear that Allwine was the *third* man whom the Surgeon had murdered. From the others he had taken a kidney and a liver.

These murders were linked to those of the women by the fact that at least one of the male victims had been chloroformed.

Copycat. Misguided imitator. Out there somewhere in New Orleans, an envious fool had been inspired by Roy's murders without understanding the purpose of them.

For a moment, he was offended. Then he realized that the copycat, inevitably less intelligent than Roy himself, would eventually screw up, and the police would pin *all* these killings on the guy. The copycat was Roy's get-out-of-jail-free card.

CHAPTER 22

THE PROJECTION BOOTH might have seemed too small for two men as large—in different ways—as Jelly Biggs and Deucalion. Nevertheless, it became the space they shared when they preferred not to be alone.

The booth was cozy, perhaps because of Jelly's collection of paperback books, perhaps because it felt like a high redoubt above the fray of life.

For extended periods of his long existence, Deucalion had found solitude appealing. One of those periods had ended in Tibet.

Now, with the discovery that Victor was not dead, solitude disturbed Deucalion. He wanted companionship.

As former carnies, he and Jelly had a world of experience in common, tales to tell, nostalgic reminiscences to share. In but one day they found that they fell into easy conversation, and Deucalion suspected that in time they would become true friends.

Yet they fell into silences, as well, for their situation was similar to that of soldiers in a battlefield trench, in the deceptive calm before the mortar fire began. In this condition, they had profound questions to ponder before they were ready to discuss them.

Jelly did his thinking while reading mystery novels of which he was inexpressibly fond. Much of his life, imprisoned in flesh, he had lived vicariously through the police, the private investigators, and the amateur detectives who populated the pages of his favorite genre.

In these mutual silences, Deucalion's reading consisted of the articles about Victor Helios, alias Frankenstein, that Ben had accumulated. He pored through them, trying to accustom himself to the bitter, incredible truth of his creator's continued existence, while also contemplating how best to destroy that pillar of arrogance.

Again and again, he caught himself unconsciously fingering the ruined half of his face until eventually Jelly could not refrain from asking how the damage had been done.

"I angered my maker," Deucalion said.

"We all do," Jelly said, "but not with such consequences."

"My maker isn't yours," Deucalion reminded him.

A life of much solitude and contemplation accustomed Deucalion to silence, but Jelly needed background noise even when reading a novel. In a corner of the projection booth, volume low, stood a TV flickering with images that to Deucalion had no more narrative content than did the flames in a fireplace.

Suddenly something in one of the droning newscast voices caught his attention. *Murders. Body parts missing.*

Deucalion turned up the volume. A homicide detective named Carson O'Connor, beseiged by reporters outside the city library, responded to most of their questions with replies that in different words all amounted to *no comment.*

When the story ended, Deucalion said, "The Surgeon . . . How long has this been going on?"

As a mystery novel aficionado, Jelly was interested in true crime stories, too. He not only knew all the gory details of the Surgeon's murder spree; he also had developed a couple of theories that he felt were superior to any that the police had thus far put forth.

Listening, Deucalion had suspicions of his own that grew from his unique experience.

Most likely, the Surgeon was an ordinary serial killer taking souvenirs. But in a city where the god of the living dead had taken up residence, the Surgeon might be something worse than the usual psychopath.

Returning the clippings to the shoe box, rising to his feet, Deucalion said, "I'm going out."

"Where?"

"To find his house. To see in what style a self-appointed god chooses to live these days."

CHAPTER 23

ILLEGALLY PARKED IN Jackson Square, the hood of the plainwrap sedan served as their dinner table.

Carson and Michael ate corn-battered shrimp, shrimp étouffée with rice, and corn maque choux from take-out containers.

Strolling along the sidewalk were young couples hand-in-hand. Musicians in black suits and porkpie hats hurried past, carrying instrument cases, shouldering between slower-moving older Cajun men in chambray shirts and Justin Wilson hats. Groups of young women showed more skin than common sense, and drag queens enjoyed the goggling of tourists.

Somewhere good jazz was playing. Through the night air wove a tapestry of talk and laughter.

Carson said, "What pisses me off about guys like Harker and Frye—"

"This'll be an epic list," Michael said.

"—is how I let them irritate me."

"They're cheesed off because no one makes detective as young as we did."

"That was three years ago for me. They better adjust soon."

"They'll retire, get shot. One way or another, we'll eventually have *our* chance to be the old cranks."

After savoring a forkful of corn maque choux, Carson said, "It's all about my father."

"Harker and Frye don't care about what your father did or didn't do," Michael assured her.

"You're wrong. Everyone expects that sooner or later it'll turn out I carry the dirty-cop gene, just like they think he did."

Michael shook his head, "I don't for a minute think you carry the dirty-cop gene."

"I don't give a shit what you think, Michael, I *know* what you think. It's what everyone else thinks that makes this job so much harder for me than it ought to be."

"Yeah, well," he said, pretending offense, "I don't give a shit that *you* don't give a shit what I think."

Chagrined, Carson laughed softly. "I'm sorry, man. You're one of a handful of people I *do* care what they think of me."

"You wounded me," he said. "But I'll heal."

"I've worked hard to get where I am." She

sighed. "Except where I am is eating another meal on my feet, in the street."

"The food's great," he said, "and I'm glittering company."

"Considering the pay, why *do* we work so hard?"

"We're genuine American heroes."

"Yeah, right."

Michael's cell phone rang. Licking Creole tartar sauce off his lips, he answered the call: "Detective Maddison." When he hung up moments later, he said, "We're invited to the morgue. No music, no dancing. But it might be fun."

CHAPTER 24

CARESSED BY CANDLELIGHT, the chased surfaces of classic silver seemed perpetually about to melt.

With five movers and shakers and their spouses gathered in his dining room, Victor looked forward to stimulating conversation that he could guide subtly into channels that would serve his interests long after the mayor, the city councilman, the university president, and the others had left his table. To Victor, every social occasion was primarily an opportunity to influence political and cultural leaders, discreetly advancing his agenda.

Initially, of course, the talk was of frivolous things, even among such accomplished guests. But Victor fancied himself to be as capable of light chatter as anyone and could enjoy this witty froth because it sharpened his anticipation for meatier discussion.

William and Christine served the soup, the butler holding the tureen while the maid ladled a creamy pink richness into the bowls.

This was Erika's third dinner party in the five weeks since she had risen from the tank, and she exhibited some improvement in her social skills, though less than he had hoped.

He saw her frown as she noticed that the flower arrangements were different from those that she had painstakingly created. She possessed the good sense to say nothing of the change.

When his wife glanced at him, however, Victor said, "The roses are perfect," so she would learn from her error.

City Councilman Watkins, whose once-patrician nose had begun subtly to deform as inhaled cocaine ate away supporting cartilage, used one hand to fan the rising aroma from the bowl to his nostrils. "Erika, the soup smells delicious."

John Watkins's opponent in the next election— Bobby Moreau—was one of Victor's people. With all the dirt about Watkins that Victor could provide, Bobby would romp to victory at the polls. In the months until then, however, it was necessary to flatter Watkins with dinner invitations and to work with him.

"I love lobster bisque," said Pamela Watkins. "Is this your recipe, Erika?"

"No. I found it in a magazine, but I added some spices. I doubt I've improved it, probably the opposite, but I like even lobster bisque to have a little bite."

"Oh, it's divine," the university president's wife declared after her first taste.

This compliment, at once echoed by others, brought a glow of pride to Erika's face, but when she herself raised a spoonful to her mouth, she took it with a soft, protracted slurp.

Appalled, Victor watched her dip the spoon into the bowl once more.

Soup had not been on the menu at either of their previous dinner parties, and Victor had taken a meal with Erika only twice otherwise. Her faux pas surprised and unsettled him.

She sucked in the second spoonful no less noisily than she had the first.

Although none of the guests appeared to notice this ghastly play of tongue and lips, Victor took offense that as his wife she should risk being mocked. Those who might laugh at her behind her back would also laugh at him.

He announced, "The bisque is curdled. William, Christine, please remove it at once."

"Curdled?" the mayor's wife asked, bewildered. "Not mine."

"Curdled," Victor insisted as the servants quickly retrieved the soup bowls. "And you don't want to eat a lobster dish when it might be in any way off."

Stricken, Erika watched as the bowls were removed from the table.

"I'm sorry, Erika," Victor said, into an awkward silence. "This is the first time I've ever found fault with your cooking—or with anything about you."

John Watkins protested, "Mine was delicious."

Although she might not have understood the cause of Victor's action, Erika recovered quickly. "No, John. You've always got my vote for city council. But in culinary matters, I trust Victor. His palate is as refined as any chef's."

Victor felt his clenched jaw relaxing into a genuine smile. In part, Erika had redeemed herself.

CHAPTER 25

THE GRAY VINYL-TILE FLOOR squeaked under Carson's and Michael's shoes. Although subtle, the sounds seemed loud in the otherwise silent hallway.

The forensic pathology unit appeared to be deserted. At this hour, staffing should have been reduced but not this drastically.

They found Jack Rogers where he said he'd be—in Autopsy Room Number 2. With him were the professionally fileted corpse of Bobby Allwine, supine upon a guttered steel table, and a lanky young assistant whom Jack introduced as Luke.

"Trumped up an excuse to send the rest of the night staff home," Jack said. "Didn't want to take a chance of some chatterbox getting a glimpse of what we've got here."

"And what do we have?" Carson asked.

"A miracle," Jack said. "Except I get a squamous feeling, like it's too dark a miracle to have anything to do with God. That's why only Luke and I are here. Luke isn't a gossiping jackass, are you, Luke?"

"No, sir."

Luke's slightly protuberant eyes, long nose, and longer chin gave him a scholarly look, as if books exerted such an attraction on him that they had pulled his features toward the contents of their pages.

Potbellied, with a hound-dog face full of sags and swags that added years to his true age, Jack Rogers looked older now than he usually did. Although his excitement was palpable, his face had a gray tinge.

"Luke's got a good eye for physiological anomalies," Jack said. "He knows his guts."

Luke nodded, taking pride in his boss's praise. "I've just always been interested in viscera since I was a kid."

"With me," Michael said, "it was baseball."

Jack said, "Luke and I completed every phase of the internal examination. Head, body cavities, neck, respiratory tract—"

"Cardiovascular system," Luke continued,

"gastrointestinal tract, biliary tract, pancreas, spleen, adrenals—"

"Urinary tract, reproductive tract, and musculoskeletal system," Jack concluded.

The cadaver on the table certainly appeared to have been well explored.

If the body had not been so fresh, Carson would have wanted to grease her nostrils with Vicks. She could tolerate this lesser stench of violated stomach and intestines.

"Every phase revealed such bizarre anatomy," Jack said, "we're going back through again to see what we might've missed."

"Bizarre? Such as?"

"He had two hearts."

"What do you mean two hearts?"

"Two. The number after one, before three. Uno, *dos*."

"In other words," Luke said earnestly, "twice as many as he should have had."

"We got that part," Michael assured him. "But at the library, we saw Allwine's chest open. You could have parked a Volkswagen in there. If everything's missing, how do you know he had two hearts?"

"For one thing, the associated plumbing," Jack said. "He had the arteries and veins to serve a double pump. The indicators are numerous. They'll all be in my final report. But that's not the only thing weird about Allwine."

"What else?"

"Skull bone's as dense as armor. I burnt out two electric trepanning saws trying to cut through it."

"He had a pair of livers, too," said Luke, "and a twelve-ounce spleen. The average spleen is seven ounces."

"A more extensive lymphatic system than you'll ever see in a textbook," Jack continued. "Plus two organs—I don't even know what they are."

"So he was some kind of freak," Michael said. "He looked normal on the outside. Maybe not a male model, but not the Elephant Man, either. Inside, he's all screwed up."

"Nature is full of freaks," Luke said. "Snakes with two heads. Frogs with five legs. Siamese twins. You'd be surprised how many people are born with six fingers on one hand or the other. But that's not like"—he patted Allwine's bare foot—"our buddy here."

Having trouble getting her mind around the meaning of all this, Carson said, "So what are the odds of this? Ten million to one?"

Wiping the back of his shirt sleeve across his damp brow, Jack Rogers said, "Get real, O'Connor. Nothing like this is possible, period. This isn't mutation. This is *design*."

For a moment she didn't know what to say, and perhaps for the first time ever, even Michael was at a loss for words.

Anticipating them, Jack said, "And don't ask me what I mean by *design*. Damn if I know."

"It's just," Luke elaborated, "that all these things look like they're meant to be . . . improvements."

Carson said, "The Surgeon's other victims . . . you didn't find anything weird in them?"

"Zip, zero, nada. You read the reports."

Such an aura of unreality had descended upon the room that Carson wouldn't have been entirely surprised if the eviscerated cadaver had sat up on the autopsy table and tried to explain itself.

Michael said, "Jack, we'd sure like to embargo your autopsy report on Allwine. File it here but don't send a copy to us. Our doc box is being raided lately, and we don't want anyone else to know about this for . . . say forty-eight hours."

"And don't file it under Allwine's name or the case number where it can be found," Carson suggested. "Blind file it under . . ."

"Munster, Herman," Michael suggested.

Jack Rogers was smart about a lot more things than viscera. The bags under his eyes seemed to darken as he said, "This isn't the only weird thing you've got, is it?"

"Well, you know the crime scene was strange," Carson said.

"That's not all you've got, either."

"His apartment was a freak's crib," Michael revealed. "The guy was as psychologically weird as anything you found inside him."

"What about chloroform?" Carson asked. "Was it used on Allwine?"

"Won't have blood results until tomorrow," Jack said. "But I'm not going out on a limb when I say we won't find chloroform. This guy couldn't have been overcome by it."

"Why not?"

"Given his physiology, it wouldn't have worked as fast on him as on you or me."

"How fast?"

"Hard to say. Five seconds. Ten."

"Besides," Luke offered, "if you tried to clamp a chloroform-soaked cloth over his face, Allwine's reflexes would have been faster than yours . . . or mine."

Jack nodded agreement. "And he would have been *strong*. Far too strong to have been restrained by an ordinary man for a moment, let alone long enough for the chloroform to work."

Remembering the peaceful expression on Bobby Allwine's face when his body lay on the library floor, Carson considered her initial perception that he had welcomed his own murder. She could make no more sense of that hypothesis, however, than she had done earlier.

Moments later, outside in the parking lot, as she and Michael approached the sedan, the light of the moon seemed to ripple through the thick humid air as it might across the surface of a breeze-stirred pond.

Carson remembered Elizabeth Lavenza, handless, floating facedown in the lagoon.

Suddenly she seemed half-drowned in the murky fathoms of this case, and felt an almost panicky need to thrash to the surface and leave the investigation to others.

CHAPTER 26

TO ALL OUTWARD APPEARANCES, Randal Six, Mercy-born and Mercy-raised, has been in various degrees of autistic trance all day, but inwardly he has passed those hours in turmoil.

The previous night, he dreamed of Arnie O'Connor, the boy in the newspaper clipping, the smiling autistic. In the dream, he requested the formula for happiness, but the O'Connor boy mocked him and would not share his secret.

Now Randal Six sits at his desk, at the computer on which he occasionally plays competitive crossword puzzles with gamers in far cities. Word games are not his purpose this evening.

He has found a site on which he can study maps of the city of New Orleans. Because this site also offers a city directory of all property owners, he has been able to learn the address of Detective Carson O'Connor, with whom the selfish Arnie resides.

The number of blocks separating Randal from their house is daunting. So much distance, so many people, untold obstacles, so much *disorder.*

Furthermore, this web site offers three-dimensional maps of the French Quarter, the Garden District, and several other historic areas of the city. Every time hc makes use of these more elaborate guides, he is quickly overcome by attacks of agoraphobia.

If he responds with such terror to the *virtual* reality of the cartoonlike dimensional maps, he will be paralyzed by the vastness and chaos of the world itself if ever he steps beyond these walls.

Yet he persists in studying the three-dimensional maps, for he is motivated by intense desire. His desire is to find happiness of the kind that he believes he has seen in the smile of Arnie O'Connor.

In the virtual reality of New Orleans on his computer screen, one street leads to another. Every intersection offers choices. Every block is lined with businesses, residences. Each of them is a choice.

In the real world, a maze of streets might lead him a hundred or a thousand miles. In that journey, he would be confronted with tens of thousands or even hundreds of thousands of *choices.*

The enormity of this challenge overwhelms him once more, and he retreats in a panic to a corner, his back to his room. He cannot move forward. Nothing confronts him except the junction of two walls.

His only choices are to stay facing the corner or turn to the larger room. As long as he doesn't turn, his fear subsides. Here he is safe. Here is order: the simple geometry of two walls meeting.

In time he is somewhat calmed by this pinched vista, but to be fully calmed, he needs his crosswords. In an armchair, Randal Six sits with another collection of puzzles.

He likes crosswords because there are not multiple right choices for each square; only *one* choice will result in the correct solution. All is predestined.

Cross YULETIDE with CHRISTMAS, cross CHRISTMAS with MYRRH. . . . Eventually every square will be filled; all words will be complete and will intersect correctly. The predestined solution will have been achieved. Order. Stasis. Peace.

As he fills the squares with letters, a startling thought occurs to Randal. Perhaps he and the selfish Arnie O'Connor are *predestined* to meet.

If he, Randal Six, is predestined to come face to face with the other boy and to take the precious secret of happiness from him, what seems now like a long harrowing journey to the O'Connor house will prove to be as simple as crossing this small room.

He cannot stop working the crossword, for he desperately needs the temporary peace that its completion will bring him. Nevertheless, as he reads the clues and inks the letters in the empty squares, he considers the possibility that finding happiness by relieving Arnie O'Connor of it might prove to be not a dream but a *destiny*.

CHAPTER 27

DRIVING AWAY FROM the medical examiner's office, into a world transformed by what they had just learned, Carson said, "Two hearts? Strange new organs? Designer freaks?"

"I'm wondering," Michael said, "if I missed a class at the police academy."

"Did Jack smell sober to you?"

"Unfortunately, yeah. Maybe he's nuts."

"He's not nuts."

"People who were perfectly sane on Tuesday sometimes go nuts on Wednesday."

"What people?" she asked.

"I don't know. Stalin."

"Stalin was not perfectly sane on Tuesday. Besides, he wasn't insane, he was evil."

"Jack Rogers isn't evil," Michael said. "If he's not

drunk, insane, or evil, I guess we're going to have to believe him."

"You think somehow Luke might be hoaxing old Jack?"

"Luke 'been-interested-in-viscera-since-I-was-a-kid'? First of all, it would be a way elaborate hoax. Second, Jack is smarter than Luke. Third, Luke—he's got about as much sense of humor as a grave-yard rat."

A disguise of clouds transformed the full moon into a crescent. The pale flush of streetlamps on glossy magnolia leaves produced an illusion of ice, of a northern climate in balmy New Orleans.

"Nothing is what it seems," Carson said.

"Is that just an observation," Michael asked, "or should I worry about being washed away by a flood of philosophy?"

"My father wasn't a corrupt cop."

"Whatever you say. You knew him best."

"He never stole confiscated drugs out of the evidence lockup."

"The past is past," Michael advised.

Braking to a stop at a red traffic light, she said, "A man's reputation shouldn't have to be destroyed forever by lies. There ought to be a hope of justice, redemption."

Michael chose respectful silence.

"Dad and Mom weren't shot to death by some drug dealer who felt Dad was poaching on his territory. That's all bullshit."

She hadn't spoken aloud of these things in a long time. To do so was painful.

"Dad had discovered something that powerful people preferred to keep secret. He shared it with Mom, which is why she was shot, too. I know he was troubled about something he had seen. I just don't know what it was."

"Carson, we looked at the evidence in his case a hundred times," Michael reminded her, "and we agreed it's too airtight to be real. No file of evidence is ever braided that tight unless it's concocted. In my book, it's proof of a frame. But that's the problem, too."

He was right. The evidence had been crafted not only with the intent of convicting her father postmortem, but to leave no clue as to the identity of those who had crafted it. She had long sought the one loose thread that would unravel it, but no such thread could be found.

As the traffic light turned green, Carson said, "We're not far from my place. I'm sure Vicky's got everything under control, but I feel like I ought to check on Arnie, if that's okay."

"Sure. I could use some of Vicky's bad coffee."

CHAPTER 28

IN THE MASTER BEDROOM of the Helios estate, all was not well.

What Victor wanted from sex exceeded mere pleasure. Furthermore, he did not merely *want* to be satisfied but fully *expected* to be. His expectation was in fact a demand.

According to Victor's philosophy, the world had no dimension but the material. The only rational response to the forces of nature and of human civilization was to attempt to dominate them rather than be humbled by them.

There were serfs and there were masters. He himself would never wear a slave's collar.

If there was no spiritual side to life, then there could be no such thing as love except in the minds of fools; for love is a state of spirit, not of flesh. In his view, tenderness had no place in a sexual relationship.

At its best, sex was a chance for the dominant person to express control of the submissive partner. The fierceness of the dominance and the completeness of the submission led to satisfaction of greater intensity than love could have provided even if love had existed.

Erika Four, like the three before her and like the other brides that he had made for himself, was not a partner in the traditional sense of marriage. To Victor, she was an accoutrement that allowed him to function more effectively in social situations, a defense against the annoyance of women who saw in him the prospect of wealth by marriage, and an instrument of pleasure.

Because pleasure and power were synonymous to him, the intensity of his satisfaction was directly proportional to the cruelty with which he used her. He was often *very* satisfied.

Like all of his modern creations, in a crisis she could block the perception of pain at will. During sex, he did not permit her to do so. Her submission would be more satisfyingly complete and genuine if she were made to suffer.

If he struck her particularly hard, the evidence would be gone in hours, for like all his people, she healed rapidly. Bleeding lasted less than a minute. Cuts healed without scars in a few hours. Bruises sustained in the night would have faded by dawn.

Most of his people were psychologically engineered to be utterly incapable of humiliation, for shame in all its shades grew from an acceptance of the belief that Moral Law lay at the heart of creation. In the war against ordinary humanity, which he would one day launch, he required soldiers without moral compunctions, so certain of their superiority that no ruthlessness would be beyond them.

He allowed Erika humility, however, because from humility arose a quality of innocence. Although he was not entirely sure why this should be the case, the mildest abuse of a delicate sensibility was more thrilling than committing savageries against a woman who lacked all innocence.

He forced her to endure the things that most shamed her because, ironically, the greater her shame and self-disgust, the further she would lower herself and the more obedient she would become. He had made her strong in many ways, but not so strong that he could not break her will and mold her as he wished.

He valued subservience in a wife more if it had been beaten into her than if it had been engineered in the tank, for in the latter case, her slavish obedience felt mechanical and dull.

Although he could remember a time, centuries ago in his youth, when he had felt differently about women and marriage, he could not recall or understand why that young Victor had felt the way he did, what belief had motivated him. He didn't actually try to understand, however, because he had for a long time taken this different road, and there was no going back.

Young Victor had also believed in the power of the human will to bend nature to its desires; and it was that aspect of his early self with which Victor could still identify. All that mattered was the triumph of the will.

What was wrong here in the bedroom was that for once his will failed to bend reality to its desire. He wanted sexual satisfaction, but it eluded him.

His mind kept straying back to the dinner party, to the sight and sound of Erika noisily sucking soup from spoon.

At last he rolled off her, onto his back, defeated.

They stared at the ceiling in silence until she whispered, "I'm sorry."

"Maybe the fault is mine," he said, meaning that perhaps he had made some mistake in the creation of her.

"I don't excite you."

"Usually, yes. Not tonight."

"I'll learn," she promised. "I'll improve."

"Yes," he said, for that was what she must do if she hoped to keep her role, but he had begun to doubt that Erika Four would be the final Erika.

"I'm going to the hospital," he said. "I'm in a creative mood."

"The Hands of Mercy." She shuddered. "I think I dream of it."

"You don't. I spare all of you from dreams of your origins."

"I dream of someplace," she persisted. "Dark and strange and full of death."

"There's your proof that it's not the Hands of Mercy. My labs are full of life."

Both bored with Erika and troubled by the direction of her musings, Victor rose from the bed and went naked into the bathroom.

A jewel in this mounting of gold-plated fixtures and marble-clad walls, he looked at himself in the beveled mirrors and saw something much more than human.

"Perfection," he said, though he knew that he was just shy of that ideal.

Looping through his torso, embedded in his flesh, entwining his ribs, spiraling around his spine, a flexible metallic cord and its associated implants converted simple electrical current—to which he submitted himself twice a day—into a different energy, a stimulating charge that sustained a youthful rate of cellular division and held biological time at bay.

His body was a mass of scars and strange excrescences, but he found them beautiful. They were the consequences of the procedures by which he'd gained immortality; they were the badges of his divinity.

One day he would clone a body from his DNA, enhance it with the many improvements he had developed, expedite its growth, and with the assistance of surgeons of his making, he'd have his brain transferred to that new home.

When that work was finished, he would be the model of physical perfection, but he would miss his scars. They were proof of his persistence, his genius, and the triumph of his will.

Now he got dressed, looking forward to a long night in his main laboratory at the Hands of Mercy.

CHAPTER 29

WHILE CARSON CHECKED on her castle-building brother, Michael stood at a kitchen counter with a mug of Vicky's coffee.

Having just finished cleaning the oven, Vicky Chou said, "How's the java?"

"As bitter as bile," he said.

"But not acidic."

"No," he admitted. "I don't know how you manage to make it bitter without it being acidic, but you do."

She winked. "My secret."

"Stuff's as black as tar. This isn't a mistake. You actually *try* to get it like this, don't you?"

"If it's so terrible," she said, "why do you always drink it?"

"It's a test of my manhood." He took a long swallow that made his face pucker. "I've been doing a lot of thinking lately, but you'll tell me to shut up, you don't want to know."

Washing her hands at the sink, she said, "I *have* to listen to you, Michael. It's part of my job description."

He hesitated but then said, "I've been thinking how things might be if Carson and I weren't partners."

"What things?"

"Between her and me."

"Is there something between you and her?"

"The badge," he said mournfully. "She's too solid a cop, too professional to date a partner."

"The bitch," Vicky said drily.

Michael smiled, sampled the coffee, grimaced. "Problem is, if I changed partners so we could date, I'd miss kicking ass and busting heads together."

"Maybe that's how the two of you relate best."

"There's a depressing thought."

Vicky clearly had more to say, but she clammed up when Carson entered the kitchen.

"Vicky," Carson said, "I know you're good about keeping doors locked. But for a while, let's be even more security conscious."

Frowning, Vicky asked, "What's wrong?"

"This weird case we're on...it feels like...if we're not careful, it could come home to us, right here." She glanced at Michael. "Does that sound paranoid?"

"No," he said, and finished the rest of the bitter coffee as though the taste of it would make their unsatisfying relationship seem sweeter by comparison.

❧

IN THE CAR AGAIN, as Carson swung away from the curb, Michael popped a breath mint in his mouth to kill the sour stench of Vicky's death brew. "Two hearts . . . organs of unknown purpose . . . I can't get *Invasion of the Body Snatchers* out of my head, pod people growing in the basement."

"It's not aliens."

"Maybe not. Then I think . . . weird cosmic radiation, pollution, genetic engineering, too much mustard in the American diet."

"Psychological profiles and CSI techs won't be worth a damn on this one," Carson said. She yawned. "Long day. Can't think straight anymore. What if I just drive you home and we call it a wrap?"

"Sounds swell. I've got a new pair of monkey-pattern jammies I'm eager to try on."

She took a ramp to the expressway, headed west toward Metairie. The traffic was mercifully light.

They rode in silence for a while, but then he said, "You know, if you ever want to petition the chief of detectives to reopen your dad's case and let us take a whack at it, I'm game."

She shook her head. "Wouldn't do it unless I had

something new—a fresh bit of evidence, a different slant on the investigation, something. Otherwise, we'd just be turned down."

"We sneak a copy of the file, review the evidence on our own time, look into it until we turn up the scrap we need."

"Right now," she said wearily, "we don't really have any time of our own."

As they exited the expressway, he said, "The Surgeon case will break. Things will ease up. Just remember, I'm ready when you are."

She smiled. He loved her smile. He didn't see enough of it.

"Thanks, Michael. You're a good guy."

He would have preferred to hear her say that he was the love of her life, but "good guy" was at least a starting point.

When she pulled to the curb in front of his apartment house, she yawned again and said, "I'm beat. Exhausted."

"So exhausted, you can't wait to go straight back to Allwine's apartment."

Her smile was smaller this time. "You read me too well."

"You wouldn't have stopped to check on Arnie if you intended to go home after dropping me off."

"I should know better than to bullshit a homicide dick. It's those black rooms, Michael. I need... to work them alone."

"Get in touch with your inner psychic."

"Something like that."

He got out of the car, then leaned in through the open door. "Ditch the twelve-hour days, Carson. There's no one you've got to prove anything to. Not anyone on the force. Not your dad."

"There's me."

He closed the door and watched her drive away. He knew that she was tough enough to take care of herself, but he worried about her.

He almost wished that she were more vulnerable. It half broke his heart that she didn't need him desperately.

CHAPTER 30

ROY PRIBEAUX ENJOYED the date more than he expected. Usually it was an annoying interlude between the planning of the murder and the commission of it.

Candace proved to be shy but charming, genuinely sweet with a dry, self-deprecating sense of humor.

They had coffee in a riverfront café. When they fell at once into easy conversation about a host of subjects, Roy was surprised but also pleased. The lack of any initial awkwardness would more quickly disarm the poor thing.

After a while she asked him exactly what he'd meant the previous night when he'd called himself *a Christian man*. Of what denomination, what commitment?

He knew at once that this was the key with which to unlock her trust and win her heart. He had used the Christian gambit in a couple of other instances, and with the right woman, it had worked as well as the expectation of great sex or even of love.

Why he, an Adonis, should be interested in a schlump like her—that mystery fed her suspicion. It made her wary.

If she believed, however, that he was a man of genuine moral principle who sought a virtuous companion and not just a good hump, she would see him as one with higher standards than physical beauty. She would convince herself that her lovely eyes were enough physical beauty for him and that what he really prized was her innocence, her chastity, her personality, and her piety.

The trick was to divine the brand of Christianity that she had embraced, then convince her that they shared that particular flavor of the faith. If she was a Pentecostal, his approach would have to be far different from that required if she was a Catholic, and *much* different from the worldly and ironic style that he must assume if she was Unitarian.

Fortunately, she proved to be an Episcopalian, which Roy found markedly easier to fake than one of the more passionate sects. He might have been lost if she'd been a Seventh Day Adventist.

She proved to be a reader, too, and especially a fan of C. S. Lewis, one of the finest Christian writers of the century just past.

In his quest to be a Renaissance man, Roy had read Lewis: not all of his many books, but enough. *The Screwtape Letters. The Problem of Pain. A Grief Observed.* Thankfully they had been short volumes.

Dear Candace was so enchanted to have a handsome and interested man as a conversationalist that she overcame her shyness when the subject turned to Lewis. She did most of the talking, and Roy needed only to insert a quote here and a reference there to convince her that his knowledge of the great man's work was encyclopedic.

Another fortunate thing about her being an Episcopalian was that her denomination did not forbid drink or the joy of sensuous music. From the café, he talked her into a jazz club on Jackson Square.

Roy had a capacity for alcohol, but one potent hurricane erased whatever lingering caution Candace might otherwise have harbored.

After the jazz club, when he suggested they take a walk on the levee, her only concern was that it might be closed at this hour.

"It's still open to pedestrians," he assured her. "They just don't keep it lit for the roller skaters and fishermen."

Perhaps she would have hesitated to stroll the unlighted levee if he hadn't been such a strong man, and so good, and capable of protecting her.

They walked toward the river, away from the shopping district and the crowds. The full moon provided more light than he would have liked but also enough to allay any of Candace's lingering concern about their safety.

A brightly decorated riverboat chattered by, its great paddle wheel splashing through warm water. Passengers stood on the decks, sat at tables. This late-night river cruise wouldn't stop at any nearby docks. Roy had checked the schedules, always planning ahead.

They ambled to the end of the pavement atop the breakwater of boulders. Fishermen were more likely to come this far in daylight. As he expected, here in the night, he and Candace were alone.

The lights of the receding riverboat painted serpentine ribbons of oily color on the dark water, and Candace thought this was pretty, and in fact so did Roy, and they watched it for a moment before she turned to him, expecting a chaste kiss, or even one not so chaste.

Instead, he squirted her in the face with the squeeze bottle of chloroform that he had withdrawn from a jacket pocket.

He had found this saturation technique to be far quicker, more effective, and less of a struggle than a soaked cloth. The fluid penetrated her nostrils, splashed her tongue.

Choking, gasping for breath and thereby inhaling the anesthetic, Candace dropped as suddenly and as hard as if she had been shot.

She fell on her side. Roy rolled her onto her back and knelt next to her.

Even in the insistent silvery moonlight, they presented a low profile to anyone who might look this way from a craft on the river. Glancing back the way they had come, Roy saw no other late strollers.

From an inside jacket pocket, he produced a stiletto and a compact kit of scalpels and other instruments.

He didn't need larger tools for this one. The eyes would be simple to extract, though he must be careful not to damage the part of them that he considered to be perfectly beautiful.

With the stiletto, he found her heart and conveyed her from sleep to death with only the faintest liquid sound.

Soon the eyes were his, safely in a small plastic bottle full of saline solution.

On his way back to the lights and the jazz, he was surprised when he suddenly had a taste for cotton candy, not a treat that he had ever before craved. But of course the red wagon was closed and might not open for days.

CHAPTER 31

A NINETEENTH-CENTURY stonemason had chiseled HANDS OF MERCY into a limestone block above the hospital entrance. A weathered image of the Virgin Mary overlooked the front steps.

The hospital had closed long ago, and after the building had been sold to a shell corporation controlled by Victor Helios, the windows had been bricked shut. Steel doors had been installed at every entrance, equipped with both mechanical and electronic locks.

A tall wrought-iron fence surrounded the oak-shaded property, like a stockpile of spears from a full Roman legion. To the rolling electric gate was affixed a sign: PRIVATE WAREHOUSE / NO ADMITTANCE.

Hidden cameras surveyed the grounds, the

perimeter. No nuclear weapons storage depot had a larger or more dedicated security force, or one more discreet.

The forbidding structure stood silent. No beam of light escaped it, though here the new rulers of the Earth were designed and made.

A staff of eighty lived and worked within these walls, assisting in experiments in a maze of laboratories. In rooms that had once held hospital patients, newly minted men and women were housed and rapidly educated until they could be infiltrated into the population of the city.

The armored doors of certain other rooms were locked. The creations within them needed to be restrained while being studied.

Victor conducted his most important work in the main laboratory. This vast space had a techno sensibility with some Art Deco style and a dash of Wagnerian grandeur. Glass, stainless steel, white ceramic: All were easy to sterilize if things got . . . messy.

Sleek and arcane equipment, much of which he himself designed and built, lined the chamber, rose out of the floor, depended from the ceiling. Some of the machines hummed, some bubbled, some stood silent and menacing.

In this windowless lab, if he put his wristwatch in a drawer, he could labor long hours, days, without a break. Having improved his physiology and metabolism to the point that he needed little or no sleep, he was able to give himself passionately to his work.

Tonight, as he arrived at his desk, his phone rang. The call came on line five. Of eight lines, the last four—rollovers that served a single number—were reserved for messages and inquiries from those creations with which he had been gradually populating the city.

He picked up the handset. "Yes?"

The caller, a man, was struggling to repress the emotion in his voice, more emotion than Victor ever expected to hear from one of the New Race: "Something is happening to me, Father. Something strange. Maybe something wonderful."

Victor's creations understood that they must contact him only in a crisis. "Which one are you?"

"Help me, Father."

Victor felt diminished by the word *father*. "I'm not your father. Tell me your name."

"I'm confused . . . and sometimes scared."

"I asked for your name."

His creations had not been designed to have the capability to deny him, but this one refused to identify himself: "I've begun to *change*."

"You must tell me your *name*."

"Murder," said the caller. "Murder . . . excites me."

Victor kept the growing concern out of his voice. "No, your mind is fine. I don't make mistakes."

"I'm changing. There's so much to learn from murder."

"Come to me at the Hands of Mercy."

"I don't think so. I've killed three men . . . without remorse."

"Come to me," Victor insisted.

"Your mercy won't extend to one of us who has . . . fallen so far."

A rare queasiness overcame Victor. He wondered if this might be the serial killer who enchanted the media. One of his own creations, breaking programming to commit murder *for no authorized reason*?

"Come to me, and I'll provide whatever guidance you need. There is only compassion for you here."

The electronically disguised voice denied him again. "The most recent one I killed . . . was one of yours."

Victor's alarm grew. One of his creations killing another *by its own decision*. Never had this happened before. A programmed injunction against suicide was knit tightly into their psyches, as was a stern commandment that permitted murder for just two reasons: in self-defense or when instructed by their maker to kill.

"The victim," Victor said. "His name?"

"Allwine. They found his corpse inside the city library this morning."

Victor caught his breath as he considered the implications.

The caller said, "There was nothing to learn from Allwine. He was like me inside. I've got to find it elsewhere, in others."

"Find what?" Victor asked.

"What I need," said the caller, and then hung up.

Victor keyed in *69—and discovered that the caller's phone was blocked for automatic call-back.

Furious, he slammed down the handset.

He sensed a setback.

CHAPTER 32

FOR A WHILE AFTER Victor left for the Hands of Mercy, Erika remained in bed, curled in the fetal position that she'd never known in the creation tank. She waited to see if her depression would pass or thicken into the darker morass of discouragement.

The flux of her emotional states sometimes seemed to have little relation to the experiences from which they proceeded. After sex with Victor, depression always followed without fail, and understandably; but when it *should* have ripened into something like despondency, it sometimes did not. And though her future seemed so bleak that her despondency should have been unshakable, she often shook it off.

Remembering verses by Emily Dickinson could

lift her out of gloom: *"Hope" is the thing with feathers— / That perches in the soul— / And sings the tune without the words— / And never stops at all.*

The art on Victor's walls was abstract: oddly juxtaposed blocks of color that loomed oppressively, spatterings of color or smears of gray on black that to Erika seemed like chaos or nullity. In his library, however, were large books of art, and sometimes her mood could be improved simply by immersing herself in a single painting by Albert Bierstadt or Childe Hassam.

She has been taught that she is of the New Race, posthuman, improved, superior. She is all but impervious to disease. She heals rapidly, almost miraculously.

Yet when she needs solace, she finds it in the art and music and poetry of the mere humanity that she and her kind are intended to replace.

When she has been confused, has felt lost, she's found clarity and direction in the writings of imperfect humanity. And the writers are those of whom Victor would especially disapprove.

This puzzles Erika: that a primitive and failed species, infirm humanity, should by its works lift her heart when none of her own kind is able to lift it for her.

She would like to discuss this with others of the New Race, but she is concerned that one of them will think her puzzlement makes her a heretic. All are obedient to Victor by design, but some view him with such reverential fear that they will interpret her questions as doubts, her doubts as betrayals, and will then in turn betray her to her maker.

And so she keeps her questions to herself, for she knows that in a holding tank waits Erika Five.

Abed, with the smell of Victor lingering in the sheets, Erika finds this to be one of the times when poetry will prevent depression from ripening toward despair. *If I shouldn't be alive / When the Robins come / Give the one in Red Cravat / A Memorial crumb.*

She smiled at Dickinson's gentle humor. That smile might have led to others if not for a scrabbling noise under the bed.

Throwing back the sheets, she sat up, breath held, listening.

As though aware of her reaction, the scrabbler went still—or if not still, at least silent, creeping now without a sound.

Having neither heard nor seen any indication of a rat when she and Victor had returned to the bedroom following the departure of their guests, Erika had assumed that she'd been mistaken in thinking one had been here. Or perhaps it had found its way into a wall or a drain and from there to another place in the great house.

Either the vermin was back or it had been here all along, quiet witness to the terrible tax Victor placed upon Erika's right to live.

A moment passed, and then a sound issued

from elsewhere in the room. A short-lived furtive rustle.

Shadows veiled the room, were lifted only where the light of a single bedside lamp could reach.

Naked, Erika slipped out of bed and stood, poised and alert.

Although her enhanced eyes made the most of available light, she lacked the penetrating night vision of a cat. Victor was conducting cross-species experiments these days, but she was not one of them.

Desirous of more light, she moved toward a reading lamp beside an armchair.

Before she reached the lamp, she sensed more than heard a thing on the floor scurry past her. Startled, she pulled her left foot back, pivoted on her right, and tried to sight the intruder along the path that instinct told her it must have taken.

When there was nothing to be seen—or at least nothing that she could see—she continued to the reading lamp and switched it on. More light revealed nothing that she hoped to find.

A clatter in the bathroom sounded like the small waste can being knocked over.

That door stood ajar. Darkness lay beyond.

She started toward the bathroom, moving quickly but coming to a stop short of the threshold.

Because members of the New Race were immune to most diseases and healed rapidly, they were afraid of fewer things than were ordinary human beings. That didn't mean they were utter strangers to fear.

Although hard to kill, they were not immortal, and having been made in contempt of God, they could have no hope of a life after this one. Therefore, they feared death.

Conversely, many of them feared *life* because they had no control of their destinies. They were indentured servants to Victor, and there was no sum they could work off to gain their freedom.

They feared life also because they could not surrender it if the burden of serving Victor became too great. They had been created with a deeply embedded psychological injunction against suicide; so if the void appealed to them, they were denied even that.

Here but a step from the bathroom threshold, Erika experienced another kind of fear: of the unknown.

That which is abnormal to nature is a monster, even if it might be beautiful in its way. Erika, created not by nature but by the hand of man, was a lovely monster but a monster nonetheless.

She supposed that monsters should not fear the unknown because, by any reasonable definition, they were part of it. Yet a tingle of apprehension traced the contours of her spine.

Instinct told her that the rat was not a rat, that instead it was a thing unknown.

From the bathroom came a *clink,* a clatter, a

metallic rattle, as if something had opened a cabinet and set about exploring the contents in the dark.

Erika's two hearts beat faster. Her mouth went dry. Her palms grew damp. In this vulnerability, but for the double pulse, she was so human, regardless of her origins.

She backed away from the bathroom door.

Her blue silk robe was draped over the armchair. With her gaze fixed on the bathroom door, she slipped into the robe and belted it.

Barefoot, she left the suite, closing the hall door behind her.

As the midnight hour came, she descended through the house of Frankenstein, to the library where, among the many volumes of human thought and hope, she felt safer.

CHAPTER 33

AT VICTOR'S SUMMONS, they came to him in the main lab, two young men as ordinary in appearance as any in New Orleans.

Not all the men of the New Race were handsome. Not all the women were beautiful.

For one thing, when at last he had secretly seeded enough of his creations in society to exterminate the Old Race, humanity would put up a better defense if it could identify its enemy by even the most subtle telltales of appearance. If all members of the New Race looked like gorgeous fodder for the box-office battlefields of Hollywood, their beauty would make them objects of suspicion, subject them to testing and interrogation, and ultimately expose them.

Their infinite variety, on the other hand, would ensure the winning of the war. Their variety, their physical superiority, and their ruthlessness.

Besides, though he sometimes crafted specimens breathtaking in appearance, this enterprise was not fundamentally about beauty. It was at root about power and the establishment of a New Truth.

Consequently, the young men he summoned might be considered extraordinary in appearance only because, considering what they were inside, they looked so common. Their names were Jones and Picou.

He told them about Bobby Allwine in a drawer at the morgue. "His body must disappear tonight. And all confirming evidence—tissue samples, photographs, video."

"The autopsy report, tape recordings?" asked Jones.

"If they're easily found," Victor said. "But by themselves, they confirm nothing."

Picou said, "What about the medical examiner, anyone who might have been there when the body was opened?"

"For now, let them live," Victor said. "Without the body or any evidence, all they'll have is a wild story that'll make them sound like drunks or druggies."

Although they were intellectually capable of

greater work than this garbage detail, neither Jones nor Picou complained or found their assignments demeaning. Their patient obedience was the essence of the New Race.

In the revolutionary civilization that Victor was making, as in Aldous Huxley's *Brave New World,* everyone in the social order would have a rank. And all would be content, without envy.

Huxley ordered his world with Alphas at the top, the ruling elite, followed by Betas and Gammas. Brute laborers were designated Epsilons, born to their positions in a designed society.

To Huxley, this vision had been a dystopia. Victor saw it more clearly: utopia.

He'd once met Huxley at a cocktail party. He considered the man to be an officious little prig who worried ridiculously about science becoming a juggernaut and more dogmatic than any religion could hope to be, crushing everything human from humanity. Victor found him to be rich in book knowledge, light on experience, and boring.

Nevertheless, Huxley's nightmare vision served well as Victor's ideal. He would make the Alpha class almost equal to himself, so they would be challenging company and capable of carrying out his plans for the day after humanity had been liquidated, when the Earth would serve as a platform for great accomplishments by a race of post-humans who would work together as industriously as a *hive*.

Now these two Epsilons, Oliver Jones and Byron Picou, set out like two good worker bees, eager to fulfill the roles for which they had been designed and built. They would steal Allwine's remains and dispose of them in a landfill that operated in higher ground outside the city.

The landfill was owned by Victor through another shell company, and it employed only members of the New Race. He regularly required a secure disposal site to bury forever those interesting but failed experiments that must never be discovered by ordinary humans.

Under those mountains of garbage lay a city of the dead. If ever they fossilized and were excavated by paleontologists a million years hence, what mysteries they would present, what nightmares they would inspire.

Although problems existed with the comparatively small hive—as yet only two thousand of the New Race—that he had established here in New Orleans, they would be solved. Week by week he made advances in his science and increased the number in his implacable army. He would soon begin to mass produce the tanks, creating his people not in a laboratory but by the many thousands in much larger facilities that might accurately be called *farms*.

The work was endless but rewarding. The Earth

had not been made in a day, but he had the necessary patience to *re*make it.

Now he was thirsty. From a lab refrigerator, he got a Pepsi. A little plate of chocolate chip cookies was in the fridge. He adored chocolate chip cookies. He took two.

CHAPTER 34

SOMEONE HAD PUT a police seal on Bobby Allwine's apartment door. Carson broke it.

This was a minor infraction, considering that the place was not actually a crime scene. Besides, she was, after all, a cop.

Then she used a Lockaid lock-release gun, sold only to police agencies, to spring the deadbolt. She eased the thin pick of the gun into the keyway, under the pin tumblers, and pulled the trigger. She pulled it four times before lodging all the pins at the shear line.

The Lockaid gun was more problematic than breaking the seal. The department owned several. They were kept in the gun locker with spare weapons. You were supposed to requisition one, in writing, through the duty officer each time that you had a legal right to use it.

No detective was authorized to carry a Lockaid gun at all times. Because of a screwup in the requisition process, Carson had come into permanent possession of one—and chose not to reveal that she had it.

She had never used it in violation of anyone's rights, only when it was legal and when precious time would be saved by dispensing with a written requisition. In the current instance, she couldn't violate the rights of Bobby Allwine for the simple reason that he was dead.

Although she liked those old movies, she wasn't a female Dirty Harry. She'd never yet bent a rule far enough to break it, not in a situation of true importance.

She could have awakened the superintendent and gotten a pass key. She would have enjoyed rousting the rude old bastard from his bed.

However, she remembered how he'd looked her up and down, licking his lips. Without Michael present, roused from sleep perhaps induced by wine, the super might try to play grab-ass.

Then she would have to reacquaint him with the effect of a knee to the gonads. That might necessitate an arrest, when all she wanted was to meditate on the meaning of Allwine's black-on-black apartment.

She switched on the living-room ceiling fixture,

closed the door behind her, and put the Lockaid gun on the floor.

At midnight, even with a light on, the blackness of the room proved so disorienting that she had half an idea what an astronaut might feel during a space walk, tethered to a shuttle, on the night side of Earth.

The living room offered nothing but the black vinyl armchair. Because it stood alone, it seemed a little like a throne, one that had been built not for earthly royalty but for a middle-rank demon.

Although Allwine had not been killed here, Carson sensed that getting a handle on the psychology of this particular victim would contribute to her understanding of the Surgeon. She sat in his chair.

Harker claimed that the black rooms expressed a death wish, and Carson grudgingly conceded that his interpretation made sense. Like a stopped clock, Harker could be right now and then, although not as often as twice a day.

A death wish did not, however, entirely explain either the décor or Allwine. This black hole was also about *power,* just as real black holes, in far reaches of the universe, exert such gravitational pull that not even light can escape them.

These walls, these ceilings, these floors had not been painted by a man in a state of despair; despair enervated and did not inspire action. She could more easily imagine Allwine blackening these walls in an energetic anger, in a frenzy of rage.

If that was true, then at what had his rage been directed?

The arms of the chair were wide and plumply padded. Under her hands, she felt numerous punctures in the vinyl.

Something pricked her right palm. From the padding beneath a puncture, she extracted a pale crescent: a broken-off fingernail.

A closer look revealed scores of curved punctures.

The chair and the room chilled her as deeply as if she had been sitting on a block of ice in a cooler.

Carson hooked her hands, spread her fingers. She discovered that each of her nails found a corresponding slit in the vinyl.

The upholstery was thick, tough, flexible. Extreme pressure would have been required for fingernails to puncture it.

Logically, despair would not produce the intensity of emotion needed to damage the vinyl. Even rage might not have been sufficient if Allwine had not been, as Jack Rogers had said, inhumanly strong.

She rose, wiping her hands on her jeans. She felt unclean.

In the bedroom, she switched on the lights. The pervasive black surfaces soaked up the illumination.

Someone had opened one of the black blinds. The apartment was such a grim world unto itself that the streetlamps, the distant neon, and the glow of the city seemed out of phase with Allwine's realm, as if they should have existed in different, isolated universes.

Beside the bed, she opened the nightstand drawer, where she discovered Jesus. His face looked out at her from a litter of small pamphlets, His right hand raised in blessing.

From among perhaps a hundred pamphlets, she selected four and discovered that they were memorial booklets of the kind distributed to mourners at funerals. The name of the deceased was different on each, though all came from the Fullbright Funeral Home.

Nancy Whistler, the librarian who had found Allwine's body, said he went to mortuary viewings because he felt at peace there.

She pocketed the four booklets and closed the drawer.

The smell of licorice hung on the air as thick as it had been earlier in the day. Carson couldn't shake the disturbing idea that someone had recently been burning the black candles that stood on a tray on the windowseat.

She crossed to the candles to feel the wax around the wicks, half expecting it to be warm. No. Cold and hard, all of them.

Her impression of the scene beyond the window was unnerving but entirely subjective. Enduring New Orleans hadn't changed. In the grip of creeping paranoia, however, she saw not the festive city that she knew, but an ominous metropolis, an alien place of unnatural angles, throbbing darkness, eerie light.

A reflection of movement on the glass pulled her focus from the city to the surface of the pane. A tall figure stood in the room behind her.

She reached under her jacket, placing her hand upon the 9mm pistol in her shoulder holster. Without drawing it, she turned.

The intruder was tall and powerful, dressed in black. Perhaps he had entered from the living room or from the bathroom, but he seemed to have materialized out of the black wall.

He stood fifteen feet away, where shadows hid his face. His hands hung at his sides—and seemed as big as shovels.

"Who're you?" she demanded. "Where'd you come from?"

"You're Detective O'Connor." His deep voice had a timbre and a resonance that in another man would have conveyed only self-assurance but that, combined with his size, suggested menace. "You were on TV."

"What're you doing here?"

"I go where I want. In two hundred years, I've learned a great deal about locks."

His implication left Carson no choice but to draw her piece. She pointed the muzzle at the floor, but said, "That's criminal trespass. Step into the light."

He did not move.

"Don't be stupid. Move. Into. The. Light."

"I've been trying to do that all my life," he said as he took two steps forward.

She could not have anticipated his face. Handsome on the left, somehow *wrong* on the right side. Over that wrongness, veiling it, was an elaborate design reminiscent of but different from a Maori tattoo.

"The man who lived here," the intruder said, "was in despair. I recognize his pain."

Although he had already stopped, he *loomed* and could have been upon her in two strides, so Carson said, "That's close enough."

"He was not made of God ... and had no soul. He agonized."

"You have a name? Very carefully, very slowly, show me some ID."

He ignored her order. "Bobby Allwine had no free will. He was in essence a slave. He wanted to die but couldn't take his own life."

If this guy was correct, Harker had nailed it. Each razor blade in the bathroom wall marked a failed attempt at self-destruction.

"We have," the intruder said, "a built-in proscription against suicide."

"We?"

"Allwine was full of fury, too. He wanted to kill his maker. But we are also designed to be incapable of raising a hand against him. I tried long ago ... and he nearly killed me."

Every modern city has its crazies, and Carson thought she knew all the tropes, but this guy had a different edge from what she had encountered before, and a disturbing intensity.

"I tried going to his house to study it from a distance ... but if I'd been seen, he might have finished me. So I came here. The case interested me, because of the missing heart. I was in part made from such stolen essentials."

Whether this hulk was the Surgeon or not, he didn't sound like the kind of citizen who made the city safer by being on the streets.

She said, "Too weird. Spread your arms, get on your knees."

Although it must have been a trick of light, she thought a luminous pulse passed through his eyes as he said, "I bow to no one."

CHAPTER 35

I BOW TO NO ONE.

No suspect had ever challenged her in such a poetic fashion.

Wound tight, wary, edging sideways from the window because her back felt exposed, she said, "I wasn't *asking.*"

She took a two-hand grip on the pistol, pointed it at him.

"Will you shoot me in the heart?" he asked. "You'll need two rounds."

Allwine lying on the autopsy table. Chest open. The associated plumbing for two hearts.

"I came here thinking Allwine was an innocent man," he said, "torn open to provide the heart for another . . . experiment. But it's not that simple anymore."

He moved, and for an instant she thought he was coming at her: "Don't be stupid."

Instead he went past her to the window. "Every city has its secrets, but none as terrible as this. Your quarry isn't a crazed murderer. Your real enemy is his maker . . . and mine, too."

Still reeling from his apparent claim to have two hearts, she said, "What do you mean, I'll need two rounds?"

"His techniques are more sophisticated now. But he created me with bodies salvaged from a prison graveyard."

When he turned away from the window, facing Carson again, she glimpsed that subtle pulse of luminosity passing through his eyes.

"My one heart from a mad arsonist," he said. "The other from a child molester."

Their positions had been reversed. His back was to the window, hers to the bathroom door. Suddenly she wondered if he'd come alone.

She put herself at an angle to him, trying to watch him directly while keeping the bathroom threshold in her peripheral vision.

This put the door to the living room behind her. She could not cover every approach by which she might be assaulted, overwhelmed.

"My hands were taken from a strangler," he said. "My eyes from an ax murderer. My life force from a thunderstorm. And that strange storm gave me gifts that Victor couldn't grant. For one thing . . ."

He moved so fast that she did not see him take a step. He was at the window but then *right in her face*.

Not since her first days at the police academy, when she'd been in training, had Carson been out-maneuvered, overpowered. Even as he seemed to materialize in front of her, he boldly wrenched the pistol out of her hand—a shot discharged, shattering a window—and then he was around her, behind her.

She *thought* he went behind her, but when she turned, he seemed to have vanished.

Even dressed in black in this black room, he could not make a shadow of himself. He was too big to play chameleon in a dark corner.

His unmistakable voice came from the window-seat—"I'm not the monster anymore"—but when Carson spun to face him, he wasn't there.

Again he spoke, seemingly from the doorway to the living room—"I'm your best hope"—yet when she turned a third time in search of him, she was still alone.

She didn't find him in the living room, either, though she did recover her service pistol. The weapon lay on the floor beside the Lockaid lock-release gun, which she had left there earlier.

The door to the public hallway stood open.

Wishing that her thudding heart would quiet, she ejected the magazine. The telltale gleam of brass confirmed that the weapon was loaded but for the one expended round.

Slamming the magazine into the pistol, she cleared the doorway fast, staying low, weapon in front of her.

The corridor was deserted. She held her breath but did not hear any footsteps thundering down the stairs. All quiet.

Considering the shot that had accidentally discharged, she could be reasonably sure that someone in the apartment across the hall was watching her through the fish-eye lens in that door.

She stepped back into the black hole, snatched up the Lockaid gun, and pulled the door shut. She left the building.

As she reached the bottom of the stairs, she realized that she had not switched off the lights in the apartment. To hell with it. Allwine was too dead to care about his electric bill.

CHAPTER 36

IN A CORNER of the main lab, Randal Six had been strapped in a cruciform posture at the center of a spherical device that resembled one of those exercise machines that could rotate a person on any imaginable axis, the better to stress all muscles equally. This, however, was not an exercise session.

Randal would not move the machine; the machine would move him, and not for the purpose of building mass or maintaining muscle tone. From head to both feet, to the tip of every finger on both hands, he was locked into a precisely determined position.

A rubber wedge in his mouth prevented him from biting his tongue if he suffered convulsions. A chin strap did not allow him to open his mouth and perhaps accidentally swallow the wedge.

These precautions would also effectively muffle his screams.

The Hands of Mercy had been insulated against the escape of any sound that might attract attention. A researcher involved in cutting-edge science, however, Victor could not be too cautious.

And so . . .

The brain is an electrical apparatus. Its wave patterns can be measured with an EEG machine.

After Randal Six had been extensively educated by direct-to-brain data downloading but while the boy had remained unconscious in the forming tank, Victor had established in his creation's brain electrical patterns identical to those found in several autistic people that he had studied.

His hope had been that this would result in Randal being "born" as an eighteen-year-old autistic of a severe variety. This fond hope had been realized.

Having imposed autism upon Randal, Victor sought to restore normal brain function through a variety of techniques. Thus far he had not been successful.

His purpose in reverse-engineering Randal's release from autism was *not* to find a cure. Finding a cure for autism interested him not at all, except that it might be a source of profits if he chose to market it.

Instead, he pursued these experiments because if he could impose and relieve autism at will, he should be able to learn to impose *selected degrees* of it. This might have valuable economic and social benefits.

Imagine a factory worker whose productivity is low due to the boring, repetitive nature of his job. Selective autism might be a means by which said worker could be made to focus *intently* on the task with an obsession that would make him as productive as—but cheaper than—a robot.

The lowest level of Epsilons in the precisely ranked social strata of Victor's ideal society might be little more than machines of meat. They would waste no time in idle chatter with their fellow workers.

Now he threw the switch that activated the spherical device in which Randal Six was strapped. It began to rotate, three revolutions on one axis, five on another, seven on yet another, slowly at first but steadily gaining speed.

A nearby wall contained a high-resolution nine-foot-square plasma screen. A colorful ultrasound display revealed the movement of blood through Randal Six's cerebral veins and arteries as well as the subtlest currents in his cerebrospinal fluid as it circulated between the meninges, through the cerebral ventricles, and in the brain stem.

Victor suspected that with the properly calculated application of extreme centrifugal and centripetal forces, he could establish unnatural conditions in cerebral fluids that would improve his chances of converting Randal's autism-characteristic brain-waves into normal cerebral electrical patterns.

As the machine spun faster, faster, the subject's groans and terrified wordless pleas escalated into screams of anguish and agony. His shrieks would have been annoying if not for the wedge in his mouth and the chin strap.

Victor hoped to achieve a breakthrough before he tested the boy to destruction. So much time would have been wasted if he had to start all over again with Randal Seven.

Sometimes Randal bit the rubber wedge so hard for so long that his teeth sank in it to the gum line, whereafter it had to be cut out of his locked jaws in pieces. This sounded as if it might be one of those occasions.

CHAPTER 37

A WHITE PICKET FENCE met white gateposts inlaid with seashells. The gate itself featured a unicorn motif.

Under Carson's feet, the front walkway twinkled magically as flecks of mica in the flagstones reflected moonlight. Moss between the stones softened her footsteps.

Almost thick enough to feel, the fragrance of the magnolia-tree flowers swagged the air.

The windows of the fairy-tale bungalow were flanked by blue shutters from which had been cut star shapes and crescent moons.

Trellises partially enclosed the front porch, entwined by leafy vines graced with trumpetlike purple blooms.

Kathleen Burke, who lived in this little oasis of

fantasy, was a police psychiatrist. Her work demanded logic and reason, but in her private life, she retreated into gentle escapism.

At three o'clock in the morning, the windows revealed no lights.

Carson rang the bell and then at once knocked on the door.

A soft light bloomed inside, and quicker than Carson expected, Kathy opened the door. "Carson, what's up, what's wrong?"

"It's Halloween in August. We gotta talk."

"Girl, if you were a cat, you'd have your back up and your tail tucked."

"You're lucky I didn't show up with a load in my pants."

"Oh, that's an elegant thing to say. Maybe you've been partnered too long with Michael. Come in. I just made some hazelnut coffee."

Entering, Carson said, "I didn't see any lights."

"At the back, in the kitchen," Kathy said, leading the way.

She was attractive, in her late thirties, molasses-black with Asian eyes. In Chinese-red pajamas with embroidered cuffs and collar, she cut an exotic figure.

In the kitchen, a steaming mug of coffee stood on the table. Beside it lay a novel; on the cover, a woman in a fantastic costume rode the back of a flying dragon.

"You always read at three in the morning?" Carson asked.

"Couldn't sleep."

Carson was too edgy to sit. She didn't pace the kitchen so much as twitch back and forth in it. "This is your home, Kathy, not your office. That matters—am I right?"

Pouring coffee, Kathy said, "What's happened? What're you so jumped up about?"

"You're not a psychiatrist here. You're just a friend here. Am I right?"

Putting the second mug of coffee on the table, returning to her own chair, Kathy said, "I'm always your friend, Carson—here, there, anywhere."

Carson stayed on her feet, too wound up to sit down. "None of what I tell you here can end up in my file."

"Unless you killed someone. Did you kill someone?"

"Not tonight."

"Then spit it out, girlfriend. You're getting on my nerves."

Carson pulled a chair out from the table, sat down. She reached for the mug of coffee, hesitated, didn't pick it up.

Her hand was trembling. She clenched it into a fist. Very tight. Opened it. Still trembling.

"You ever see a ghost, Kathy?"

"I've taken the haunted New Orleans tour, been to the crypt of Marie Laveau at night. Does that count?"

Clutching the handle of the mug, staring at her white knuckles, Carson said, "I'm serious. I mean any weird shit you can't wrap your head around. Ghosts, UFO, Big Foot . . ." She glanced at Kathy. "Don't look at me that way."

"What way?"

"Like a psychiatrist."

"Don't be so defensive." Kathy patted the book with the dragon on the cover. "I'm the one reads three fantasy novels a week and wishes she could actually *live* in one."

Carson blew on her coffee, tentatively took a sip, then a longer swallow. "I need this. Haven't slept. No *way* I'll sleep tonight."

Kathy waited with professional patience.

After a moment, Carson said, "People talk about the unknown, the mystery of life, but I've never seen one squirt of mystery in it."

"Squirt?"

"Squirt, drop, spoonful—whatever. I *want* to see mystery in life—who doesn't?—some mystical meaning, but I'm a fool for logic."

"Until now? So tell me about your ghost."

"He wasn't a ghost. But he sure was *something*. I've been driving around the past hour, maybe longer, trying to find the right words to explain what happened. . . ."

"Start with *where* it happened."

"I was at Bobby Allwine's apartment—"

Leaning forward, interested, Kathy said, "The

Surgeon's latest victim. I've been working up a profile on the killer. He's hard to figure. Psychotic but
controlled. No obvious sexual component. So far he
hasn't left much forensic evidence at the scene. No
fingerprints. A garden-variety psychopath isn't usually so prudent."

Kathy seemed to realize that she had seized the
wheel of the conversation. Relinquishing it, she sat
back in her chair.

"Sorry, Carson. We were talking about your
ghost."

Kathy Burke could probably keep her police
work separate from their friendship, but she would
find it more difficult to take off her psychiatrist hat
and keep it off when she heard what Carson had
come here to tell her.

*A giant with a strangely deformed face, claiming to
have been made from the body parts of criminals, claiming
to have been brought to life by lightning, capable of such
nimbleness of movement, such uncanny stealth, such inhuman speed that he could be nothing less than supernatural
and, therefore, might be what he claimed to be . . .*

"Hello? Your ghost?"

Instead of replying, Carson drank more coffee.

"That's it?" Kathy asked. "Just the tease, and
then good-bye?"

"I feel a little guilty."

"Good. I was ready for some spooky dish."

"If I tell you as a friend, I compromise you professionally. You'll need to report my ass for an OIS investigation."

Kathy frowned. "Officer involved shooting? Just how serious is this, Carson?"

"I didn't smoke anybody. Didn't even wing him, as far as I know."

"Tell me. I won't report you."

Carson smiled affectionately. "You'd do the right thing. You'd report me, all right. And you'd write me up an order for some couch time."

"I'm not as righteous as you think I am."

"Yes, you are," Carson said. "That's one reason I like you."

Kathy sighed. "I'm all primed for a campfire tale, and you won't spook me. Now what?"

"We could make an early breakfast," Carson suggested. "Assuming you've got any real food here in elfland."

"Eggs, bacon, sausages, hash browns, brioche toast."

"All of the above."

"You're going to be one of those blimp cops."

"Nah. I'll be dead long before that," Carson said, and more than half believed it.

CHAPTER 38

ROY PRIBEAUX LIKED TO RISE well before dawn to undertake his longevity regimen—except on those occasions when he had been up late the previous night murdering someone.

Nothing was quite as luxurious as lingering in bed with the knowledge that a new piece of the ideal woman had so recently been wrapped, bagged, and stored in the freezer. One felt the satisfaction of accomplishment, the swelling pride of work well done, which made an extra hour in the sheets seem justified and therefore sweet.

Getting Candace's eyes and preserving them had not required him to be out as late as he'd been on other harvests, but he still would have lazed in bed if he hadn't been amazingly energized by the fact that *his collection was complete.* The perfect eyes had been the last item on his list.

He slept deeply but for just a few hours, every minute in the arms of rapturous dreams, and sprang out of bed profoundly rested and with enthusiasm for the day ahead.

An array of high-end exercise machines occupied a portion of his loft. In shorts and tank top, he followed a circuit of weight machines that brought a burn to every muscle group in graduated sets ending in his maximum resistance. Then he worked up a positively tropical sweat on the treadmill and the ski trainer.

His morning shower always took a while. He lathered with two soaps: first an exfoliating bar with a loofa sponge, followed by a moisturizing bar and soft cloth. For the most complete cleanliness achievable and perfect follicle health, he used two natural shampoos, followed by a cream conditioner that he rinsed out after precisely thirty seconds.

The sun finally rose as he applied a skin-conditioning lotion from his neck to the bottoms of his feet. He did not neglect a single square inch of his magnificently maintained body, and used a spatula-style sponge to reach the middle of his back.

This lotion wasn't merely a moisturizer, but also a youthenizing emollient rich in free-radical-scavenging vitamins. If he had left the bottoms of his feet untreated, he'd have been an immortal walking on a dying man's soles, a thought that made him shudder.

After applying the usual series of revitalizing substances to his face—including a cream enriched with liquified monkey embryos—Roy regarded his reflection in the vanity mirror with satisfaction.

For a few years, he had succeeded in fully arresting the aging process. More exciting, he had recently begun to reverse the effects of time, and week by week he had watched himself grow younger.

Others deluded themselves into thinking they were rolling back the years, but Roy knew his success was real. He had arrived at the most perfectly effective combination of exercise, diet, nutritional supplements, lotions, and meditation.

The final key ingredient had been purified New Zealand lamb's urine, of which he drank four ounces a day. With a lemon wedge.

This turning back of the clock was highly desirable, of course, but he reminded himself that he could youthenize himself too far. If he reversed himself to the condition of a twenty-year-old and stayed there for a hundred years, that would be good; but if he got carried away and made himself twelve again, that would be bad.

He had not enjoyed his childhood and adolescence the first time around. Repeating any portion of them, even if solely in physical appearance, would be a glimpse of Hell.

After Roy dressed, as he stood in the kitchen,

washing down twenty-four capsules of supplements with grapefruit juice prior to preparing breakfast, he was abruptly struck by the realization that his life now had no purpose.

For the past two years, he had been collecting the anatomical components of the perfect woman, first in a variety of locations far removed from New Orleans, then lately and with particular frenzy here in his own backyard. But as of Candace, he had them all. Hands, feet, lips, nose, hair, breasts, eyes, and so much more—he had forgotten nothing.

Now what?

He was surprised that he had not thought further than this. Being a man of leisure, he had a lot of time on his hands; being an immortal, he had eternity.

This thought proved suddenly daunting.

Now he slowly realized that during the years of searching and harvesting, he had superstitiously and unconsciously assumed that when his collection was complete, when the freezer was filled with all the jigsaw pieces of the most perfectly beautiful woman, then a living woman, embodying every one of those features and qualities, would magically come into his life. He had been engaged on a kind of hoodoo quest with the purpose of shaping his romantic destiny.

Perhaps this mojo would work. Perhaps this very afternoon, as he strolled the Quarter, he would come face to face with her dazzling, bewitching self.

If the days passed without this desired encounter, however, days and weeks and months... what then?

He yearned to share his perfection with a woman who would be his equal. Until that moment came, life would be empty, without purpose.

An uneasiness overcame him. He tried to quell it with breakfast.

As he ate, he became fascinated with his hands. They were more than beautiful male hands; they were exquisite.

Oh, but until he found his goddess—not in pieces but whole and alive, without fault or deficiency—his flawless hands would not be able to caress the perfection that was their erotic destiny.

His uneasiness grew.

CHAPTER 39

AT DAYBREAK, with the rising sun not yet at an angle to fire the stained-glass windows, Our Lady of Sorrows sheltered a congregation of shadows. The only light came from the illuminated stations of the cross and from the candles in the ruby-red glass votive cups.

The humidity and early heat ripened the fragrances of incense, tallow, and lemon-scented wax. Inhaling this mélange, Victor imagined he would be sweating it through every pore for the rest of the day.

His footsteps on the marble floor echoed from the groin vaults overhead. He liked the crisp coldness of this sound, which he fancied spoke truth to the cloying atmosphere of the church.

With the first Mass of the day still half an hour away, the only person present, other than Victor, was Patrick Duchaine. He waited, as instructed, on a pecan pew in the front row.

The man rose nervously, but Victor said, "Sit, sit," not quite in the tone he might use to decline a courtesy, but in a tone rather like the one in which he might speak with impatience to a vexing dog.

At sixty, Patrick had white hair, an earnest grandfatherly face, and eyes moist with perpetual compassion. His looks alone inspired the trust and affection of his parishioners.

Add to appearances a gentle, musical voice. A warm, easy laugh. Furthermore, he had the genuine humility of a man who knew too well his place in the scheme of things.

Father Duchaine was the image of an unassailably good priest to whom the faithful would give their hearts. And to whom they would confess their sins without hesitation.

In a community with many Catholics—practicing and not—Victor found it useful to have one of his people manning the confessional in which some of the city's more powerful citizens went to their knees.

Patrick Duchaine was one of those rare members of the New Race who had been cloned from the DNA of an existing human being rather than having been designed from scratch by Victor. Physiologically, he had been improved, but to the eye he was the Patrick Duchaine who had been born of man and woman.

The real Father Duchaine had donated to a Red Cross blood drive, unwittingly providing the material from which he could be replicated. These days, he rotted under tons of garbage, deep in the landfill, while his Doppelgänger tended to the souls at Our Lady of Sorrows.

Replacing real human beings with replicas entailed risks that Victor seldom wished to take. Although the duplicate might look and sound and move exactly like its inspiration, the *memories* of the original could not be transferred to him.

The closest relatives and friends of the replaced individual were certain to notice numerous gaps in his knowledge of his personal history and relationships. They wouldn't imagine he was an imposter, but they would surely think that he was suffering from a mental or physical ailment; they would press him to seek medical attention.

In addition, out of concern, they would watch him closely and would not entirely trust him. His ability to blend in with society and to carry out his work in the service of the New Race would be compromised.

In the case of the priest, he'd had no wife, of course, and no children. His parents were dead, as was his only brother. While he had many friends and parishioners to whom he was close, no *intimate* family existed to note his memory gaps throughout the day.

In the lab Victor raised this Father Duchaine from spilled blood before the real Father Duchaine had died, a trick more complicated than the one that the man from Galilee had performed with Lazarus.

Sitting in the front pew beside his priest, Victor said, "How do you sleep? Do you dream?"

"Not often, sir. Sometimes... a nightmare about the Hands of Mercy. But I can never recall the details."

"And you never will. That's my gift to you—no memory of your birth. Patrick, I need your help."

"Anything, of course."

"One of my people is having a serious crisis of the mind. I don't know who he is. He called me... but he is afraid to come to me."

"Perhaps... not afraid, sir," the priest said. "Ashamed. Ashamed that he has failed you."

That statement troubled Victor. "How could you suggest such a thing, Patrick? The New Race has no capacity for shame."

Only Erika had been programmed to know shame, and only because Victor found her more erotic in the throes of it.

"Shame," he told Patrick, "isn't a virtue. It's a

weakness. No Natural Law requires it. We *rule* nature . . . and transcend it."

The priest evaded Victor's gaze. "Yes, sir, of course. I think what I meant was . . . maybe he feels a sort of . . . regret that he hasn't performed to your expectations."

Perhaps the priest would need to be watched closely or even subjected to a day-long examination in the lab.

"Search the city, Patrick. Spread the word among my people. Maybe they've seen one of their kind behaving oddly. I'm charging you and a few other key people with this search, and I know that you *will* perform up to my expectations."

"Yes, sir."

"If you find him and he runs . . . kill him. You know how your kind can be killed."

"Yes, sir."

"Be cautious. He's already killed one of you," Victor revealed.

Surprised, the priest met his eyes again.

"I'd prefer to have him alive," Victor continued. "But at least I need his body. To study. Bring him to me at the Hands of Mercy."

They were near enough to the rack of votive candles that the pulsing crimson reflections of the flames crawled Patrick's face.

This inspired Victor to ask "Do you sometimes wonder if you're damned?"

"No, sir," the priest answered, but with a hesitation. "There is no Hell or Heaven. This is the one life."

"Exactly. Your mind is too well made for superstition." Victor rose from the pew. "God bless you, Patrick." When the priest's eyes widened with surprise, Victor smiled and said, "That was a joke."

CHAPTER 40

WHEN CARSON PICKED UP Michael at his apartment house, he got in the car, looked her over, and said, "Those are yesterday's clothes."

"Suddenly you're a fashion critic."

"You look . . . rumpled."

As she pulled away from the curb, she said, "Rumpled, my ass. I look like a cow pie in a bad wig."

"You didn't get any sleep?"

"Maybe I'm done with sleep forever."

"If you've been up more than twenty-four hours, you shouldn't be driving," he said.

"Don't worry about it, Mom." She took a tall Starbucks cup from between her thighs, drank through a straw. "I'm so wired on caffeine, I've got the reflexes of a pit viper."

"Do pit vipers have quick reflexes?"

"You want to get in a pit with one and see?"

"You *are* wound tight. What's happened?"

"Saw a ghost. Scared the crap out of me."

"What's the punch line?"

What she hadn't been able to say to Kathy Burke, she could say to Michael. In police work, partners were closer than mere friends. They had better be. They daily trusted each other with their lives.

If you couldn't share everything with your partner, you needed a new partner.

Nevertheless, she hesitated before she said, "He seemed to walk out of walls, disappear into them. Big sucker, but he moves quicker than the eye."

"Who?"

"You listening to *anything* I'm saying? The ghost, that's who."

"You spiking that coffee with something?"

"He said he's made from pieces of criminals."

"Slow down. You're driving too fast."

Carson accelerated. "The hands of a strangler, one heart from a mad arsonist, one from a child molester. His life force from a thunderstorm."

"I don't get it."

"Neither do I."

BY THE TIME Carson parked in front of Fullbright's Funeral Home, she had told Michael everything that happened in Allwine's apartment.

His face revealed no skepticism, but his tone of voice was the equivalent of raised eyebrows: "You were tired, in a weird place—"

"He took a *gun* away from me," she said, which might have been the essence of her astonishment, the one thing about the experience that had seemed the most supernatural. "No one takes a gun away from me, Michael. *You* want to try?"

"No. I enjoy having testicles. All I'm saying is that he was dressed in black, the apartment is black, so the disappearing trick was probably just a trick."

"So maybe he manipulated me, and I saw what he wanted me to see. Is that it?"

"Doesn't that make more sense?"

"Sure damn does. But if it was a trick, he should be headlining a magic act in Vegas."

Looking at the funeral home, Michael said, "Why're we here?"

"Maybe he didn't really move faster than the eye, and maybe he didn't *in fact* vanish into thin air, but he was dead-on when he said Allwine was in despair, wanted to die . . . but couldn't kill himself."

From a pocket she withdrew the four memorial booklets and handed them to Michael.

"Bobby had like a hundred of these," she continued, "in a drawer of his nightstand. All from different funerals at this place. Death appealed to him."

She got out of the car, slammed the driver's door, and met Michael on the sidewalk.

He said, "'Life force from a thunderstorm.' What the hell does that mean?"

"Sometimes like a soft lightning throbs through his eyes."

Hurrying at her side, Michael said, "You've always been stone solid until now, like Joe Friday with no Y chromosome. Now you're Nancy Drew on a sugar rush."

Like so many things in New Orleans, the mortuary seemed as much a dream place as a reality. It had once been a Gothic Revival mansion and no doubt still served as the mortician's residence as well as his place of business. The weight of the lavish rococo millwork must have been only a few pounds shy of the critical load needed to buckle the eaves, implode the walls, and collapse the roof.

Live oaks dating to the plantation era shaded the house, while camellias, gardenias, mimosa, and tea roses cast a scene-saturating perfume. Bees buzzed lazily from bloom to bloom, too fat and happy to sting, besotted by rich nectar.

At the front door, Carson rang the bell. "Michael, don't you sometimes sense there's more to life than the grind—some amazing secret you can almost see from the corner of your eye?" Before he could reply, she plunged on: "Last night I saw something amazing...something I can't put into words. It's almost like UFOs exist."

"You and me—we've put guys in psych wards who talk like that."

A bearish, dour-looking man answered the door and acknowledged in the most somber tones that he was indeed Taylor Fullbright.

Flashing her police ID, Carson said, "Sir, I'm sorry I didn't call ahead, but we're here on a rather urgent matter."

Brightening at the discovery that they were not a bereaved couple in need of counseling, Fullbright revealed his true convivial nature. "Come in, come in! I was just cremating a customer."

CHAPTER 41

FOR A LONG TIME after the session in the spinning rack, Randal Six lies on his bed, not sleeping—for he seldom sleeps—facing the wall, his back to the room, shutting out the chaos, allowing his mind slowly, slowly to grow still.

He does not know the purpose of the treatment, but he is certain that he cannot endure many more of those sessions. Sooner than later, he will suffer a massive stroke; the failure of an inner vessel will do what a bullet to his armored skull cannot as easily achieve.

If a cerebral aneurysm does not finish him, he will surely trade the developmental disability called autism for genuine psychosis. He will seek in madness the peace that mere autism is not always able to ensure.

In his darkest moments, Randal wonders whether the spinning rack is a treatment, as Father has repeatedly called it, or if it might be intended as torture.

Not born of God and alienated from belief, this is the closest he can come to a blasphemous thought: that Father is a cruel rather than a caring maker, that Father himself is psychotic and his entire enterprise an insane endeavor.

Whether Father is sincere or deceitful, whether his project is genius or dementia, Randal Six knows that he himself will never find happiness in the Hands of Mercy.

Happiness lies streets away, a little less than three miles from here, at the home of one Carson O'Connor. In that house lies a secret to be taken if it isn't freely offered: the cause of Arnie O'Connor's smile, the reason for the moment of joy captured in the newspaper photo, no matter how brief it might have been.

As soon as possible, he must get to the O'Connor boy, before the cerebral aneurysm that kills him, before the spinning rack whirls him into madness.

Randal is not locked in his room. His autism, which is at times complicated by agoraphobia, keeps him this side of the threshold more securely than could locks or chains.

Father often encourages him to explore from end to end of the building, even floors above and below this one. Adventurousness will be a first proof that his treatments are working.

No matter where he goes in the building, he cannot leave, for the exterior doors are wired to a security system. He would be caught before he escaped the grounds . . . and might be punished with a very long session in the spinning rack.

Anyway, when he occasionally leaves his room and wanders the halls, he never dares to go far, never a fraction as far as Father would like to see him travel. Sometimes even a distance of thirty feet presents him with an overload of sights and sounds that brings him trembling to his knees.

In his self-isolation, he nonetheless sees. He hears. He learns. He knows of a way out of Mercy that will not trigger an alarm.

He may not have sufficient fortitude to reach that special door, let alone to confront the busier world beyond. But his despondency has recently advanced to desperation, and the reckless action that is the whip of desperation may lash into him a kind of courage.

He will leave this coming night, in little more than twelve hours.

CHAPTER 42

THE QUIET RECEIVING FOYER featured a baroque frieze instead of traditional crown moldings: deeply carved acanthus leaves punctuated every two feet and at the corners by the heads of angels alternating with gargoyles or perhaps mocking demons.

Inlaid in the forest-green marble floor, a foot-wide circular work of marquetry employed lighter marbles to portray mythological beings—gods, goddesses, and demigods—in perpetual pursuit. Even without dropping to his knees, Michael could see that some of the pursuit involved sexual fondling.

Only in New Orleans would either of these elements have seemed suitable to a funeral home. The house had probably been built around 1850 by nouveau riche newcomers who hadn't been welcome in the Creole sections of town. In this city, time eventually conferred dignity on what had once been outrageous as well as on what had been classic from the day it had been erected.

Studying a photo of Bobby Allwine that Carson had given him, Taylor Fullbright said, "This is the very gentleman, yes. I felt sorry for the poor soul—so many of his friends were dying. Then I realized he didn't know any of the deceased."

Carson said, "He—what?—just got a thrill being around dead people?"

"Nothing that kinky," said Fullbright. "He just . . . seemed to be at peace around them."

"That's what he said—he was at peace?"

"The only thing I can remember he said was 'Death can be as much a gift as a curse,' which is often true."

"Did you confront him about coming to all these viewings?"

"Confrontation isn't my style, Detective. Some funeral directors are solemn to the point of seeming stern. I'm more of a hugger and a consoler. Mr. Allwine and his friend, they were never a problem. More melancholy than weird."

Carson's phone rang, and when she stepped away to answer it, Michael said to Fullbright, "He came with a friend? Can you give us a description?"

Smiling, nodding, as affable as a cartoon bear, the mortician said, "I can see him as clear in memory as if he were standing here. He was ordinary to a fault. Average height. A little heavier than average weight. Middle-aged. Brown hair—or maybe blond. Blue or green eyes, maybe hazel."

With a sarcasm that sounded like earnest praise, Michael said, "Amazing. That's as good as a photo."

Pleased, Fullbright said, "I've got a sharp eye for detail."

Putting away her phone, Carson turned to Michael: "Jack Rogers wants to see us at the morgue."

"You might mention to the coroner," Fullbright said, "that while I don't extend commissions to those who send us business, I do offer discounts for referrals."

"I can't wait to tell him," Michael said. Pointing to the marble marquetry at their feet, he asked, "Who's that figure?"

"The one with the winged feet? That's Mercury."

"And that one next to him?"

"Aphrodite," said Fullbright.

"Are they . . . ?"

"Engaged in sodomy?" the mortician asked jovially. "Indeed they are. You'd be amazed how many mourners notice and are cheered by it."

"I *am* amazed," Michael agreed.

CHAPTER 43

THE LONGER ROY PRIBEAUX roamed his expansive loft apartment, gazing out of the tall windows, brooding about his future, the more troubled he became.

When a brief midmorning shower pelted the panes, blurring the city, he felt as if his future also blurred further, until it was a meaningless smear. He might have cried if crying had been his thing.

Never in his young—and getting steadily younger—life had he been without a purpose and a plan. Meaningful work kept the mind sharp and the heart uplifted.

Meaningful work, having a worthwhile purpose, was as crucial to longevity and to enduring youthfulness as were megadoses of Vitamin C and Coenzyme Q_{10}.

Without a purpose to inspire him, Roy feared that in spite of a perfect diet, ideally balanced nutritional supplements, an array of exotic emollients, and even purified lamb's urine, he would begin to grow old mentally. The more he brooded, the more it seemed that the path to senility loomed before him, as steep as a luge chute.

Mind and body were inextricably linked, of course, so a year of mental senescence would inevitably lead to lines at the corners of his eyes, the first gray hairs at his temples. He shuddered.

He tried to muster the desire to take a walk, but if he spent the day in the Quarter, among the throngs of celebratory tourists, and if he failed to encounter the radiant goddess of his destiny, his uneasiness would deepen.

Because he himself was very close to perfect, perhaps now that he had collected all the parts of an ideal woman, he should make it his goal to refine himself that final degree. He could now focus on achieving the perfect metabolism until he ceased to excrete wastes.

Although this was a noble undertaking, it didn't promise as much *fun* as the quest he had recently completed.

Finally, out of desperation, he found himself wondering—indeed *hoping*—that he had erred when he concluded that he had completed his collection. He might have overlooked an anatomical feature that, while minor, remained essential to beauty's jigsaw.

For a while he sat at the kitchen table with da Vinci's famous anatomical charts and several old *Playboy* centerfolds. He studied the female form from every angle, looking for a morsel that he might have overlooked.

When he made no discovery that allowed him to cry *Eureka,* he began to consider the possibility that he had not been sufficiently specific in his collecting. Was it possible that he had collected from too macro a perspective?

Were he to take Elizabeth Lavenza's lovely pale hands from the freezer and review them critically, he might be surprised to find that they were perfect, yes, in every detail *but one.* Perhaps she had a single thumb that fell short of perfection.

Perhaps the lips he had harvested were not *both* perfect as he had remembered. The upper might be perfect, the lower *not quite*.

If he needed to set out on a search for the perfect left thumb to marry to Elizabeth's otherwise faultlessly fair hands, if he must find a bee-stung lower lip to match the exquisite upper already in his possession, then his quest had not been completed, after all, and he would for a while have meaningful . . .

"No," he declared aloud. "That way lies madness."

Soon he would be reduced to harvesting one toe per donor and killing for mere eyelashes. A thin line separated serious homicidal purpose from buffoonery.

Realizing that a blind alley lay before him, Roy might at that moment have fallen into a swoon of despair, even though at heart he was an optimistic person. Fortunately, he was saved by a new thought.

From his nightstand he retrieved his original list of wanted anatomical delights. He had drawn a line through every item as he acquired it, concluding with EYES.

The list was long, and perhaps early in the quest he had crossed off an item out of wishful thinking, before he had taken possession of it. His memory of certain periods in his past was somewhat hazy, not because of any mental deficiency, but solely because he was such a tomorrow-oriented person, focused on the future in which he would grow younger and closer to perfection.

He vaguely recalled, over the years, killing a woman or two for an ideal feature, only to discover, in the intimate presence of the corpse, that the wanted item was minutely flawed and therefore not worth harvesting. Perhaps more than a woman or two. Maybe as many as four had disappointed him. Maybe five.

He supposed it was possible that he had crossed off an item or two on his list only to discover, after the kill, that he had been too easy in his judgment— and then in his busyness had forgotten to restore the needed item to the list.

Either to confirm or eliminate this possibility, he needed to compare the contents of his special freezer to his original list.

Despondency quickly faded and a happy anticipation filled him. He opened a bottle of apple juice and sectioned a raisin muffin to sample as he worked.

All the appliances in his roomy kitchen boasted stainless-steel finishes, including the ovens, microwave, dishwasher, icemaker, Sub-Zero refrigerator, and two enormous freezers.

In the first freezer he stored the parts of the perfect woman. He playfully referred to this as the *love locker.*

The second freezer contained an assortment of dairy-free, soy-based ice creams, free-range chicken breasts, and quarts of rhubarb puree. In the event that a major act of terrorism led to a disruption in the distribution of vital nutritional supplements, he also stored five-pound packages of powdered saw palmetto, St. John's wort, bee pollen, and other items.

When he lifted the lid on the first freezer, a cloud of frosted air wafted past him, crisp with a faint scent vaguely like that of frozen fish. He saw at once that the freezer contained items that did not belong with his collection.

His larger treasures—legs and arms—were tightly sealed in multiple layers of Reynolds Plastic Wrap. The smaller lovelies were sealed first in One-Zip bags and then in Tupperware containers with dependably tight lids.

Now he found among his collection three containers that were not Tupperware. They were cheap knockoffs of that desired brand: opaque plastic bottoms with ugly green lids.

This discovery mystified him. Although certain events in the more distant past might be blurry in his memory, these unacceptable containers were set atop the rest of his collection; they could have been placed here only recently. Yet he had never seen them before.

Curious but not yet alarmed, he took the three containers from the freezer. He put them on a nearby counter.

When he opened them, he found what might have been human organs. The first resembled liver. The second might have been a heart. With no real interest in things internal, he couldn't guess whether the third item was a kidney, spleen, or something even more arcane.

Pausing for some raisin muffin and apple juice, he could not avoid considering that these three specimens might be the souvenirs taken by the *other* killer currently making the news in New Orleans.

Being a Renaissance man who had educated himself in a variety of disciplines, Roy knew more than a little about psychology. He could not help but give some consideration now to the concept of multiple personalities.

He found it interesting to consider that he might be both the original killer *and* the copycat, might have murdered three men while in a fugue state, and that even now, confronted with evidence, he couldn't remember popping or chopping them. Interesting...but in the end not convincing. He and himself, working separately, were not, together, the Surgeon.

The true explanation eluded him, but he knew that it would prove to be more bizarre than multiple personalities.

Instinct drew his attention to the second freezer.

If the first had contained the unexpected, might not the second hold surprises, too? He might find gallons of high-fat ice cream and pounds of bacon among the herbs and health foods.

Instead, when he opened the lid and blinked away the initial cloud of frosted air, he discovered Candace's eyeless corpse jammed atop the supplements and foodstuffs.

Roy was certain that he had not brought this cotton-candy person home with him.

CHAPTER 44

LIKE THE SOMEWHAT disheveled medical examiner himself, Jack Rogers's private office was a classic example of managed chaos. The desktop overflowed with papers, notebooks, folders, photos. Books were jammed in the shelves everywhichway. Nevertheless, Jack would be able to find anything he needed after mere seconds of searching.

Only partly because of sleep deprivation and too much coffee, Carson's mind felt as disordered as the office. "Bobby Allwine's *gone?*"

Jack said, "The cadaver, the tissue samples, the autopsy video—all gone."

"What about the autopsy report and photos?" Michael asked. "Did you file them under 'Munster, Herman' like I suggested?"

"Yeah. They found them, took them."

"They thought to look under 'Munster, Herman'?" Michael asked in disbelief. "Since when do grave robbers double as trivia mavens?"

"Judging by the mess in the file room," Jack said, "I think they just tore through all the drawers till they got what they wanted. We could have filed it under 'Bell, Tinker,' and they would have found it. Anyway, they weren't grave robbers. They didn't dig Allwine out of the ground. They took him from a morgue drawer."

"So they're bodysnatchers," Michael said. "Getting the term right doesn't change the fact that your ass is in a sling, Jack."

"It feels like a barbed-wire thong," Jack said. "Losing evidence in a capital case? Man, there goes the pension."

Trying to make sense of the situation, Carson said, "Did the city cut your security budget or what?"

Jack shook his head. "We're as tight as a prison here. It has to be an inside job."

Simultaneously, Carson and Michael looked at Luke, who sat on a stool in a corner.

"Hey," he said, "I never stole a dime in my life, let alone a dead guy."

"Not Luke," Jack Rogers assured them. "He couldn't have pulled it off. He'd have screwed up."

Luke winced. "Thanks, I guess."

"Luke and I were here for a while after you two left, but not all night. We hit a wall, needed sleep. Because I'd sent home the night staff to keep the lid on this, the place was deserted."

"You forget to lock up?" Carson asked.

Jack glowered at her. "No way."

"Signs of forced entry?"

"None. They must've had keys."

"Somebody knew what you'd find in Allwine," she said, "because maybe he's not unique. Maybe there're others like him."

"Don't go off in the Twilight Zone again," Michael half warned, half pleaded.

"At least one other," she said. "The friend he went to funerals with. Mr. Average Everything."

Almost simultaneous with a knock, the door opened, and Frye, Jonathan Harker's partner, entered. He looked surprised to see them.

"Why so glum?" he asked. "Did somebody die?"

Weariness and caffeine sharpened Carson's edge. "What don't you understand about 'buzz off'?"

"Hey, I'm not here about your case. We're on that liquor-store shooting."

"Yeah? Is that right? Is that what you were doing yesterday at Allwine's apartment—looking for clues in the liquor-store shooting?"

Frye pretended innocence. "I don't know what you're talking about. O'Connor, you're wound as tight as a golf ball's guts. Get a man, relieve some tension."

She wanted to shoot him accidentally.

As if reading her mind, Michael said, "A gun can always go off accidentally, but you'd have to explain why you drew it in the first place."

CHAPTER 45

COMFORTABLE IN HER ROBE, ensconced in a wing-back chair, Erika spent the night and the morning with no company but books, and even took her breakfast in the library.

Reading for pleasure, lingering over the prose, she nevertheless covered a hundred pages an hour. She was, after all, an Alpha-class member of the New Race, with superb language skills.

She read Charles Dickens's *A Tale of Two Cities,* and when she finished it, she did something that she had not done before in her weeks of life. She wept.

The story was about the power of love, the nobility of self-sacrifice, and the horrors of revolution in the name of political ideology, among other things.

Erika understood the concept of love and found it appealing, but she didn't know if she would ever *feel* it. The New Race was supposed to value reason, to eschew emotion, to reject superstition.

She had heard Victor say that love was superstition. One of the Old Race, he'd made himself New. He claimed that perfect clarity of mind was a pleasure greater than any mere sentiment.

Nevertheless, Erika found herself intrigued by the concept of love and longed to experience it.

She found hope in the fact that she was capable of tears. Her built-in disposition toward reason at the expense of emotion had not prevented her from identifying with the tragic lawyer who, at the end of Dickens's novel, went to the guillotine in place of another man.

The lawyer had sacrificed himself to ensure that the woman he loved would have happiness with the man *she* loved. That man was the one whose name the lawyer had assumed and in whose place he had been executed.

Even if Erika was capable of love, she would not be capable of self-sacrifice, for it violated the proscription against suicide that had been embedded in every member of the New Race. Therefore, she was in awe of this capacity in ordinary human beings.

As for revolution... A day would come when Victor would give the command, and the New Race living secretly among the Old would pour down upon humanity a storm of terror unprecedented in history.

She'd not been created to serve in the front lines of that war, only to be a wife to Victor. When the time came, she supposed that she would be as ruthless as her maker had created her to be.

If they knew what she was, ordinary humans would consider her a monster. Members of the Old Race weren't her brothers and sisters.

Yet she admired much about them and, in truth, envied some of their gifts.

She suspected that it would be a mistake to let Victor know that her interest in the arts of the Old Race had evolved into admiration. In his view, they deserved only contempt. If she could not sustain that contempt, Erika Five could always be activated.

As noon drew near, when she was certain that the household staff had cleaned the master suite and made the bed, she went upstairs.

If the maids had found something extraordinary or just peculiar in the bedroom, if they had uncovered even a few rat droppings, she would have been told. Whatever had been in the bedroom the previous night must not be there now.

She prowled the suite anyway, listening for furtive sounds, looking behind furniture.

In the night, gripped by a surprising fear of the

unknown, she had retreated. Fear, an important survival mechanism, had not been entirely denied to the New Race.

Superstition, on the other hand, was uncontestable proof of a weak mind. Victor had no tolerance for superstition. Those with weak minds would be recalled, terminated, replaced.

The most innocent-seeming superstition—such as a belief that ill fortune attended every Friday the thirteenth—could open a door in the mind to consideration of larger supernatural issues. The most essential purpose of Victor's revolution was to complete the work of modernity and create a race of absolute materialists.

Erika searched the suite to quell the quasi-superstitious dread that had seized her the previous night and that still lingered. When she found nothing untoward, her confidence returned.

She enjoyed a long hot shower.

Members of the New Race, even Alphas like her, were encouraged to develop a keen appreciation for simple physical pleasures that could serve as an inoculation against emotions. Emotions themselves could be a form of pleasure, but also an antirevolutionary force.

Sex was among the approved pleasures, pure animal sex divorced from affection, from love. Sex between members of the New Race was also divorced from reproduction; they were engineered to be sterile.

Each new man and woman owed his or her existence to the direct action of Victor. The family was an antirevolutionary institution. Family fostered emotion.

Victor trusted no one but Victor to create life only for purely intellectual, solely rational reasons. Life from the lab will one day entirely replace life from the loins.

Shower completed, Erika opened the door of the stall, fished a towel from the nearby rack, stepped onto the bath mat—and discovered that she'd had a visitor. The splash of water and the clouds of steam had masked the movements of the intruder.

On the mat lay a scalpel. Stainless steel. Sparkling.

The scalpel must be one of Victor's. He owned collections of surgical instruments acquired at various times during his two-century crusade.

Victor, however, had not put this blade on her bath mat. Nor had any member of the household staff. Someone else had been here. Something else.

Steam swirled around her. Yet she shivered.

CHAPTER 46

FOLLOWING THEIR STOP at the morgue, Michael made a play for the car keys, but Carson as usual took the wheel.

"You drive too slow," she told him.

"You drive too asleep."

"I'm fine. I'm cool."

"You're both," he agreed, "but you're not fully awake."

"Unconscious, I wouldn't drive as slow as you."

"Yeah, see, I don't want to test that claim."

"You sound like your father's a safety engineer or something."

"You *know* he's a safety engineer," Michael said.

"What's a safety engineer do, anyway?"

"He engineers safety."

"Life is inherently unsafe."

"That's why we need safety engineers."

"You sound like probably your mother was obsessed with safe toys when you were growing up."

"As you know perfectly well, she's a product-safety analyst."

"God, you must have had a boring childhood. No wonder you wanted to be a cop, get shot at, shoot back."

Michael sighed. "None of this has anything to do with whether you're fit to drive or not."

"I am not only fit to drive," Carson said, "I am God's gift to Louisiana highways."

"I hate it when you get like this."

"I am what I am."

"What you are, Popeye, is stubborn."

"Look who's talking—a guy who will *never* accept that a woman can drive better than he can."

"This isn't a gender thing, and you know it."

"I'm female. You're male. It's a gender thing."

"It's a nut thing," he said. "You're nuts, I'm not, so I ought to drive. Carson, really, you need sleep."

"I can sleep when I'm dead."

The day's agenda consisted of several interviews with friends of Elizabeth Lavenza, the floater without hands who had been found in the lagoon. After the second of these, in the bookstore where Lavenza had worked as a clerk, Carson had to admit that sleep deprivation interfered with her ability as an investigator.

Returning to the sedan, she said, "Okay, I gotta grab some sack time, but what'll you do?"

"Go home, watch *Die Hard*."

"You've watched it like fifty times."

"It just gets better. Like *Hamlet*. Give me the car keys."

She shook her head. "I'll take you home."

"You'll drive me head-on into a bridge abutment."

"If that's what you want," she said, getting behind the wheel.

In the passenger's seat, he said, "You know what you are?"

"God's gift to Louisiana highways."

"Besides that. You're a control freak."

"That's just a slacker's term for someone who works hard and likes to do things *right*."

"So I'm a slacker now?" he asked.

"I didn't say that. All I'm saying, in a friendly way, is you're using their vocabulary."

"Don't drive so fast."

Carson accelerated. "How many times did your mother warn you not to run with scissors in your hand?"

"Like seven hundred thousand," he said. "But that doesn't mean you're fit to drive."

"God, you're relentless."

"You're incorrigible."

"Where'd you get *that* word? The dialogue in *Die Hard* isn't that sophisticated."

When Carson stopped at the curb in front of Michael's apartment house, he hesitated to get out. "I'm worried about you driving home."

"I'm like an old dray horse. I know the route in my bones."

"If you were *pulling* the car, I wouldn't worry, but you're gonna drive it at warp speed."

"I've got a gun, but you aren't worried about that."

"All right, all right. Drive. Go. But if you get behind a slow motorist, don't shoot him."

As she drove away, she saw him in the rearview mirror, watching her with concern.

The question wasn't whether she had fallen in love with Michael Maddison. The question was *how deeply, how irretrievably?*

Not that love was a sucking slough from which a person needed to be retrieved, like a drowner from the wild surf, like an addict from addiction. She was all for love. She just wasn't *ready* for love.

She had her career. She had Arnie. She had questions about her parents' deaths. Her life didn't have room for passion right now.

Maybe she'd be ready for passion when she was thirty-five. Or forty. Or ninety-four. But not now.

Besides, if she and Michael went to bed together, departmental regulations would necessitate a new partner for each of them.

She didn't like that many other homicide

detectives. The chances were that she'd be paired with a fathead. Furthermore, right now she didn't have the time or patience to break in a new partner.

Not that she always obeyed departmental regulations. She wasn't a by-the-book i-dotter and t-crosser.

But the rule against cops copulating with cops and then sharing an assignment struck Carson as common sense.

Not that she always deferred to her common sense. Sometimes you had to take reckless chances if you trusted your instinct and if you were human.

Otherwise you might as well leave the force and become a safety engineer.

As for being human, there was the fright figure in Allwine's apartment, who claimed not to be human, unless he believed that being cobbled together from pieces of criminals and being brought to life by lightning was not a sufficient deviation from the usual dad-makes-mom-pregnant routine to deny him human status.

Either the monster—that's what he called himself; she was not being politically incorrect—had been a figment of her imagination, in which case she was crazy, or he had been real, in which case maybe the whole world had gone crazy.

In the midst of this gruesome and impossible case, she couldn't just unzip Michael's fly and say, *I know you've been dreaming about this.* Romance was a delicate thing. It needed tender care to grow and mature into something wonderful. Right now she didn't have time for an orgasm, let alone for romance.

If she and Michael could have something meaningful together, she didn't want to ruin it by rushing into bed, especially not at a time when the pressure of work was half crushing her.

And *that* indicated how deeply and irretrievably she loved him. She was in the water over her head.

She drove all the way home without killing herself or anyone else. If she had been as awake and clearheaded as she claimed to be, she wouldn't have taken such goofy pride in this accomplishment.

Between the car and the house, the sunlight seemed bright enough to blind her. Even in her bedroom, daylight at the windows stung her bloodshot eyes and made her wince.

She shut the blinds. She closed the drapes. She considered painting the room black, but decided that would be going too far.

Fully clothed, she fell into bed and was asleep before the pillows finished compressing under her head.

CHAPTER 47

THE FOURTH TIME that Roy Pribeaux opened the freezer to see if Candace was still there, she was still there, so he decided to rule out the possibility that he might be delusional.

He had not taken his car the previous night. He lived within strolling distance of the Quarter. They had walked everywhere.

Yet he could not have carried her all the way from the levee to his loft. Although he was a strong man and getting stronger by the day, she was a heavy person.

Besides, you couldn't carry an eyeless corpse around the heart of New Orleans without drawing comment and suspicion. Not even New Orleans.

He didn't *own* a wheelbarrow. Anyway, that wouldn't have been a practical solution.

He poured another glass of apple juice to accompany what remained of the muffin.

The only credible explanation for Candace's surprise appearance was that someone had brought her here from the levee and stowed her in his food freezer. The same person had put the three plastic containers, with organs, in the other freezer, the love locker.

This meant that someone knew Roy had killed Candace.

Indeed, that someone must have *watched* him kill her.

"Spooky," he whispered.

He had not been aware of being followed. If someone had been dogging him, watching him romance Candace, the guy had been a master of surveillance, nearly as ephemeral as a ghost.

Not just *someone*. Not just anyone. Considering the human organs in the three tacky containers with ugly green lids, the perpetrator could be none other than the copycat killer.

Roy's work had inspired an imitator. The imitator had by these actions said, *Hi there. Can we be friends? Why don't we combine our collections?*

Although Roy was flattered, as any artist might be flattered by the admiration of another artist, he didn't like this development. He didn't like it at all.

For one thing, this organ-obsessed individual

was a burrower whose fascination with internals was gross and unsophisticated. He wasn't of Roy's caliber.

Besides, Roy didn't need or want the admiration of anyone. He was sufficient unto himself—until the perfect woman of his destiny entered his life.

He wondered when the copycat had visited. Candace had donated her eyes only a little more than twelve hours before he had found her in his freezer. The intruder would have had only two opportunities to bring her to the loft.

Satisfied with his life, immensely satisfied with himself, Roy had no reason for insomnia. He slept soundly every night.

The copycat, however, could not have brought such a heavy person as Candace into the loft and to the freezer while Roy slept unawares.

The kitchen was open to the dining area. The dining area flowed into the living room. Only a pony wall separated the living room from the bedroom. Sound would have traveled unobstructed, and Roy would have been awakened.

Now he went into the bathroom at the far end of the loft from the kitchen. He shut the door. He turned on the water in the shower. He switched on the vent fan.

Yes. Entirely possible. The copycat could have brought Candace into the loft when Roy had been enjoying his predawn shower.

He took long showers: the exfoliating soap with

loofa sponge, the moisturizing soap, two superb shampoos, a cream conditioner. . . .

The visitor's precise timing suggested that he knew a great deal about Roy's domestic routine. And he must have a key.

Roy had no landlord. He owned the building. He possessed the only keys to the loft.

Standing in the bathroom, surrounded by the susurrant rush of water and vent-fan blades, he was overcome by the suspicion that the copycat was in the apartment even now, preparing another surprise.

This concern had no merit, based as it was on the requirements that the copycat be omniscient and omnipresent. Yet suspicion grew into conviction.

Roy cranked off the shower, switched off the fan. He burst out of the bathroom and searched the loft. No one.

Although alone, Roy was at last alarmed.

CHAPTER 48

SHE WAS RIDING a black horse across a desolate plain under a low and churning sky.

Cataclysmic blasts of lightning ripped the heavens. Where each bright sword stabbed to earth, a giant rose, half handsome and half deformed, tattooed.

Each giant grabbed at her, trying to pull her from her mount. Each grabbed at the horse, too, at its flashing hooves, at its legs, at its silky mane.

The terrified horse screamed, kicked, faltered, broke loose, plunged forward.

Without a saddle, she clamped the mount with her knees, clutched fistfuls of its mane, held on, endured. There were more giants in the earth than the horse could outrun. Lightning, the crash of thunder, yet another golem rising, a huge hand closing around her wrist—

Carson woke in unrelieved darkness, not thrown from sleep by the nightmare but pricked from it by a sound.

Piercing the soft thrum and *shush* of the air conditioner came the sharp creak of a floorboard. Another floorboard groaned. Someone moved stealthily through the bedroom.

She had awakened on her back, in a sweat, atop the bedclothes, in the exact position in which she'd fallen into bed. She sensed someone looming over her.

For a moment she couldn't remember where she'd left her service pistol. Then she realized that she still wore her street clothes, her shoes, even her shoulder holster. For the first time in her life, she had fallen asleep while armed.

She slid a hand under her jacket, withdrew the gun.

Although Arnie had never previously entered her room in the dark and though his behavior was predictable, this might be him.

When she slowly sat up and with her left hand groped toward the nightstand lamp, the bedsprings sang softly.

Floorboards creaked, perhaps because the intruder had reacted to the noise she made. Creaked again.

Her fingers found the lamp, the switch. Light.

She saw no one in the first flush of light. At once, however, she sensed more than saw movement from the corner of her eye.

Turning her head, bringing the pistol to bear, she found no one.

At one window, draperies billowed. For a moment she attributed that movement to the air conditioner. Then the billows subsided. The draperies hung limp and still. As if someone, leaving, had brushed against them.

Carson got out of bed and crossed the room. When she pulled the draperies aside, she found the window closed. And locked.

Maybe she hadn't awakened as instantly as she'd thought. Maybe sleep had clung to her, and the dream. Maybe.

CARSON SHOWERED, changed clothes, and felt fresh but slightly disoriented. Having slept away the afternoon, she rose to the night, inner clock confused, lacking purpose.

In the kitchen, she scooped a serving of curried chicken salad from a bowl. With her dish and a fork, eating on the move, she went to Arnie's room.

The castle glorious, fit for King Arthur, seemed to have grown higher towers.

For once, Arnie was not at work upon this citadel. Instead he sat staring at a penny balanced on his right thumbnail, against his forefinger.

"What's up, sweetie?" she asked, though she expected no reply.

He met her expectation, but flipped the penny into the air. The copper winked brightly as it turned.

With quicker reflexes than he usually exhibited, the boy snatched the coin from the air, held it tightly in his right fist.

Carson had never seen him engaged in this behavior before. She watched, wondering.

Half a minute passed while Arnie stared at his clenched fist. Then he opened it and frowned as if with disappointment when he saw the penny gleaming on his palm.

As the boy flipped it and caught it in midair once more, Carson noticed a stack of bright pennies on the drawbridge to the castle.

Arnie had neither an understanding of money nor any need for it.

"Honey, where did you get the pennies?"

Opening his hand, Arnie saw the penny and frowned as before. He flipped it again. He seemed to have a new obsession.

At the open door, Vicky Chou peered in from the hallway. "How's the chicken salad?"

"Fabulous. Every day, you make me feel inadequate in a new way."

Vicky made a *de nada* gesture. "We all have our special talents. I couldn't shoot anyone the way you do."

"Anytime you need it done, you know where to find me."

"Where did Arnie get the pennies?" Vicky asked.

"That's what I was gonna ask you."

Having flipped the penny again, having found it in his palm after snatching it from the air, the boy looked puzzled.

"Arnie, where did you get the pennies?"

From his shirt pocket, Arnie withdrew a card. He sat staring at it in silence.

Aware that her brother might study the card for an hour before offering it to her, Carson gently plucked it from his fingers.

"What?" Vicky asked.

"It's a pass to someplace called the Luxe Theater. One free movie. Where would he have gotten this?"

Arnie flipped the penny again, and as he snatched it out of the air, he said, "Every city has secrets—"

Carson knew she had heard those words somewhere—

"—but none as terrible as this."

—and her blood chilled as she saw in her mind's eye the tattooed man standing at the window in Bobby Allwine's apartment.

CHAPTER 49

TWO HUNDRED YEARS of life can leave a man jaded.

If he is a genius, like Victor, his intellectual pursuits lead him always on new adventures. The mind can be kept fresh and forever engaged as it confronts and resolves increasingly complex problems.

On the other hand, repetition of physical pleasures eventually makes former delights seem dull. Boredom sets in. During the second century, a man's appetites turn increasingly toward the exotic, the extreme.

This is why Victor requires violence with sex, and the cruel humiliation of his partner. He has long ago transcended the guilt that committing acts of cruelty might spawn in others. Brutality is an aphrodisiac; the exercise of raw power thrills him.

The world offers so many cuisines that conventional sex grows boring long before favorite dishes grow bland to the tongue. Only in the past decade has Victor developed a periodic craving for foods so exotic that they must be eaten with discretion.

At certain restaurants in the city, where the owners value his business, where the waiters value his generous gratuities, and where the chefs admire his uniquely sophisticated palate, Victor from time to time arranges special dinners in advance. He is always served in a private room, where a man of his refinement can enjoy dishes so rare that they might seem repulsive to the ignorant multitudes. He has no wish to explain these acquired tastes to the boorish diners—and they are virtually always boorish—at an adjoining table.

Quan Yin, a Chinese restaurant named for the Queen of Heaven, had two private dining rooms. One was suitable for a group of eight. Victor had reserved it for himself.

He frequently ate alone. With two hundred years of experience that no one of an ordinary life span could match, he found that he was virtually always his own best company.

Teasing his appetite, allowing time to anticipate the exotic entrée, he began with a simple dish: egg drop soup.

Before he had half finished this first course, his cell phone rang. He was surprised to hear the voice of the renegade.

"Murder doesn't scare me anymore, Father."

With a note of authority that always secured obedience, Victor said, "You must talk to me about this in person."

"I'm not as troubled about murder as when I called you before."

"How did you get this number?"

The emergency contact number at Hands of Mercy, given to members of the New Race, did not transfer calls to Victor's cell phone.

Instead of answering, the renegade said, "Murder just makes me more human. They excel at murder."

"But you're better than their kind." The need to discuss this, to *debate* it, annoyed Victor. He was master and commander. His word was law, his desire obeyed, at least among his people. "You're more rational, more—"

"We're not better. There's something missing in us . . . something they have."

This was an intolerable lie. This was heresy.

"The help you need," Victor insisted impatiently, "only I am able to give."

"If I just cut open enough of them and look inside, sooner or later I'll discover what makes them . . . happier."

"That isn't rational. Come to me at the Hands of Mercy—"

"There's this girl I see sometimes, she's particularly happy. I'll find the truth in her, the secret, the thing I'm missing."

The renegade hung up.

As before, Victor pressed *69. Also as before, the call had come from a number that blocked automatic call-backs.

His special dinner had not been ruined by this development, but his bright mood had dimmed. He decided to switch from tea to wine.

Beer often went with Chinese food better than wine did. Victor was not, however, a beer man.

Unlike many Chinese restaurants, Quan Yin had an extensive cellar full of the finest vintages. The waiter—in a ruffled white tuxedo shirt, bow tie, and black tuxedo pants—brought a wine list.

As he finished his soup and waited for a salad of hearts of palms and peppers, Victor studied the list. He wavered between a wine suitable for pork and one better matched with seafood.

He would be eating neither pork nor seafood. The entrée, which he'd had before, was such a rare delicacy that any connoisseur of wine must be of several minds about the most compatible selection.

Finally he chose a superb Pinot Grigio and enjoyed the first glass with his salad.

Much ceremony accompanied the presentation of the main course, beginning with the chef himself, a Buddha-plump man named Lee Ling. He sprinkled red rose petals across the white tablecloth.

Two waiters appeared with an ornately engraved red-bronze tray on which stood a legged, one-quart copper pot filled with boiling oil. A Sterno burner under the pot kept the oil bubbling.

They put the tray on the table, and Victor breathed deeply of the aroma rising from the pot. This peanut oil, twice clarified, had been infused with a blend of pepper oils. The fragrance was divine.

A third waiter put a plain white plate before him. Beside the plate, red chopsticks. So gently as to avoid the slightest clink, the waiter placed a pair of stainless-steel tongs on the plate.

The handles of the tongs were rubberized to insulate against the heat that the steel would draw from the boiling oil. The pincer ends were shaped like the petals of lotus blossoms.

The pot of oil stood to Victor's right. Now a bowl of saffron rice was placed at the head of his plate.

Lee Ling, having retreated to the kitchen, returned with the entrée, which he put to the left of Victor's plate. The delicacy waited in a silver serving dish with a lid.

The waiters bowed and retreated. Lee Ling waited, smiling.

Victor removed the lid from the silver server. The dish had been lined with cabbage leaves briefly steamed to wilt them and make them pliable.

This rare delicacy did not appear on the menu. It was not available at all times or on short notice.

In any event, Lee Ling would prepare it only for

that one-in-a-thousand customer whom he'd known for years, whom he trusted, whom he knew to be a true gourmet. The customer must also be one so familiar with regional Chinese cuisine that he knew to request this very item.

Restaurant-licensing officials would not have approved of this offering, not even here in libertine New Orleans. No health risk was involved, but some things are too exotic even for the most tolerant of people.

In the dish, nestled in the cabbage, squirmed a double litter of live baby rats, so recently born that they were still pink, hairless, and blind.

In Chinese, Victor expressed his approval and gratitude to Lee Ling. Smiling, bowing, the chef retreated, leaving his guest alone.

Perhaps the excellent wine had restored Victor's good mood or perhaps his own extraordinary sophistication so pleased him that he could not for long remain glum. One of the secrets to leading a life full of great accomplishment was to like oneself, and Victor Helios, alias Frankenstein, liked himself more than he could express.

He dined.

CHAPTER 50

THE SECOND FLOOR of the Hands of Mercy is quiet.

Here the men and women of the New Race, fresh from the tanks, are undergoing the final stages of direct-to-brain data downloading. Soon they will be ready to go into the world and take their places among doomed humanity.

Randal Six will leave Mercy before any of them, before this night is over. He is terrified, but he is ready.

The computer maps and virtual reality tours of New Orleans have unnerved him as much as they have prepared him. But if he is to avoid the spinning rack and survive, he can wait no longer.

To make his way in the dangerous world beyond these walls, he should be armed. But he has no weapon and cannot see anything in his room that might serve as one.

If the journey is longer than he hopes, he will need provisions. He has no food in his room, only what is brought to him at mealtimes.

Somewhere in this building is a kitchen of considerable size. A pantry. There he would find the food he needs.

The prospect of searching for a kitchen, gathering food from among an overwhelming number of choices, and packing supplies is so daunting that he cannot begin. If he must provision himself, he will never leave Mercy.

So he will set out with nothing more than the clothes he wears, a fresh book of crossword puzzles, and a pen.

At the threshold between his room and the hallway, paralysis seizes him. He cannot proceed.

He knows that the floors of these two spaces are on the same plane, yet he feels certain that he will drop a killing distance if he dares cross into the corridor. What he *knows* is usually not as powerful as what he *feels,* which is the curse of his condition.

Although he reminds himself that perhaps an encounter with Arnie O'Connor is his destiny, he remains unmoved, unmoving.

His emotional weather worsens as he stands paralyzed. Agitation stirs his thoughts into confusion, like a whirl of wind sweeps autumn leaves into a colorful spiral.

He is acutely aware of how this agitation can quickly develop into a deeper disturbance, then a storm, then a tempest. He wants desperately to open the book of puzzles and put his pen to the empty boxes.

If he succumbs to the crossword desire, he will finish not one puzzle, not two, but the entire book. Night will pass. Morning will come. He will have lost forever the courage to escape.

Threshold. Hallway. With one step, he can cross the former and be in the latter. He has done this before, but this time it seems like a thousand-mile journey.

The difference, of course, is that previously he had intended to go no farther than the hallway. This time, he wants the world.

Threshold, hallway.

Suddenly *threshold* and *hallway* appear in his mind as hand-inked black letters in rows of white boxes, two entries in a crossword puzzle, sharing the letter *h*.

When he sees the two words intersecting in this manner, he more clearly recognizes that the threshold and the hallway in reality also intersect on the same plane. Crossing the first into the latter is no more difficult than filling the boxes with letters.

He steps out of his room.

CHAPTER 51

THE GEOMETRIC DESIGNS on the Art Deco facade of the Luxe Theater were given greater depth and drama by the honing glow of a streetlamp and the shadows that it sharpened.

The marquee was dark, and the theater appeared to be closed if not abandoned until Carson peered through one of the doors. She saw soft light at the refreshment counter and someone at work there.

When she tried the door, it swung inward. She stepped into the lobby.

The glass candy cases were lighted to display their wares. On the wall behind the counter, an illuminated Art Deco–style Coca-Cola clock, frost white and crimson, was a surprisingly poignant reminder of a more innocent time.

The man working behind the counter was the

giant she had met in Allwine's apartment. His physique identified him before he turned and revealed his face.

She snapped the movie pass against the glass top of the counter. "Who are you?"

"I told you once."

"I didn't get your name," she said tightly.

He had been cleaning out the popcorn machine. He turned his attention to it once more. "My name's Deucalion."

"First or last?"

"First and last."

"You work here?"

"I own the theater."

"You assaulted a police officer."

"Did I? Were you hurt?" He smiled, not sarcastically but with surprising warmth, considering his face. "Or was the damage to your self-esteem?"

His composure impressed her. His intimidating size was not the source of his confidence; he was no bully. Instead, his calm nature approached the deeper serenity that she associated with monastics in their cowled robes.

Some sociopaths were serene, too, as collected as trapdoor spiders waiting in their lairs for prey to drop on them.

She said, "What were you doing in my house?"

"From what I've seen of how you live, I think I can trust you."

"Why do I give a rat's ass whether you trust me? Stay out of my house."

"Your brother is a heavy burden. You carry him with grace."

Alarmed, she said, "You. Aren't. In. My. Life."

He put down the damp cloth with which he'd been wiping out the popcorn machine, and he turned to her again, with only the candy counter between them.

"Is that what you want?" he asked. "Is it really? If that's what you want, why did you come to hear the rest of it? Because you didn't come just to tell me to stay away. You came with questions."

His insight and his quiet amusement did not comport with the brutal look of him.

When she stood nonplussed, he said, "I mean no harm to Arnie or to you. Your enemy is Helios."

She blinked in surprise. "Helios? Victor Helios? Owns Biovision, big philanthropist?"

"He has the arrogance to call himself 'Helios,' after the Greek god of the sun. Helios . . . the life-giver. That isn't his real name." Without emphasis, without a raised eyebrow, with no apparent irony, he said, "His real name is Frankenstein."

After what he had said in Bobby Allwine's apartment, after his riff about being made from pieces of criminals and given life force by a thunderstorm, she should have expected this development. She did *not* expect it, however, and it disappointed her.

Carson had felt that Deucalion was special in some way other than his formidable size and appearance, and for reasons that she couldn't articulate to her satisfaction, she had *wanted* him to be something special. She needed to have the rug of routine pulled out from under her, to be tumbled headlong into the *mystery* of life.

Maybe mystery was a synonym for change. Maybe she needed a different kind of excitement from what the job usually supplied. She suspected, however, that she needed more meaning in her life than the homicide assignment currently gave her, though she didn't know quite what she meant by *meaning.*

Deucalion disappointed her because this Frankenstein business was just another flavor of the nutcase rants she encountered more days than not in the conduct of ordinary investigations. He'd seemed strange but substantive; now he sounded hardly different from the pinwheel-eyed ginks who thought that CIA operatives or aliens were after them.

"Yeah," she said. "Frankenstein."

"The legend isn't fiction. It's fact."

"Of course it is." Disappointment of various kinds had the same effect on her: a craving for chocolate. Pointing through the glass top of the counter, she said, "I'd like one of those Hershey's bars with almonds."

"Long ago, in Austria, they burned his laboratory to the ground. Because he created me."

"Bummer. Where are your neck bolts? Did you have them surgically removed?"

"Look at me," he said solemnly.

She gazed longingly at the Hershey's bar for a moment but at last met his gaze.

Ghostly radiance pulsed through his eyes. This time she was so close that even if she had wanted to, she could not have dismissed it as a reflection of some natural light source.

"I suspect," he said, "that stranger things than I now roam this city . . . and he's begun to lose control of them."

He stepped to the cash register, opened a drawer beneath it, and withdrew a newspaper clipping and a rolled paper tied with a ribbon.

The clipping included a photo of Victor Helios. The paper was a pencil portrait of the same man a decade younger.

"I tore this from a frame in Victor's study two centuries ago, so I would never forget his face."

"This doesn't prove anything. Are the Hershey's bars for sale or not?"

"The night I was born, Victor needed a storm. He got the storm of the century."

Deucalion rolled up his right sleeve, revealing three shiny metal disks embedded in his flesh.

Admittedly, Carson had never seen anything like this. On the other hand, this was an age when some people pierced their tongues with studs and even had the tips of their tongues split for a reptilian effect.

"Contact points," he explained. "All over my body. But something was strange about the lightning . . . such power."

He didn't mention the ragged white keloid scars that joined his wrist to his forearm.

If he was living out a Frankenstein-monster fantasy, he had gone to extremes to conform his physical appearance to the tale. This was a bit more impressive than a Star Trek fan wearing a jumpsuit and Spock ears.

Against her better judgment, even if she couldn't believe him, Carson felt herself wanting to believe *in* him.

This desire to believe surprised her, disturbed her. She didn't understand it. So *not* Carson O'Connor.

"The storm gave me life," he continued, "but it also gave me something just short of immortality."

Deucalion picked up the newspaper clipping, stared for a moment at the photo of Victor Helios, then crushed it in his fist.

"I thought my maker was long dead. But from the beginning, he's been after his own immortality—of one kind or another."

"Quite a story," she said. "Does abduction by extraterrestrials come into it at any point?"

In Carson's experience, kooks could not tolerate mockery. They reacted with anger or they accused her of being part of whatever conspiracy they believed had targeted them.

Deucalion merely threw aside the wadded clipping, withdrew a Hershey's bar from the display case, and put the candy on the counter in front of her.

Unwrapping the chocolate, she said, "You expect me to believe two hundred years? So the lightning that night, it—what?—altered his genetics?"

"No. The lightning didn't touch him. Only me. He got this far . . . some other way."

"Lots of fiber, fresh fruit, no red meat."

She couldn't tweak him.

No more of the eerie luminosity passed through his eyes, but she saw in them something else that she had never glimpsed in the eyes of another. An electrifying directness. She felt so exposed that a chill closed like a fist around her heart.

Loneliness in that gaze, and wisdom, and humility. And . . . more that was enigmatic. His eyes were a singularity, and though there was much to be read in them, she hadn't the language to understand what she read, for the soul that looked out at her through those lenses suddenly seemed as alien as that of any creature born on another world.

Chocolate cloyed in her mouth, her throat. The candy tasted oddly like blood, as if she had bitten her tongue.

She put down the Hershey's bar.

"What has Victor been doing all this time?" Deucalion wondered. "What has he been . . . making?"

She remembered Bobby Allwine's cadaver, naked and dissected on the autopsy table—and Jack Rogers's insistence that its freakish innards were the consequence not of mutation but of *design*.

Deucalion appeared to pluck a shiny quarter from the ether. He flipped it off his thumb, caught it in midair, held it for a moment in his fist. When he opened his hand, the quarter wasn't there.

Here was the trick that Arnie had been trying to imitate.

Turning over the candy bar that Carson had just put down on the glass counter, Deucalion revealed the quarter.

She sensed that this peculiar impromptu performance was meant to be more than entertainment. It was meant to convince her that the truth of him was as magical as he had presented it.

He picked up the quarter—his hands so dexterous for their great size—and flipped it high and past her head.

When she turned to follow its arc, she lost sight of the quarter high in the air.

She waited for the *ping* and clatter of the coin bouncing off the marble floor of the lobby. Silence.

When the silence endured beyond all reasonable expectation of the quarter's return, Carson looked at Deucalion.

He had another quarter. He snapped it off his thumb.

More intently than before, she tracked it—but lost it as it reached the apex of its arc.

She held her breath, waiting for the falling coin to ring off the floor, but the sound didn't come, didn't come—and then she needed to breathe.

"Am I still not in your life?" he asked. "Or do you want to hear more?"

CHAPTER 52

SCONCES SPREAD RADIANT amber fans on the walls, but at this hour the lights are dim and shadows dominate.

Randal Six has only now realized that the blocks of vinyl-tile flooring in the hallway are like the squares in a crossword puzzle. This geometry gives him comfort.

He visualizes in his mind one letter of his name with every step that he takes, spelling himself along the tile floor, block by block, toward freedom.

This is the dormitory floor, where the most recently awakened members of the New Race are housed until they are polished and ready to infiltrate the city.

Half the doors stand open. Beyond some of

them, naked bodies are locked in every imaginable sexual posture.

Especially in their early weeks, the tank-born are filled with anguish that arises from their knowledge of what they are. They also suffer intense anxiety because they come to full consciousness with the immediate understanding that, as Victor's chattel, they do not control the primary issues of their lives and possess no free will; therefore, in their beginning is their end, and their lives are mapped without hope of mystery.

They are sterile but vigorous. In them, sex has been divorced entirely from the purpose of procreation and functions solely as a vent for stress.

They copulate in groups, tangled and writhing, and it seems to Randal Six, whose autism makes him different from them, that these thrusts provide them no pleasure, only release from tension.

The sounds issuing from these orgiastic groups have no quality of joy, no suggestion of tenderness. These are bestial noises, low and rough, insistent almost to the point of violence, eager to the point of desperation.

The slap of flesh on flesh, the wordless grunts, the guttural cries that seem charged with rage—all this frightens Randal Six as he passes these rooms. He feels the urge to run but dares not step on the lines between the vinyl blocks; he must place each foot entirely in a square, which requires a deliberative pace.

The hallway increasingly seems like a tunnel, the chambers on both sides like catacombs in which the restless dead embrace in cold desire.

Heart knocking as if to test the soundness of his ribs, Randal spells his name often enough to reach an intersection of corridors. Using the final letter, he spells a crossing word—*left*—which allows him to turn in that direction.

From the letter *t,* he sidesteps four blocks, spelling *right* backward as he goes. With the letter *r* as his new beginning, he is able to spell his name and, thereby, proceed forward along this new hall, toward the choice of elevators or a stairwell.

CHAPTER 53

ERIKA TOOK DINNER alone in the master bedroom, at a nineteenth-century French marquetry table featuring a motif of autumn bounty—apples, oranges, plums, grapes, all spilling from a horn of plenty—rendered with exquisitely inlaid woods of numerous varieties.

Like all those of the New Race, her metabolism was as fine-tuned and as powerful as a Ferrari engine. This required a formidable appetite.

Two six-ounce steaks—filet mignon, prepared medium-rare—were accompanied by a rasher of crisp bacon, buttered carrots with thyme, and snow peas with sliced jicama. A separate chafing dish contained braised potatoes in blue cheese sauce. For dessert waited an entire peach cobbler with a side dish of vanilla ice cream coddled in a bowl of crushed ice.

While she ate, she stared at the scalpel that had been left on her bath mat earlier in the day. It lay across her bread plate as if it were a butter knife.

She didn't know how the scalpel related to the furtive ratlike noises that she had been hearing, but she was certain that the two were connected.

There is no world but this one. All flesh is grass, and withers, and the fields of the mind, too, are burned black by death and do not grow green again. That conviction is essential to the creed of materialism; and Erika is a soldier in the determined army that will inevitably conquer the Earth and impose that philosophy pole to pole.

Yet, though her creator forbade belief in the supernatural and though her laboratory origins suggested that intelligent life can be manufactured without divine inspiration, Erika could not shake a sense of the uncanny in these recent events. The scalpel seemed to sparkle not solely with the sheen of surgical steel but also with . . . magic.

As if by her thoughts she had opened a door between this world and another, a force inexplicable switched on the plasma TV. Erika looked up with a start as the screen came alive.

The cordless Crestron panel, by which the TV was controlled, currently lay on Victor's nightstand, untouched.

Some bodiless Presence seemed to be channel

surfing. Images flipped rapidly across the screen, faster, faster.

As Erika put down her fork and pushed her chair back from the table, the Presence selected a dead channel. A blizzard of electronic snow whitened the big screen.

Sensing that something bizarre—and something of significance—was about to happen, she rose to her feet.

The voice—deep, rough, and ominous—came to her out of the dead channel, through the Dolby SurroundSound speakers in the ceiling: *"Kill him. Kill him."*

Erika moved away from the table, toward the TV, but halted after two steps when it seemed unwise to get too close to the screen.

"Shove the scalpel in his eye. Into his brain. Kill him."

"Who are you?" she asked.

"Kill him. Thrust it deep, and twist. Kill him."

"Kill whom?"

The Presence did not answer.

She repeated her question.

On the plasma screen, out of the snow, a pale ascetic face began to form. For a moment, she assumed this must be the face of a spirit, but as it developed character, she recognized Victor, eyes closed and features relaxed, as though this were his death mask.

"Kill him."

"He made me."

"To use."

"I can't."

"You're strong."

"Impossible."

"Kill him."

"Who are you?"

"Evil," said the voice, and she knew that this Presence was not speaking of itself, but of Victor.

If she participated in this conversation, she would inevitably consider betraying Victor even if only to make an argument that it was impossible to raise a hand against him. The mere act of *thinking* about killing her maker could bring her own death.

Every thought creates a unique electrical signature in the brain. Victor had identified those signatures that represented the thought of taking violent action against him.

Implanted in Erika's brain—as in the brain of every member of the New Race—was a nanodevice programmed to recognize the thought signature of patricide, of deicide.

If ever she picked up a weapon with the intention of using it against Victor, that spy within would instantly recognize her intent. It would plunge her into a state of paralysis from which only Victor could retrieve her.

If thereafter he allowed her to live, hers would be a life of greater suffering. He would fill all her days with imaginative punishment.

Consequently, she moved now to the Crestron touch panel on the nightstand and used it to switch off the TV. The plasma screen went dark.

Waiting with the control in hand, she expected the TV to switch itself on again, but it remained off.

She did not believe in spirits. She *must* not believe. Such belief was disobedience. Disobedience would lead to termination.

The mysterious voice urging murder was best left mysterious. To pursue an understanding of it would be to chase it off a cliff, to certain death.

When she realized that she was trembling with fear, Erika returned to her chair at the table.

She began to eat again, but now her appetite was of the nervous variety. She ate voraciously, trying to quell a hunger that food could never satisfy: a hunger for meaning, for freedom.

Her tremors—and the fear of death they represented—surprised her. There had been times since her "birth" six weeks ago when she had thought death desirable.

Not now. Something had changed. When she had not been looking, that thing with feathers, hope, had come into her heart.

CHAPTER 54

ROY PRIBEAUX HAD GUNS.

He retrieved them from the closet where they were stored in custom cases. He examined them lovingly, one by one, cleaned and lubricated them as necessary, preparing them for use.

Throughout his adolescence and twenties, he had *adored* guns. Revolvers, pistols, shotguns, rifles—he had a core collection of each type of weapon.

Shortly after his twentieth birthday, when he had come into his inheritance, he bought a Ford Explorer, loaded it with his favorite firearms, and toured the South and Southwest.

Until that time, he had only killed animals.

He hadn't been a hunter. He'd never acquired a hunting license. Tramping around in the woods and fields didn't appeal to him. His prey were domestic and farm animals.

On the road at twenty, he targeted people for the first time. For several years he was carefree and happy.

As are many people in their twenties, Roy had been idealistic. He believed that he could make this a better society, a better world.

Even then, he'd realized that life was made tolerable only by the existence of beauty. Beauty in nature. Beauty in architecture and art and in objects of human manufacture. Beauty among human beings.

From childhood, he himself had been strikingly attractive, and he had been aware how the sight of him lifted people's spirits and how his company improved their moods.

He intended to make the world a happier place by eliminating ugly people wherever he found them. And he found them everywhere.

In eighteen states as far east as Alabama, as far north as Colorado, as far west as Arizona, and as far south as Texas, Roy traveled to kill. He destroyed ugly humanity where circumstances assured that he could strike without risk of apprehension.

He employed such a variety of fine weapons over such an enormous geographical area that his many scores were never linked as the work of one perpetrator. He killed at a distance with rifles, at forty yards or less with 12-gauge shotguns loaded with buckshot, and close-up with revolvers or pistols as the mood took him.

Generally he preferred the intimacy of handguns. They virtually always allowed him to get close enough to explain that he held no personal animosity toward the target.

"It's an aesthetic issue," he might say. Or "I'm sure you'll agree, dead is better than ugly." Or "I'm just doing Darwin's work to advance the beauty of the species."

Shotguns were thrilling when he had the leisure to reload and to use with increasing proximity a total of four or six Federal three-inch, ooo shells, which had tremendous penetration. He could not only remove the ugly person from the gene pool but also, with the Federal rounds, *obliterate* their ugliness and leave a corpse so ravaged that there would *have* to be a closed-casket funeral.

During those years of travel and accomplishment, Roy had known the satisfaction of noble purpose and worthwhile labor. He assumed that this would be his life's work, with no need ever to learn new job skills or to retire.

Over time, however, he reluctantly came to the conclusion that so many ugly people inhabited the world that his efforts alone could not ensure prettier future generations. In fact, the more people he killed, the uglier the world seemed to become.

Ugliness has the momentum of a tsunami. It is the handmaiden to entropy. One man's resistance, while admirable, cannot turn back the most titanic forces of nature.

Eventually he returned to New Orleans, to rest and to reconsider his mission. He purchased this building and rebuilt the loft into an apartment.

He began to suspect that he had too long associated with too many ugly people. Although he had killed them all, sparing humanity the further sight of them, perhaps their ugliness had somehow tainted Roy himself.

For the first time, his reflection in a mirror disquieted him. Being brutally honest, he had to admit that he was still beautiful, certainly in the top one tenth of one percent of the most beautiful people in the world, but perhaps not as beautiful as he had been before he had set out in his Explorer to save humanity from ugliness.

Being a forward-looking and determined person, he had not fallen into despair. He developed a program of diet, exercise, nutritional supplementation, and meditation to regain fully his former splendor.

As any mirror now revealed, he succeeded. He was breathtaking.

Nevertheless, he often thought of those years of rehabilitation as the Wasted Years, because while he restored himself, he had no time to kill anyone. And no reason to kill them.

Roy was a goal-driven person with a deep desire to contribute to society. He didn't kill just to kill. He needed a purpose.

When he had struck upon the idea of harvesting and preserving the ideal parts of a perfect woman, he rejoiced that his life had meaning once more.

Eventually he might anonymously donate the collection to a great museum. The academics and critics who championed modern art would at once recognize the value and brilliance of his assembled woman.

First he must find that elusive living female who was perfect in every detail and who was destined to be his mate. Until then he would need the collection in order to lay it out and, item by item, compare his beloved to all those pieces of perfection, to be certain that in every way she measured up to his highest standard.

No doubt his longed-for Venus would soon cross his path—another reason why he couldn't tolerate the intrusion of the copycat killer into his life. That poor fool's use of tacky, low-quality Tupperware imitations provided proof enough that his appreciation for beauty in all things was so inadequate that no friendship could ever flower between him and Roy.

Now, in preparation for the copycat's next visit, Roy loaded various pistols and revolvers. He secreted a weapon in each area of his expansive apartment.

In the bathroom, a Browning Hi-Power 9mm in the drawer where he kept his colognes.

Under a pillow on his bed, a Smith & Wesson Chief's Special, one of the best small-frame .38 Special revolvers ever made.

Under a living-room sofa cushion, a Glock Model 23 loaded with .40 Smith & Wesson ammo.

Concealed at two points among the array of exercise machines were a pair of SIG P245s.

In the kitchen, Roy placed a Springfield Trophy Match 1911-A1 in the bread box, next to a loaf of low-fat seven-grain with raisins.

When Roy closed the drop door on the bread box and turned, a sizable stranger stood in the kitchen with him, a red-faced, boiled-looking guy with mean blue eyes.

How the intruder had gotten in and moved so quietly, Roy didn't know, but this must be the copycat. The guy wasn't aggressively ugly, but he wasn't half pretty, either, just homely, so there could be no chance whatsoever of a friendship between him and Roy.

The fierce expression on the copycat's face suggested he had no interest in friendship, either. Maybe Roy had been mistaken to assume the copycat had come here, in the first place, out of admiration.

He noticed the intruder wore latex surgical gloves. Not a good sign.

Realizing that he wouldn't be able to turn to the bread box and retrieve the pistol quickly enough to use it, Roy struck out at his adversary with confidence, employing what he had learned during four years of instruction in Tae Kwon Do.

Although he didn't appear to be as fit as Roy, the copycat proved to be fast and strong. He not only blocked the blows but seized Roy's right hand, bent it backward, and snapped his wrist as if it were a dry branch.

The pain rocked Roy Pribeaux. He didn't handle pain well. His life had been mercifully free of it. The shock of the broken wrist robbed him of breath so completely that an attempt at a scream produced only a wheeze.

Incredibly, the copycat grabbed him by his shirt and by the crotch of his slacks, lifted him overhead as if he weighed no more than a child, and slammed him down on the edge of a kitchen counter.

Louder than the wheeze of his scream came the sound of his spine snapping.

The copycat released him. Roy slid off the counter, onto the floor.

The pain had stopped. This seemed like a good thing, until he realized that he had no feeling whatsoever below his neck.

He tried to move his left hand. He could not. Paralyzed.

Glaring down at him, the copycat said, "I don't need to cut you open and see inside. You don't have what I'm looking for. You're all dark inside, and I need the other thing."

Darkness wanted Roy, and he gave himself to it.

CHAPTER 55

JONATHAN HARKER, Mercy-born and Mercy-raised, had joined the New Orleans Police Department sixteen years ago.

All papers substantiating his identity and previous employment history had been impeccably forged. According to these records, he'd been a cop in Atlanta, Georgia.

Other members of the New Race, already seeded in the department at that time, had falsified follow-up with officials in Atlanta, facilitating his employment. Later they greased his path into the NOPD Homicide Division.

He had been a good son to Father, dutiful and dedicated...until the past year. He had lost his sense of purpose. The preparations for war against humanity, still at least a decade distant, did not excite or even interest him any longer.

For several years he had felt…incomplete. Over the preceding twelve months, this feeling had matured into a terrible emptiness, a cold and yawning void at the center of him.

He recognized in humanity a lust for life, a joy, that he did not possess. He wanted to know how this quality arose in them.

Every detail of his own physical and mental design had been direct-to-brain downloaded when Jonathan had been in the creation tank, so that he would have a proper awe of Victor, his maker. Thus it occurred to him that by studying human physiology and comparing theirs to his own, he should be able to identify what the Old Race had that he lacked, perhaps a gland that secreted a hormone or an enzyme that was required for happiness.

He began by studying human biology. He pored through medical texts.

Instead of discovering greater complexity in their bodies, he found comparative simplicity. He didn't lack anything they had; quite the contrary, they seemed less well constructed for durability than he was with his second heart and other redundant systems.

Eventually he arrived at the conviction that they *did* contain some gland or organ that allowed them the possibility of happiness but that *they themselves had not yet discovered and identified it.* Therefore he could not find it in a textbook.

Because the New Race came out of their creation tanks inculcated with a faith in their superiority to ordinary human beings, Jonathan had no doubt that through further self-education, he could find what had eluded Old Race physiologists. By cutting open enough of them and searching their innards, he would—by virtue of his sharper mind and keener eye—find the gland of happiness.

When a serial killer appeared on the scene, Jonathan recognized an opportunity. He could pursue his own dissections with caution and eventually contrive to have them attributed to the killer. He'd used chloroform on one of his first two subjects for this very purpose.

Investigating behind O'Connor and Maddison, Jonathan worked the Surgeon case twenty-four hours a day, without sleep. He had an eerie, intuitive understanding of the killer's psychology and sensed early on that his quarry had embarked on a quest for happiness similar to his own. For this reason, he found his way to Roy Pribeaux in time to watch him court and kill the cotton-candy girl.

Jonathan might have allowed Pribeaux to carry on indefinitely if not for the fact that his own circumstances had changed. Something was happening to him that promised the fulfillment for which he had long been yearning.

He had learned nothing from probing inside his first two subjects. And what he'd done to Bobby Allwine had not been part of his researches, merely an act of mercy. Bobby had wanted to die, and because Father's programmed injunction against murder had broken down in Jonathan, he had been able to oblige his friend.

Yet though he'd discovered nothing to advance his understanding of the source of human happiness, Jonathan had begun to change in a wondrous way. He felt movement within himself. Several times he had *seen* something inside him, something alive, pressing against his abdomen, as if yearning to get out.

He suspected that he was going to overcome another of Father's key restrictions on the New Race. Jonathan believed that he would soon reproduce.

Therefore, he needed to wrap up business with Pribeaux, pin all the killings to date on him, and prepare for what glory might be coming.

He intended to conduct only a single additional dissection, markedly more elaborate than the previous ones. He would dispose of this final subject in such a way that when her body was found long after the fact, she also might be linked to Roy Pribeaux.

As Pribeaux lay paralyzed and unconscious on the kitchen floor, Jonathan Harker produced a comb from his shirt pocket. He had bought it earlier in the day but had not used it himself.

He drew it through the killer's thick hair. Several loose strands had tangled in the plastic teeth.

He put the comb and these hairs in an envelope that he brought for this purpose. Evidence.

Pribeaux had regained consciousness. "Who . . . who are you?"

"Do you want to die?" Jonathan asked.

Tears swelled in Pribeaux's eyes. "No. Please, no."

"You want to live even if you'll be paralyzed for life?"

"Yes. Yes, please. I have plenty of money. I can receive the finest care and rehabilitation. Help me dispose of . . . of what's in the freezers, everything incriminating, let me live, and I'll make you rich."

The New Race was not motivated by money. Jonathan pretended otherwise. "I know the depth of your resources. Maybe we can strike a bargain, after all."

"Yes, we can, I know we can," Pribeaux said weakly but eagerly.

"But right now," Jonathan said, "I want you to be quiet. I've got work to do, and I don't want to have to listen to your whining. If you stay quiet, we'll bargain later. If you speak once, just once, I'll kill you. Do you understand?"

When Pribeaux tried to nod, he couldn't.

"All right," said Jonathan. "We're on the same page."

Pribeaux bled from his shattered wrist, but slowly and steadily rather than in arterial spurts.

With a new eyedropper that he had purchased in the same drugstore where he'd bought the comb, Jonathan suctioned blood from the puddle on the floor. He transferred a few ccs at a time to a little glass bottle that he had also brought with him.

Pribeaux's eyes followed his every move. They were moist with self-pity, bright with curiosity, wide with terror.

When he had filled the small bottle, Jonathan screwed a cap on it and stowed it in a jacket pocket. He wrapped the bloody eyedropper in a handkerchief and pocketed that, as well.

Quickly he searched the kitchen drawers until he found a white plastic garbage bag and rubber bands.

He slid the bag over Pribeaux's damaged left arm and fixed it tightly above the elbow with two rubber bands. This would make it possible to move the man without leaving a blood trail.

Effortlessly, Jonathan lifted Pribeaux and put him on the floor near the dinette set, out of the way.

He cleaned the blood from the white ceramic tiles. Fortunately, Pribeaux had sealed the grout so effectively that the blood did not penetrate.

When he was certain that not one drop or smear of blood remained and that no other evidence of violence could be found in the kitchen, he bagged the paper towels and other cleanup supplies in another garbage bag, knotted the neck of it, and secured it to his belt.

At the desk in the living room, he switched on the computer. He chose a program from the menu and typed a few lines that with great thought he had earlier composed.

Leaving the computer on, Jonathan went to the front door, opened it, and stepped onto the roomy landing at the head of the stairs that served Pribeaux's loft. He stood listening for a moment.

The businesses on the first floor had closed hours ago. Pribeaux didn't seem to have friends or visitors. Deep stillness pooled in the building.

In the apartment again, Jonathan lifted Pribeaux and carried him in his arms as though he were a child, out to the landing.

In addition to stairs, the apartment was served by the freight elevator that was original to the building. With an elbow, Jonathan pressed the call button.

Pribeaux's eyes searched Jonathan's face, desperately trying to read his intent.

Aboard the elevator, still carrying the paralyzed man, Jonathan pressed the number 3 on the control panel.

On the flat roof of the former warehouse were storage structures that required elevator service.

When Pribeaux realized they were going to the

roof, his pale face paled further, and the terror in his eyes grew frenetic. He knew now that there would be no bargain made to save his life.

"You can still feel pain in your face, in your neck," Jonathan warned him. "I will cause you the most horrific pain you can imagine, in the process of blinding you. Do you understand?"

Pribeaux blinked rapidly, opened his mouth, but dared not speak a word even of submission.

"Excruciating pain," Jonathan promised. "But if you remain silent and cause me no problem, your death will be quick."

The elevator arrived at the top of the building.

Only orange light of an early moon illuminated the roof, but Jonathan could see well. He carried the killer to the three-foot-high safety parapet.

Pribeaux had begun to weep, but not so loud as to earn him the unendurable pain that he had been promised. He sounded like a small child, lost and full of misery.

The cobblestone alleyway behind the warehouse lay forty feet below, deserted at this hour.

Jonathan dropped Pribeaux off the roof. The killer screamed but not loud or long.

In desperate physical condition *before* he had been dropped, Roy Pribeaux had no chance whatsoever of surviving the fall. The sound of him hitting the pavement was a lesson in the fragility of the human skeleton.

Jonathan left the elevator at the roof and took

the stairs to the ground floor. He walked to his car, which he had parked three blocks away.

En route, he tossed the garbage bag full of bloody paper towels in a convenient Dumpster.

In the car, he used a cell phone that just hours ago he had taken off a drug dealer whom he rousted near the Quarter. He called 911, disguised his voice, and pretended to be a junkie who, shooting up in an alley, saw a man jump from a warehouse roof.

Call completed, he tossed the phone out of the car window.

He was still wearing the latex gloves. He stripped them off as he drove.

CHAPTER 56

THE ELEVATOR IS like a three-dimensional cross-word-puzzle box, descending to the basement of the Hands of Mercy.

Randal Six had turned *left* in the second-floor hall-way, entering the elevator on his fourth step; there-fore, the letter that this box contains—and from which he must proceed when he reaches the lower level—is *t*.

When the doors open, he says, "Toward," and steps *o-w-a-r-d* into the corridor.

A life of greater mobility is proving easier to achieve than he had expected. He is not yet ready to drive a car in the Indianapolis 500, and he may not even be ready for a slow walk in the world beyond these walls, but he's making progress.

Years ago, Father had conducted some of his

most revolutionary experiments on this lowest floor of the hospital. The rumors of what he created here, which Randal has overheard, are as numerous as they are disturbing.

A battle seems to have been fought on this level. A section of the corridor wall has been broken down, as if something smashed its way out of one of the rooms.

To the right of the elevator, half the width of the passageway is occupied by organized piles of rubble: broken concrete blocks, twisted rebar in mare's nests of rust, mounds of plaster, steel door frames wrenched into peculiar shapes, the formidable steel doors themselves bent in half . . .

According to Hands of Mercy legend, something had gone so wrong down here that Father wished always to keep the memory of it clear in his mind and, therefore, made no repairs and left the rubble instead of having it hauled away. Dozens of the New Race had perished here in an attempt to contain . . . something.

Because Father enters and exits Mercy every day on this level, he is regularly confronted with the evidence of the terrible crisis that apparently almost led to the destruction of his life's work. Some even dare to speculate that Father nearly died here, though to repeat this claim seems like blasphemy.

Turning away from the rubble, Randal Six uses

the last letter of *toward* to spell *determination* in a new direction.

By a series of side steps that spell small words, alternating with forward steps that spell long words, he comes to a door at the end of the hallway. This is not locked.

Beyond is a storage room with rows of cabinets in which are kept hard-copy backup files of the project's computerized records.

Directly opposite the first door stands another. That one will be locked. Through it, Father comes and goes from Mercy.

Randal Six navigates the tile floor in this room by means of crosswords, at last settling in a hiding place between rows of file cabinets, near the second door but not within sight of it.

Now he must wait.

CHAPTER 57

FROM THE LUXE, Carson went to Homicide, settled at the computer on her desk, and launched her web browser.

There was no graveyard shift in Homicide. Detectives worked when the investigation required, night or day, but they tended to be in-office less as the day waned, on call but not sitting desks in the wee hours. At the moment, though the night was not yet that late, she sat alone in the corpse-chasers' corner.

Reeling from what Deucalion had told her, Carson wasn't sure what to believe. She found it surprisingly difficult to *dis*believe any of his story regardless of the fact that it was fantastic to the point of insanity.

She needed to get background on Victor Helios. With the World Wide Web, she was able to unwrap a fictitious biography more easily than in the days when a data chase had to be done on foot or through cooperating officers in other jurisdictions.

She typed in her search string. In seconds, she had scores of hits. Helios, the visionary founder of Biovision. Helios, the local mover and shaker in New Orleans politics and society. Helios, the philanthropist.

At first she seemed to have a lot of material. Quickly, however, she found that for all his wealth and connections, Helios didn't so much swim the waters of New Orleans society as skim across the surface.

In the city for almost twenty years, he made a difference in his community, but with a minimum of exposure. Scores of people in local society got more press time; they were omnipresent by comparison to Helios.

Furthermore, when Carson attempted to track the few facts about Helios's past, prior to New Orleans, they trailed away like wisps of evaporating mist.

He had gone to university "in Europe," but nothing more specific was said about his alma mater.

Though he inherited his fortune, the names of his parents were never mentioned.

He was said to have greatly enlarged that fortune

with several financial coups during the dot-com boom. No details were provided.

References to "a New England childhood" never included the state where he had been born and raised.

One thing about the available photos intrigued Carson. In his first year in New Orleans, Victor had been handsome, almost dashing, and appeared to be in his late thirties. In his most recent photos, he looked hardly any older.

He had adopted a more flattering hairstyle—but he had no less hair than before. If he'd had plastic surgery, the surgeon had been particularly skilled.

Eight years ago, he had returned from an unspecified place in New England with a bride who appeared to be no older than twenty-five. Her name was Erika, but Carson could find no mention of her maiden name.

Erika would be perhaps thirty-three now. In her most recent photos, she looked not a day older than in those taken eight years previously.

Some women were fortunate enough to keep their twenty-something looks until they were forty. Erika might be one of those.

Nevertheless, the ability of *both* her and her husband to defy the withering hand of time seemed remarkable. If not uncanny.

"They got him, O'Connor."

Startled, she looked up from the computer and

saw Tom Bowmaine, the watch commander, at the open door to the hallway, on the farther side of the Homicide bullpen.

"They got the Surgeon," Tom elaborated. "Dead. He took a header off a roof."

CHAPTER 58

ONE BLOCK OF THE ALLEYWAY had been cordoned off to preserve as much evidence as possible for the CSI crew. Likewise the roof of the building and the freight elevator.

Carson climbed the stairs to Roy Pribeaux's apartment. The jake outside the door knew her; he let her into the loft.

She half expected to find Harker or Frye, or both. Neither was present. Another detective, Emery Framboise, had been in the area and had caught the call.

Carson liked Emery. The sight of him didn't raise a single hair on the back of her neck.

He was a young guy—thirty-four—who dressed the way certain older detectives had once dressed before they decided they looked like throwbacks to the lost South of the 1950s. Seersucker suits, white rayon shirts, string ties, a straw boater parked dead-flat on his head.

Somehow he made this retro look seem modern, perhaps because he himself was otherwise entirely of a modern sensibility.

Carson was surprised to see Kathy Burke, friend and shrink, with Emery in the kitchen. Primarily Kathy conducted mandatory counseling sessions with officers involved in shootings and in other traumatic situations, though she also wrote psychological profiles of elusive perpetrators like the Surgeon. She seldom visited crime scenes, at least not this early in the game.

Kathy and Emery were watching two CSI techs unload the contents of one of two freezers. Tupperware containers.

As Carson joined Kathy and Emery, one of the techs read a label on the lid of a container. "Left hand."

She would have understood the essence of the situation without hearing those two words, because the raised lid of the second freezer revealed the eyeless corpse of a young woman.

"Why aren't you home reading about swashbuckling heroines and flying dragons?" Carson needled.

"There's a different kind of dragon dead in the

alleyway," Kathy said. "I wanted to see his lair, see if my profile of him holds any water."

"Right hand," a tech said, taking a container from the freezer.

Emery Framboise said, "Carson, looks like you've just been saved a ton of casework."

"I suppose it wasn't an accident he went off the roof?"

"Suicide. He left a note. Probably heard you and Michael were on his trail, figured he was a dead man walking."

"Do homicidal sociopaths commit suicide?" Carson wondered.

"Rarely," Kathy said. "But it's not unheard of."

"Ears," said one of the CSI techs, removing a small container from the freezer, and his partner read the label on another: "Lips."

"I disappointed my mother," Emery said. "She wanted me to be an airline pilot like my dad. At times like this, I think maybe I *would* be better off high in the night, up where the sky is clean, flying San Francisco to Tokyo."

"Yeah," Carson said, "but then what airline pilot is ever going to have stories like this to tell his grandkids when he tucks them into bed? Where's the suicide note?"

Kathy said, "I'll show you."

In the living room, a computer stood on a corner desk. White letters on a field of blue offered a peculiar farewell:

Killed what I wanted. Took what I needed. Now
I leave when I want, how I want, and go where
I want—one level below Hell.

"The taunting tone is typical for a sociopath,"
Kathy said. "The suggestion that he's earned a
princely place in Hell isn't unique, either, but usually if he's playing out a satanic fantasy, you find
occult literature, posters. We haven't come across
any of that yet."

Only half listening, chilled by a sense of déjà vu,
of having seen this message before, Carson stared at
the screen, reading the words twice, three times,
four.

As she read, she extracted a latex glove from a
jacket pocket, pulled it on her right hand, and then
keyed in a print request.

"There was a time," Kathy said, "if a suicide note
wasn't handwritten, it was suspicious. But these
days, they often use their computers. In some cases
they e-mail suicide notes to friends and relatives
just before offing themselves. Progress."

Stripping off the glove, waiting impatiently for
the printer to produce a hard copy, Carson said,
"Down there in the alley, is there enough left of his
face to get a good photograph?"

"No," Kathy said. "But his bedroom's full of
them."

Was it ever. On both nightstands and on the
dresser were a dozen or more photos of Roy

Pribeaux, mostly glamour shots by professional photographers, each in an expensive, ornamental silver frame.

"He doesn't seem to have been lacking in self-esteem," Kathy said drily.

CHAPTER 59

JENNA PARKER, TWENTY-FIVE, lived for parties. She seemed to be invited to one every night.

This evening, she obviously had taken a few pre-party toots of something, getting primed for a late-night bash, for she was buzzed when she came out of her apartment, singing tunelessly.

With or without drugs, Jenna was perpetually happy, walking on sunshine even when the day offered only rain.

On this rainless night, she seemed to float a quarter inch off the floor as she tried to lock her door. The proper relationship of a key to a key-hole seemed to elude her, and she giggled when, three times in a row, she failed the simple insertion test.

Maybe she wasn't merely buzzed but fully stung.

She succeeded on the fourth try, and the dead-bolt snapped shut with a solid *clack*.

"Sheryl Crowe," Jonathan Harker said from the doorway of his apartment, across the hall from hers.

She turned, saw him for the first time, and broke into a sunny grin. "Johnny!"

"You sound like Sheryl Crowe when you sing."

"Do I really?"

"Would I lie?"

"Depends on what you want," she said coyly.

"Now, Jen, have I ever come on to you?"

"No. But you will."

"When will I?"

"Later. Sooner. Maybe now."

She'd been to his apartment a couple times for pasta dinners, and he'd been to her place for take-out, since she didn't cook even pasta. These had been strictly neighborly occasions.

He didn't want sex from Jenna Parker. He wanted to learn from her the secret of happiness.

"I told you—it's just you remind me of my sister."

"Sister. Yeah, right."

"Anyway, I'm almost old enough to be your father."

"When has that ever mattered to a man?"

"We aren't all swine," he said.

"Oh. Sorry, Johnny. Jeez, I didn't mean to sound . . . mean. I'm just floatin' so high inside that I'm not always down there where the words come out."

"I noticed. Why do you ever use drugs, anyway? You're happy when you're sober. You're always happy."

She grinned, came to him, and pinched his cheek affectionately. "You're right. I love life. I'm always happy. But it's no crime to want to be even happier now and then."

"Actually," he said, "if I were in Vice instead of Homicide, maybe I'd have to consider it a crime."

"You'd never arrest me, Johnny. Probably not even if I killed someone."

"Probably not," he agreed, and squirted her in the mouth and nostrils with chloroform solution.

Her gasp of surprise did what a blow across the backs of her knees would have done: dropped her to the floor. She sputtered, wheezed, and passed out.

He had taken the squeeze bottle from Roy Pribeaux's apartment. It was one of three he had found there.

Later he would leave it with her dead body. Her remains wouldn't be found for months, so their condition wouldn't enable CSI to date her death after Pribeaux's. The bottle would be one of several pieces of evidence identifying her as his final victim.

Now Jonathan lifted her effortlessly, carried her into his apartment, and kicked the door shut behind them.

Of the four apartments here on the fourth floor, one stood vacant. Paul Miller, in 4-C, was away at a sales conference in Dallas. Only Jonathan and Jenna were in residence. No one could have witnessed the assault and abduction.

Jenna wouldn't be missed for a day or two. By then, he would have opened her top to bottom, would have found the special something that she had and that he was missing, and would have disposed of her remains.

He was taking all these precautions not because he feared going to prison but because he feared that Father would identify him as the renegade.

In his bedroom, Jonathan had pushed the bed into a corner. He had stacked the other furniture atop it to create sufficient space for the makeshift autopsy table that he had prepared for her.

Plastic sheeting covered the floor. At the head and foot of the table stood lamps that were bright enough to reveal the source of her happiness whether it was nestled in a tangle of guts or embedded in the cerebellum.

Putting her on the table, he noticed that she was bleeding from one nostril. She'd cracked her nose against the floor when she had fallen. The bleeding wasn't serious. The nose injury wasn't what would kill her.

Jonathan checked her pulse. Steady.

He was relieved. He'd been concerned that she

had inhaled too much chloroform, that maybe she'd suffered chemical suffocation or anaphylactic shock.

He wanted her to be alive through this procedure. For some of it, he needed her to be awake and responsive.

CHAPTER 60

IN THE BASEMENT of Mercy, hiding behind a row of file cabinets, Randal Six hears noise from beyond the walls of his world: first, the hollow sound of a door falling shut in another room.

According to what Randal has overheard while seeming to be lost in his autism, only Father enters and leaves through the outer door of this chamber. Now, after a late dinner, as he often does, Father must be returning with the intention of working through the night.

Crouched at the end of the cabinet row, Randal cocks his head and listens intently. After a moment, he hears the electronic tones of the numbers being entered in an electric-lock keypad on the far side of the outer file-room door.

The ten tones that represent numbers—zero

through nine—on telephone, security-system, electric-lock, and other keypads are universal. They do
not vary from one manufacturer to another.

He learned this from an educational web site
maintained by one of the nation's largest commu-
nications companies. Having downloaded these
tones in preparation for this odyssey, he has
replayed them hundreds of times until he can
unfailingly identify any code by the tones that
comprise it.

Because the file-room door intervenes, the tones
are muffled. If he didn't have the enhanced hearing
of the New Race, Randal might not be able to identify the code: 368284.

A soft *burrrrr* indicates that the circuit engaging
the lock has been broken.

Although the door is not in Randal's line of
sight, the creak of hinges suggests that Father has
opened it. Footsteps on vinyl tile reveal that Father
has entered the file room.

Out of view of the main aisle, Randal suddenly
wonders to what degree, if any, Father's senses might
have been enhanced—and he holds his breath lest
the faintest exhalation reveal his presence.

Without hesitation, Father's footsteps cross the
room.

The outer door falls shut behind him, and the
burrrrr of the disengaged lock is cut short by the
hard *snap* of the bolt.

The inner door opens, closes, and Father is now

gone into the basement corridor where piles of rubble remind him of a bad day here at the bottom of Mercy.

Patience is a virtue that Randal has in spades. He does not move at once from hiding, but waits a few minutes until Father is almost certainly on another floor, far out of hearing.

Vinyl square by vinyl square, he spells himself to the outer door. Here, as on the other side, there is a keypad. He enters the code: 368284.

The electric lock releases. He puts his hand on the door but cannot find the courage to open it.

Beyond, there is no Mercy. All is new and full of bewildering choices.

He delays so long that the electric lock engages once more.

He enters the code in the keypad. The lock releases: *burrrrr.*

He tells himself to open the door. He cannot.

The lock engages once more.

Trembling, he stands before the door, terrified to go through it, but also terrified to remain on this side.

Into his tortured mind comes the memory of the newspaper photo: Arnie O'Connor, autistic but smiling. Arnie is clearly happier than Randal has ever been or ever will be.

A bitter, caustic sense of injustice floods through Randal. This emotion is so intense that he fears it will dissolve him from the inside out if he does not take action to secure for himself the happiness that Arnie O'Connor enjoys.

The little snot. The hateful little worm, selfishly keeping the secret of happiness. What right does *he* have to be happy when a child of Father, superior in every way, lives in misery more than Mercy?

Again he enters the code. *Burrrrr.*

He pushes on the door. It opens.

Randal Six spells himself across the threshold, out of Mercy, into the unknown.

CHAPTER 61

THROUGH THE DOOR, Carson heard scary-movie music. She rang the bell, rang it again before the first series of chimes quite finished echoing through the apartment beyond.

In undershirt, jeans, and stocking feet, Michael answered the door. Tousled hair. Puffy face. Eyes heavy-lidded from the weight of a sleep not fully cast off. He must have dozed in his big green-leatherette recliner.

He looked adorable.

Carson wished he was grungy. Or slovenly. Or geeky. The last thing she wanted to feel toward a partner was physical attraction.

Instead, he looked as cuddly as a teddy bear. Worse, the sight of him filled her with a warm, agreeable feeling consisting largely of affection but not without an element of desire.

Shit.

"It's just ten o'clock," she said, pushing past him into the apartment, "and you're asleep in front of the TV. What're those orange crumbs on your T-shirt? Cheez Doodles?"

"Exactly," he said, following her into the living room. "Cheez Doodles. You *are* a detective."

"Can I assume you're sober?"

"Nope. Had two diet root beers."

He yawned, stretched, rubbed at his eyes with the back of one fist. He looked edible.

Carson tried to derail that train of thought. Indicating the massive green recliner, she said, "That is the ugliest lump of a chair I've ever seen. Looks like a fungus scraped out of a latrine in Hell."

"Yeah, but it's *my* fungus from Hell, and I love it."

Pointing to the TV, she said, *"Invasion of the Body Snatchers?"*

"The first remake."

"You've seen it like what—ten times?"

"Probably twelve."

"When it comes to glamour," she said, "you're the Cary Grant of your generation."

He grinned at her. She knew why. Her curmudgeonly attitude did not fool him. He sensed the effect that he had on her.

Turning away from him as she felt her face flush,

Carson picked up the remote control and switched off the TV. "The case is breaking. We've gotta move."

"Breaking how?"

"Guy jumped off a roof, smashed himself into alley jam, leaving a freezer full of body parts. They say he's the Surgeon. Maybe he is—but he didn't kill them all."

Sitting on the edge of the recliner, tying his shoes, Michael said, "What—he's got a kill buddy or a copycat?"

"Yeah. One or the other. We dismissed that idea too easily."

"I'll grab a clean shirt and a jacket," he said.

"Maybe change the Cheez Doodle T while you're at it," she said.

"Absolutely. I wouldn't want to embarrass you in front of some criminal scum," he said, and stripped off the T-shirt as he left the room.

He knew exactly what he was doing: giving her a look. She took it. Good shoulders, nice abs.

CHAPTER 62

ERIKA ROAMED the silent mansion, pausing frequently to study Victor's collection of European and Asian antiques.

As they did every night, the nine members of the household staff—butler, maids, chef, cleaning crew, gardeners—had retired to their quarters above the ten-car garage at the back of the property.

They lived dormitory-style, the sexes integrated. They were provided with a minimum of amenities.

Victor seldom needed servants after ten o'clock—even on those nights when he was home—but he preferred not to allow his household staff, all members of the New Race, to lead lives separate from the mansion. He wanted them to be available twenty-four hours a day. He insisted that the only focus of their lives should be his comfort.

Erika was pained by their circumstances. They were essentially hung on a rack, like tools, to await the next use he had for them.

The fact that her circumstances were not dissimilar to theirs *had* occurred to her. But she enjoyed a greater freedom to fill her days and nights with pursuits that interested her.

As her relationship with Victor matured, she hoped to be able to gain influence with him. She might be able to use that influence to improve the lot of the household staff.

As this concern for the staff had grown, she found herself less often despairing. Following her interests—and thus refining herself—was fine, but having a *purpose* proved more satisfying.

In the main drawing room, she paused to admire an exquisite pair of Louis XV ormolu-mounted boulle marquetry and ebony *bas d'armoires.*

The Old Race could create objects of breathtaking beauty unlike anything the New Race had done. This puzzled Erika; it did not seem to square with Victor's certainty that the New Race was superior.

Victor himself had an eye for the art of the Old Race. He had paid two and a quarter million for this pair of *bas d'armoires.*

He said that some members of the Old Race excelled at creating things of beauty because they were inspired by anguish. By their deep sense of loss. By their search for meaning.

Beauty came at the expense, however, of certitude,

efficiency. Creating a beautiful piece of art, Victor said, was not an admirable use of energy because it in no way furthered mankind's conquest of itself or of nature.

A race without pain, on the other hand, a race that was *told* its meaning and explicitly given its purpose by its creator, would never need beauty, because it would have an infinite series of great tasks ahead of it. Working as one, with the single-minded purpose of a hive, all members of the New Race would tame nature, conquer the challenges of Earth as ordinary humanity had failed to do, and then become the masters of the other planets, the stars.

All barriers would fall to them.

All adversaries would be crushed.

New Men and New Women would not need beauty because they would have *power*. Those who felt powerless created art; beauty was their substitute for the power they could not attain. The New Race would need no substitute.

Yet Victor collected the art and the antiques of the Old Race. Erika wondered why, and she wondered if Victor himself knew why.

She had read enough literature to be sure that Old Race authors would have called him a cruel man. But Victor's art collection gave Erika hope that in him existed a core of pity and tenderness that might with patience be tapped.

Still in the main drawing room, she came to a

large painting by Jan van Huysum, signed and dated 1732. For this still life, Victor had paid more millions.

In the painting, white and purple grapes appeared ready to burst with juice at the slightest touch. Succulent peaches and plums spilled across a table, caressed by sunshine in such a way that they seemed to glow from within.

The artist realistically portrayed this ripe bounty yet managed, subtly and without sentimentality, to suggest the ephemeral quality of even nature's sweetest gifts.

Mesmerized by van Huysum's genius, Erika was subconsciously aware of a furtive scrabbling. The noise grew louder, until at last it distracted her from the painting.

When she turned to survey the drawing room, she at once saw the source of the sound. Like a five-legged crab on some strange blind mission, a severed hand crawled across the antique Persian carpet.

CHAPTER 63

DETECTIVE DWIGHT FRYE lived in a bungalow so overgrown with Miss Manila bougainvillea that the main roof and the porch roof were entirely concealed. Floral bracts—bright pink in daylight but more subdued now—dripped from every eave, and the entire north wall was covered with a web of vine trunks that had woven random-pattern bars across the windows.

The front lawn had not been mowed in weeks. The porch steps had sagged for years. The house might not have been painted for a decade.

If Frye rented, his landlord was a tightwad. If he owned this place, he was white trash.

The front door stood open.

Through the screen door, Carson could see a muddy yellow light back toward the kitchen. When she couldn't find a bell push, she knocked, then knocked louder, and called out, "Detective Frye? Hey, Dwight, it's O'Connor and Maddison."

Frye hove into sight, backlit by the glow in the kitchen. He wove along the hall like a seaman tacking along a ship's passageway in a troublesome swell.

When he reached the front door, he switched on the porch light and blinked at them through the screen. "What do you assholes want?"

"A little Southern hospitality for starters," Michael said.

"I was born in Illinois," Frye said. "Never shoulda left."

He wore baggy pants with suspenders. His tank-style, sweat-soaked undershirt revealed his unfortunate breasts so completely that Carson knew she'd have a few nightmares featuring them.

"The Surgeon case is breaking," she said. "There's something we need to know."

"Told you in the library—I got no interest in that anymore."

Frye's hair and face glistened as if he had been bobbing for olives in a bowl of oil.

Getting a whiff of him, Carson took a step back from the door and said, "What I need to know is when you and Harker went to Bobby Allwine's apartment."

Frye said, "Older I get, the less I like the sloppy red cases. Nobody strangles anymore. They all chop and slice. It's the damn sick Hollywood influence."

"Allwine's apartment?" she reminded him. "When were you there?"

"You listening to me *at all*?" Frye asked. "I was never there. Maybe you get off on torn-out hearts and dripping guts, but I'm getting queasy in my midlife. It's *your* case, and welcome to it."

Michael said, "Never there? So how did Harker know about the black walls, the razor blades?"

Frye screwed up his face as if to spit but then said, "What razor blades? What's got you girls in such a pissy mood?"

To Michael, Carson said, "You smell truth here?"

"He reeks with it," Michael said.

"Reeks—is that some kind of wisecrack?" Frye demanded.

"I've got to admit it is," Michael said.

"I wasn't half drunk and feelin' charitable," Frye said, "I'd open this here screen door and kick your giblets clean off."

"I'm grateful for your restraint," Michael said.

"Is that some kind of sarcasm?"

"I've got to admit it is," Michael said.

Turning from the door, heading for the porch steps, Carson said, "Let's go, let's move."

"But me and the Swamp Thing," Michael said, "we're having such a nice chat."

"That's another wisecrack, ain't it?" Frye demanded.

"I've got to admit it is," Michael said as he followed Carson off the porch.

As she thought back over her encounters with Harker during the past couple of days, Carson headed toward the car at a run.

CHAPTER 64

AFTER CUFFING JENNA'S WRISTS and ankles to the autopsy table in his bedroom, Jonathan Harker used a pair of scissors to cut away her clothes.

With a damp cotton ball, he gently cleaned the blood from around her left nostril. Already, the bleeding from her nose seemed to have stopped.

Each time that she began to wake, he used the squeeze bottle to dribble two or three drops of chloroform on her upper lip, just under her nostrils. Inhaling the fumes as the fluid rapidly evaporated, she retreated again from consciousness.

When the woman was naked, Jonathan touched her where he wished, curious about his reaction. Rather, he was curious about his *lack* of a reaction.

Sex—disconnected from the power of procreation—was the primary means by which members of the New Race relieved tension. They were available to one another on request, to a degree that even the most libertine members of the Old Race would find shocking.

They were capable of performance on demand. They did not need beauty or emotion or any form of tender feeling to stimulate their desire.

Desire in them did not encompass love, merely *need*.

Young men coupled with old women, old women with young women, young girls with old men, the thin with the fat, the beautiful with the ugly, in every combination, each with the sole purpose to satisfy himself, with no obligations to the other, with no greater affection than they had toward the food they ate, with no expectation that sex would lead to a relationship.

Indeed, personal relationships between members of the New Race were discouraged. Jonathan sometimes suspected that as a species they were hardwired to be incapable of relationships in any of the ways that the Old Race experienced and defined them.

Couples committed to each other are impediments to the infinite series of conquests that is to be the uniform purpose of every member of the New Race. So are friendships. So are families.

For the world to be as one, every thinking creature must share the same drive, the same goal. They must live by a system of values so simplified as to allow no room for the concept of morality and the differences of opinion that it fosters.

Because friendships and families are distractions from the great unified purpose of the species, the ideal citizen, Father says, must be a loner in his personal life. As a loner, he is able to commit his passion fully to the triumph and the glory of the New Race.

Touching Jenna as he wished, unable to stir within himself the need that passed for desire, Jonathan suspected that his kind were also hardwired to be incapable of—or at least disinterested in—sex with members of the Old Race.

With their basic education via direct-to-brain data downloading comes a programmed contempt for the Old Race. Contempt, of course, can lead to a sense of righteous domination that includes sexual exploitation. This does not happen with the New Race, perhaps because their programmed contempt for nature's form of humanity includes a subtle element of disgust.

Among those created in the tanks, only Father's wife was allowed desire for one of the Old Race. But in a sense, he was not of the Old Race anymore, but was the god of the New.

Caressing Jenna, whose body was lovely and whose exterior form could pass for that of any woman of the New Race, Jonathan not only remained detumescent but also became vaguely repulsed by her.

How strange that this lesser creature, who was the dirty link between lower animals and the superior New Race, nevertheless might have within her the thing that Jonathan himself seemed to be missing, the organ or the gland or the neural matrix that enabled her to be happy nearly all the time.

The time had come to cut.

When she groaned and her eyelids fluttered, he applied a few more drops of chloroform to her upper lip, and she subsided.

He rolled a wheeled IV rack beside the table. From it hung a bag of glucose-saline solution.

He tied a rubber-tube tourniquet around Jenna's right arm and found a suitable blood vessel. He inserted an intravenous cannula by which the glucose-saline would be infused into her bloodstream, and removed the tourniquet.

The drip line between the solution bag and the cannula featured a drug port. He inserted a large, full syringe of a potent sedative, which he would be able to administer in multiple, measured doses, as required.

To keep Jenna perfectly still during dissection, he must put her in deep sedation. When he wanted her awake to answer questions that he might have about what he found inside her, he could deny her the sedative.

Because she might cry out even during sedation and alarm the residents in the apartment below, Jonathan now wadded a rag and stuffed it in her mouth. He sealed her lips with duct tape.

When he pressed the tape in place, Jenna's eyes fluttered, opened. For a moment she was confused, disoriented—and then not.

As her eyes widened with terror, Jonathan said, "I know that your kind can't turn off physical pain at will, as we can. So I'll wake you as seldom as possible to get your explanation of what I find inside you."

CHAPTER 65

WITH A SUCTION-ADHERED emergency beacon on the roof above the driver's door, Carson cruised fast on surface streets.

Struggling to absorb everything she had told him, Michael said, "The guy you saw in Allwine's apartment, he owns a movie theater?"

"The Luxe."

"The nutcase who says he's made from parts of criminals and brought alive by lightning—he owns a movie theater? I would have thought a hot-dog stand. A tire-repair shop."

"Maybe he's not a nutcase."

"A hamburger joint."

"Maybe he's what he says he is."

"A beauty salon."

"You should've seen what he did with those quarters."

"I can tie a knot in a cherry stem using my tongue," Michael said, "but that doesn't make me supernatural."

"I didn't say he was supernatural. He says part of what the lightning brought him that night, in addition to life, was . . . an understanding of the quantum structure of the universe."

"What the hell does that mean?"

"I don't know," she admitted. "But somehow it explains how he makes the coins vanish."

"Any half-good magician can make a coin vanish, and they're not all wizards of quantum physics."

"This was more than cheap magic. Anyway, Deucalion said some of their kind are sure to have a strong death wish."

"Carson—what kind?"

Instead of answering his question, aware that she must lead him a careful step at a time toward her ultimate revelation, Carson said, "Allwine and his friend were in the library, poring through aberrant psychology texts, trying to understand their anguish."

"Don't drive so fast."

Accelerating, Carson said, "So the books weren't pulled off the shelves in a struggle. There *wasn't* a struggle. That's why the scene was so neat in spite of the apparent violence."

"Apparent? Allwine's *heart* was cut out."

"Hearts. Plural. But he probably *asked* his friend to kill him."

"'Hey, pal, do me a favor and cut my heart out?' He couldn't just slit his own wrists, take poison, bore himself to death with multiple viewings of *The English Patient?*"

"No. Deucalion said their kind are built to be incapable of suicide."

With a sigh of frustration, Michael said, "Their kind. Here we go again."

"The proscription against suicide—it's there in the original diary. I saw it. After the coins, after I started to accept . . . then Deucalion showed me."

"Diary? Whose diary?"

She hesitated.

"Carson?"

"This is going to be a real test."

"What test?"

"A test of you, me, our partnership here."

"Don't drive so fast," he cautioned.

This time, she didn't react to his admonition by accelerating. She didn't slow down, either, but she didn't pump up more speed. A little concession to help win him over.

"This is weird stuff," she warned.

"What—I don't have a capacity for weird? I have a fabulous capacity for weird. *Whose diary?*"

She took a deep breath. "Victor's diary. Victor Frankenstein." When he stared at her in flabbergasted silence, she said, "Maybe this sounds crazy—"

"Yeah. Maybe."

"But I think the legend is true, like Deucalion says. Victor Helios is Victor Frankenstein."

"What have you done with the *real* Carson O'Connor?"

"Deucalion—he was Victor's first . . . I don't know . . . his first creation."

"See, right away, I start getting geeky Renaissance Fair vibes from the name. It sounds like the Fourth Musketeer or something. What kind of name is Deucalion, anyway?"

"He named himself. It's from mythology. Deucalion was the son of Prometheus."

"Oh, of course," Michael said. "Deucalion Prometheus, son of Fred Prometheus. I remember him now."

"Deucalion is his only name, first and last."

"Like Cher."

"In classic mythology, Prometheus was the brother of Atlas. He shaped humans out of clay and gave them the spark of life. He taught humanity several arts, and in defiance of Zeus, he gave us the gift of fire."

"Maybe I wouldn't have fallen asleep in school so often if my teacher had been driving the classroom at eighty miles an hour. For God's sake, slow down."

"Anyway, Deucalion has Victor's original diary. It's written in German, and it's full of anatomical drawings that include an improved circulatory system with two hearts."

"Maybe if you give it to Dan Rather and *Sixty Minutes,* they'll do a segment on it, but it sounds like a forgery to me."

She wanted to punch him. To temper that impulse, she reminded herself of how cuddly he had looked back at his apartment.

Instead of hitting him, she pumped the brakes and slid the plainwrap sedan to the curb in front of Fullbright's Funeral Home.

"A good cop has to have an open mind," she said.

"Agreed. But it doesn't help much to have one *so* open that the wind blows through with a mournful, empty sound."

CHAPTER 66

LIFE IN THE HOUSE of Victor Frankenstein was certain to involve more macabre moments than life in the house of Huckleberry Finn.

Nevertheless, the sight of a severed hand crawling across the drawing-room carpet amazed even Erika, a man-made woman equipped with two hearts. She stood transfixed for perhaps a minute, unable to move.

No science could explain an ambulatory hand. This seemed to be a supernatural manifestation as surely as would be an ectoplasmic human figure floating above a séance table.

Yet Erika felt less fear than amazement, less amazement than wonder. Her heart beat faster the longer that she watched the hand, and a not-unpleasant thrill made her tremble.

Instinctively, she knew that the hand was aware of her. It had no eyes, no sense other than touch—and should not possess a sense of touch, either, considering that it had no nervous system, no *brain*—yet somehow it *knew* that she was watching it.

This must have been the thing that she'd heard moving furtively through the bedroom, under the bed, the thing rattling the contents of the bathroom cabinet. The thing that had left the scalpel on her bath mat.

That last thought led her to the realization that the hand must be merely the tool of whatever entity had spoken to her through the television screen and had encouraged her to kill Victor. As it used the TV, it used the hand.

As it used the hand, it wished to use her as agent to destroy the man it had called *evil*.

There is no world but this one.

Erika reminded herself that she was a soul-free soldier in the army of materialism. Belief in something more than the eyes can see was punishable by termination.

As if it were the hand of a blind man exploring the patterns on the Persian carpet, the beast with five fingers felt its way past furniture, toward the double doors that separated the drawing room from the downstairs hall.

The thing did not wander aimlessly. By all appearances, it moved with purpose.

One of the two doors to the hallway stood open. The hand paused there, waiting.

Erika suspected that it not only moved with purpose but also that it wanted her to follow. She stepped toward it.

The hand crabbed forward once more, crawled across the threshold and into the hallway.

CHAPTER 67

EVEN AS THE NIGHT ticked toward the dark start of a new day, lights were on at the back of the funeral home.

Insistently thumbing the bell push, Michael said, "See, another thing that doesn't make sense is why Victor Frankenstein would turn up in New Orleans, of all places."

Carson said, "Where would you expect him to set up shop—Baton Rouge, Baltimore, Omaha, Las Vegas?"

"Somewhere in Europe."

"Why Europe?"

"He's European."

"Once was, yeah, but not now. As Helios, he doesn't even speak with an accent."

"The whole creepy Frankenstein shtick—it's totally European," Michael insisted.

"Remember the mobs with pitchforks and torches storming the castle?" Carson asked. "He can't go back there ever."

"That was in the *movies,* Carson."

"Maybe they're more like documentaries."

She knew she sounded crazy. The bayou heat and humidity had finally gotten to her. Maybe if you cut open her skull, you'd find Spanish moss growing on her brain.

She said, "Where is the most recombinant-DNA work being done, the most research into cloning? Where are the most discoveries in molecular biology taking place?"

"According to the tabloids I read, probably in Atlantis, a few miles under the surface of the Caribbean."

"It's all happening here in the good old USA, Michael. If Victor Frankenstein is alive, this is where he'd want to be, right where the most science is being done. And New Orleans is plenty creepy enough to please him. Where else do they bury all their dead in mausoleums aboveground?"

The porch light came on. A deadbolt turned with a rasp and a clack, and the door opened.

Taylor Fullbright stood before them in red silk pajamas and a black silk robe on the breast of which was appliquéd an image of Judy Garland as Dorothy.

As convivial as ever, Fullbright said, "Why, hello again!"

"I'm sorry if we woke you," Carson apologized.

"No, no. You didn't. I finished embalming a customer half an hour ago, worked up an appetite. I'm making a pastrami and tongue sandwich, if you'd like one."

Michael said, "No thanks. I'm full of Cheez Doodles, and she's full of inexplicable enthusiasm."

"We don't need to come in," Carson said, showing him first the silver-framed photo of Roy Pribeaux. "Have you ever seen him before?"

"Quite a handsome fellow," said Fullbright. "But he looks a bit smug. I know the type. They're always trouble."

"More trouble than you can imagine."

"But I don't know him," Fullbright said.

From a nine-by-twelve manila envelope, Carson extracted a police-department file photo of Detective Jonathan Harker.

"This one I know," said the funeral director. "He was Allwine's funeral buddy."

CHAPTER 68

JENNA PARKER, party girl, not for the first time naked in front of a man, but for the first time unable to excite sexual interest, wept. Her sobs were more pathetic for being muffled by the rag in her mouth and the lip-sealing duct tape.

"It's not that I don't find you attractive," Jonathan told her. "I do. I think you're a fine example of your species. It's just that I'm of the New Race, and having sex with you would be like you having sex with a monkey."

For some reason, his sincere explanation made her cry harder. She was going to choke on her sobs if she wasn't careful.

Giving her a chance to adjust to her circumstances and to get control of her emotions, he fetched a physician's bag from a closet. He put it on a stainless-steel cart, and rolled the cart to the autopsy table.

From the black bag he extracted surgical instruments—scalpels, clamps, retractors—and lined them up on the cart. They had not been sterilized, but as Jenna would be dead when he was done with her, there was no reason to guard against infection.

When the sight of the surgical instruments excited the woman to greater weeping, Jonathan realized that fear of pain and death might be the sole cause of her tears.

"Well," he told her, "if you're going to cry about *that,* then you're going to have to cry, because there's nothing I can do about it. I can't very well let you go now. You'd tell."

After emptying the bag, he set it aside.

On the bed lay a thin but tough plastic raincoat, one of those that could be wadded up and stored in a zippered case no larger than a tobacco pouch. He intended to wear it over his T-shirt and jeans to minimize cleanup when he had finished with Jenna.

As Jonathan shook the raincoat to unfurl it, a familiar throb, a shifting and turning within him, made him gasp with surprise, with excitement.

He threw aside the raincoat. He pulled up his T-shirt, exposing his torso.

In his abdomen, the Other pressed against the caging flesh, as if testing the walls of its confinement. It writhed, it bulged.

He had no concern that it would burst out of him and perhaps kill him in the process. That was not how the birth would occur. He had studied various methods of reproduction, and he had developed a theory that he found convincing.

Seeing this movement within Jonathan, Jenna stopped crying in a blink—and started to scream into the rag, the duct tape.

He attempted to explain to her that this was nothing to fear, that this was his ultimate act of rebellion against Father and the start of the New Race's emancipation.

"He denies us the power to reproduce," Jonathan said, "but I am reproducing. It's going to be like parthenogenesis, I think. When the time comes, I'll divide, like an ameba. Then there will be two of me—I the father, and my son."

When Jenna thrashed, desperately but stupidly trying to wrench loose of her restraints, Jonathan worried that she would tear out the IV drip. Eager to proceed with her dissection, he didn't want to have to waste time reinserting the cannula.

He carefully pressed the plunger of the syringe in the drug port and delivered a couple ccs of the sedative.

Her thrashing quickly quieted to a trembling. She grew still. She slept.

Inside Jonathan, the Other grew still, as well. His stretched torso regained its natural shape.

Smiling, he slid one hand down his chest and abdomen. "Our time is coming."

CHAPTER 69

TURNING AWAY FROM the front door of Fullbright's Funeral Home, Michael wanted to sprint to the car and climb in behind the wheel. He would have done it, too, would have seized control—if he'd had a key.

Mere possession of the driver's seat would mean nothing to Carson. She wouldn't give him her key. Unless she *chose* to ride shotgun, she'd walk before she'd give up the wheel.

The plainwrap came with two sets of keys. Carson had both.

Michael had frequently considered requisitioning another set from the motor pool. He knew she'd consider that betrayal.

So she drove again. Clearly, there were no safety engineers in her family.

At least he was distracted from consideration of their speed by the need to get his mind around the cockamamie story she wanted him to believe. "Man-made men? Science just isn't that far along yet."

"Maybe most scientists aren't, but Victor is."

"Mary Shelley was a *novelist*."

"She must've based the book on a true story she heard that summer. Michael, you *heard* what Jack Rogers told us. Not a freak. Bobby Allwine was *designed*."

"Why would he be creating monsters to be security guards like Bobby Allwine? Doesn't that seem goofy?"

"Maybe he creates them to be all kinds of things—cops, like Harker. Mechanics. Pilots. Bureaucrats. Maybe they're all around us."

"Why?"

"Deucalion says—to take our place, to destroy God's work and replace it with his own."

"I'm not Austin Powers, and neither are you, and it's hard to swallow that Helios is Dr. Evil."

Impatiently, she said, "What happened to your imagination? Have you watched so many movies, you can't imagine for yourself anymore, you have to have Hollywood do it for you?"

"Harker, huh? From homicide cop to homicidal robot?"

"Not robot. Engineered or cloned or grown in a

vat—I don't know how. It's no longer parts of corpses animated by lightning."

"One man, even a genius, couldn't—"

She interrupted him: "Helios is an obsessed, demented visionary at work for two centuries, with a huge family fortune."

Preoccupied with a new thought, she let their speed fall.

After a silence, Michael said, "What?"

"We're dead."

"I don't feel dead."

"I mean, if Helios *is* who Deucalion says, if he has achieved all of this, if his creations are seeded through the city, we don't have much of a chance against him. He's a genius, a billionaire, a man of enormous power—and we're squat."

She was scared. He could hear fear in her voice. He had never known her to be afraid. Not like this. Not without a gun in her face and some dirtbag's finger on the trigger.

"I just don't buy this," he said, though he half did. "I don't understand why *you* buy it."

With an edge, she said, "If I buy it, homey, isn't that good enough for you?"

When he hesitated to reply, she braked hard and pulled to the curb. Pissed, she switched off the light and got out of the car.

In the movies, when they saw a body with two hearts and organs of unknown purpose, they knew *right away* it was aliens or something.

Even though he hadn't met Deucalion, Michael didn't know why he was resisting the usual movie conclusion to be made from what Jack Rogers had found inside Bobby Allwine. Besides, someone had stolen Allwine's corpse and the autopsy records, which seemed to indicate a vast conspiracy of some kind.

He got out of the car.

They were in a residential neighborhood, under a canopy of live oaks. The night was hot. The moon seemed to be melting down through the branches of the trees.

Michael and Carson regarded each other across the roof of the sedan. Her lips were tight. Usually they looked kissable. They didn't look kissable now.

"Michael, I told you what I saw."

"I've jumped off cliffs with you before—but this one's pretty damn high."

She said nothing at first. What might have been a wistful look came over her face. Then: "Some mornings it's hard to get up knowing Arnie will still be...Arnie."

Michael moved toward the front of the car. "All of us want things we maybe aren't ever going to get."

Carson remained at the driver's door, not giving an inch. "I want meaning. Purpose. Higher stakes. I want things to *matter* more than they do."

He stopped in front of the sedan.

Staring up through the oaks at the creamy moon,

she said, "This is real, Michael. I know it. Our lives will never be the same."

He recognized in her a yearning for change so strong that even *this*—a trading of the world they knew for another that had even more terror in it—was preferable to the status quo.

"Okay, okay," he said. "So where's Deucalion? If any of this is real, then it's his fight more than ours."

She lowered her gaze from the moon to Michael. She moved toward the front of the car.

"Deucalion is incapable of violence against his maker," she said. "It's like the proscription against suicide. He tried two hundred years ago, and Victor nearly finished him. Half his face . . . so damaged."

They stood face to face.

He wanted to touch her, to place a hand on her shoulder. He restrained himself because he didn't know what a touch might lead to, and this was not a moment for even more change.

Instead, he said, "Man-made men, huh?"

"Yeah."

"You're sure?"

"Honestly? I don't know. Maybe I just *want* to be sure."

Heat, humidity, moonlight, the fragrance of jasmine: New Orleans sometimes seemed like a fever dream, but never more than now.

"Frankenstein alive," he said. "It's just a *National Enquirer* wet dream."

A harder expression pinched her eyes.

Hastily Michael said, "I *like* the *National Enquirer.* Who in his right mind would believe the *New York Times* anymore? Not me."

"Harker's out there," she reminded him.

He nodded. "Let's get him."

CHAPTER 70

IN A MANSION as large as this, a severed hand had to do a lot of crawling to get where it wanted to go.

When previously it had scuttled unseen through the bedroom, the hand, judging by the sound of it, had moved as fast as a nervous rat. Not now.

The concept of a *weary* severed hand, exhausted from relentless creeping, made no sense.

Neither did the concept of a *confused* severed hand. Yet this one paused from time to time, as though it were not sure of the correct direction, and once it even retraced the path that it had taken and chose another route.

Erika persisted in the conviction that she was witnessing an event of supernatural character. No science she knew could explain this crawling marvel.

Although Victor had long ago trafficked in such

parts as this, making jigsaw men from graveyard fragments, he had not used such crude methods in a long time.

Besides, the hand did not end in a bloody stump. It terminated in a round stub of smooth skin, as though it had never been attached to an arm.

This detail, if nothing else, seemed to confirm its supernatural origins.

In time, with Erika in patient attendance, the hand made its way to the kitchen. There it halted before the pantry door.

She waited for it to do something, and then she decided that it was in need of her assistance. She opened the pantry door, switched on the light.

As the determined hand crawled toward the back wall of the pantry, Erika realized that it must wish to lead her into Victor's studio. She knew of the studio's existence but had never been there.

His secret work space lay beyond the back wall of the pantry. Most likely, a hidden switch would cause the food-laden shelves to swing inward like a door.

Before she could begin to search for the switch, the shelves in fact slid aside. The hand on the floor had not activated them; some other entity was at work.

She followed the hand into the hidden room and saw on the center worktable a Lucite tank filled with a milky solution, housing a man's severed head. Not a fully realized head, but something like a crude model of one, the features only half formed.

Bloodshot blue eyes opened in this travesty of a human face.

The thing spoke to Erika in a low, rough voice exactly like that of the entity who, through the TV, had urged her to kill Victor: "Look at what I am . . . and tell me if you can that he's not evil."

CHAPTER 71

WHEN SHE PARKED in front of Harker's apartment house, Carson got out of the car, hurried to the back, and grabbed the pistol-grip, pump-action shotgun from the trunk.

Michael joined her as she loaded. "Hey. Wait. I don't pretend to be a SWAT team."

"If we try to take Harker into custody like he's an ordinary wack job, we'll be two dead cops."

A guy in a white van across the street had noticed them. Michael didn't want to make a scene, but he said, "Gimme the shotgun."

"I can take the kick," she assured him.

"We're not going in that way."

She slammed the trunk and moved toward the sidewalk.

Michael moved with her, trying reason where *gimme* didn't work. "Call for backup."

"How're you gonna explain to Dispatch why you *need* backup. You gonna tell them we've cornered a man-made monster?"

As they reached the front door of the building, he said, "This is crazy."

"Did I say it wasn't?"

The front door opened into a shabby-genteel lobby with sixteen brass mailboxes.

Carson read the names on the boxes. "Harker's on the fourth floor. Top of the building."

Not convinced of the wisdom of this but caught up in Carson's momentum, Michael went with her to a door beyond which lay stairs that led up through a shaft too long in need of fresh paint.

She started to climb, he followed, and she warned: "Deucalion says, in a crisis, wounded, they're probably able to turn off pain."

"Do we need silver bullets?"

"Is that some kind of sarcasm?" Carson asked, mimicking Dwight Frye.

"I've got to admit it is."

The stairs were narrow. The odors of mildew and disinfectant curdled together in the stifling air. Michael told himself he wasn't getting dizzy.

"They can be killed," Carson said. "Allwine was."

"Yeah. But he *wanted* to die."

"Remember, Jack Rogers said the cranium has incredible molecular density."

"Does that mean something in real words?" he asked.

"His brain is armored against all but the highest caliber."

Gasping not from exertion but from a need for cleaner air than what the fumy stairwell offered, Michael said, "Monsters among us, masquerading as real people—it's the oldest paranoia."

"The word *impossible* contains the word *possible*."

"What's that—some Zen thing?"

"I think *Star Trek*. Mr. Spock."

At the landing between the third and fourth floors, Carson paused and pumped the shotgun, chambering a shell.

Drawing his service piece from the paddle holster on his right hip, Michael said, "So what are we walking into?"

"Scary crap. What's new about that?"

They climbed the last flight to the fourth floor, went through a fire door, and found a short hallway serving four apartments.

The wood floor had been painted a glossy battleship gray. A few feet from Harker's door lay keys on a coiled plastic ring.

Michael squatted, snared the keys. Also on the ring was a small plastic magnetic-reader membership card in a supermarket discount club. It had been issued to Jenna Parker.

He remembered the name from the mailboxes in the public foyer on the ground floor. Jenna Parker lived here at the top of the building; she was one of Harker's neighbors.

Carson whispered, *"Michael."*

He looked up at her, and she pointed with the shotgun barrel.

Closer to Harker's door than where the keys had fallen, an inch from his threshold, a dark spot marred the glossy gray planks. The spot was glossy, too, approximately the size of a quarter but oval. Dark, glossy, and red.

Michael touched it with a forefinger. Wet.

He rubbed forefinger to thumb, smelled the smear. Rising to his feet, he nodded at Carson and showed her the name on the supermarket card.

Standing to one side of the door, he tried the knob. You never knew. Most killers were far short of a genius rating on the Stanford-Binet scale. If Harker had two hearts, he still had one brain, and if he was responsible for some of the murders attributed to the Surgeon, a lot of his synapses must be misfiring. All murderers made mistakes. Sometimes they did everything but post a sign inviting arrest.

This time the door proved to be locked. Michael felt enough play in it, however, to suggest that only the latch was engaged, not the deadbolt.

Carson could have destroyed the lock with one round from her 12-gauge. A shotgun is a pretty good residential-defense weapon because the pellets won't penetrate a wall and kill an innocent person in the next room as easily as will the rounds from high-power handguns.

Although a blast to the lock wouldn't risk deadly consequences to anyone inside, Michael wasn't keen to use the shotgun.

Maybe Harker wasn't alone in there. Maybe he had a hostage.

They had to use the minimum force necessary to effect entrance, then escalate as developments required.

Michael stepped in front of the door, kicked it hard in the lock zone, but it held, and he kicked it again, kicked it a third time, each blow booming almost as loud as a shotgun, and the latch snapped. The door flew open.

Quarter-crouched and fast, Carson went through the door first, the shotgun in front of her, sweeping the muzzle left and right.

Behind her, over her shoulder, Michael saw Harker crossing the far end of the room.

"Drop it!" Carson shouted because he had a revolver.

Harker squeezed off a shot. The door frame took it.

A spray of splinters peppered Michael's brow, his hair, as Carson fired at Harker.

The primary force of the blast caught Harker in the left hip, the thigh. He reeled, crashed against the wall, but didn't go down.

As soon as she fired, still moving, Carson chambered another round and simultaneously side-stepped to the left of the door.

Coming behind her, Michael moved to the right as Harker fired a second shot. He heard the keening lament of a bullet cleaving the air, a near miss, inches from his head.

Carson fired again, and Harker staggered with the impact, but he kept moving, plunging into the kitchen, out of sight, as Carson chambered a third round.

CHAPTER 72

STANDING WITH HER BACK to the shared wall between the living room and the kitchen, Carson fished shotgun shells out of a jacket pocket.

She had the shakes. She handled the fat shells one at a time, afraid of fumbling them. If she dropped one, if it rolled under a piece of furniture . . .

Outside at the open trunk of the car, when she had loaded the 12-gauge, she almost hadn't pocketed any spare rounds. This was a finishing weapon, useful for bringing a quick end to a dangerous situation; it wasn't a piece you used for extended firefights.

Only twice before had she needed a shotgun. On each occasion a single shot—in one instance, just a warning; in the other incident, intended to wound—had put an end to the confrontation.

Apparently Harker would be as hard to bring down as Deucalion had predicted.

She only had three spare shells. She inserted them in the tube-style magazine and hoped she had enough to do the job.

Skull bone as dense as armor plating. She might blind him with a face shot, but would that matter, could he function anyway?

Two hearts. Aim for the chest. Two rapid-fire rounds, maybe three, point-blank if possible. Take out both hearts.

Across the room, Michael was staying low, using furniture for cover, moving deeper into the living room, angling for a line of sight into the kitchen, where Harker had taken cover.

Harker was only part of their problem, Jenna the other part. The blood in the hallway suggested she was in the apartment. Hurt. Maybe mortally wounded.

Small apartment. Probably three rooms, one bath. He had come out of the bedroom. Jenna might be in there.

Or she might be in the kitchen, where he had gone. He might be slitting her throat now.

Back against the wall, holding the shotgun cross-body, Carson eased toward the archway between this room and the kitchen, aware that he might be waiting to shoot her in the face the instant she showed.

They had to whack Harker quickly, get Jenna

medical help. The woman wasn't screaming. Maybe dead. Maybe dying. In this situation, time was the essence, terror the quintessence.

A noise in the kitchen. She couldn't identify it.

Rising recklessly from behind a sofa to get a better look, Michael said, "He's going out a window!"

Carson cleared the archway, saw an open casement window. Harker crouched on the sill, his back to her.

She swept the room to be sure that Jenna wasn't there to take ricochets. No. Just Harker.

Monster or no monster, shooting him in the back would earn her an OIS investigation, but she would have shot him anyway, except that he was gone before she could squeeze the trigger.

Rushing to the window, Carson expected a fire escape beyond, perhaps a balcony. She found neither.

Harker had thrown himself into the alleyway. The fall was at least thirty feet, possibly thirty-five. Far enough to acquire a mortal velocity before impact.

He lay facedown on the pavement. Unmoving.

His plunge seemed to refute Deucalion's contention that Victor's creations were effectively forbidden to self-destruct.

Below, Harker stirred. He sprang to his feet. He had known that he could survive such a fall.

When he looked up at the window, at Carson, reflected moonlight made lanterns of his eyes.

At this distance, a round—or all four rounds— from the shotgun wouldn't faze him.

He ran toward the nearest end of the alley. There he halted when, with a bark of brakes in the street beyond, a white van skidded to a stop in front of him.

The driver's door flew open, and a man got half out. From this distance, at night, Carson couldn't see his face. He seemed to have white or pale-blond hair.

She heard the driver call something to Harker. She couldn't make out his words.

Harker rounded the van, climbed in the passenger's side.

Behind the wheel again, the driver slammed his door and stood on the accelerator. Tires spun, shrieked, smoked, and left rubber behind as the vehicle raced off into the night.

The van might have been a Ford. She couldn't be certain.

Perspiration dripped from Carson's brow. She was soaked. In spite of the heat, the sweat felt cold on her skin.

CHAPTER 73

VICTOR HAD NAMED HIM Karloff, perhaps intending humor, but Erika found nothing funny about the hideous "life" that this creature had been given.

The bodiless head stood in a milky antibiotic bath, served by tubes that brought it nutrients and by others that drained metabolic waste. An array of machines attended and sustained Karloff, all of them mysterious and ominous to Erika.

The hand lay on the floor, in a corner, palm-up. Still.

Karloff had controlled that five-fingered explorer through the power of telekenesis, which his maker had hoped to engineer into him. An object of horror, he had nonetheless proved to be a successful experiment.

Self-disconnected from its sustaining machinery, the hand is now dead. Karloff can still animate it, although not for much longer. The flesh will rapidly deteriorate. Even the power of telekenesis will not be able to manipulate frozen joints and putrefying musculature.

Surely, however, Victor had not anticipated that Karloff would be able to employ his psychic ability to gain even a limited form of freedom and to roam the mansion with the desperate hope of inciting his maker's murder.

With that same uncanny power, Karloff had activated the electric mechanism that operated the secret door in the food pantry, providing entrance to Erika. With it, he had also controlled the television in the master suite, to speak with her and to encourage rebellion.

Being less of a complete creation than Erika, Karloff had not been programmed with a full understanding of Victor's mission or with knowledge of the limitations placed upon the freedom of the New Race. Now he knew that she could not act against her maker, and his despair was complete.

When she suggested that he use his power to disable the machines that supported his existence, Erika discovered that he, too, had been programmed to be incapable of self-destruction.

She struggled against despondency, her hope reduced to the shaky condition of a three-legged table. The crawling hand and the other apparitions

had not been the supernatural events that she had
longed to believe they were.

Oh, how badly she had wanted these miracles to
be evidence of another world beyond this one.
What seemed to be a divine Presence, however, had
been only the grotesque Karloff.

She might have blamed him for her deep disappointment, might have hated him, but she did not.
Instead she pitied this pathetic creature, who was
helpless in his power and condemned to a living
hell.

Perhaps what she felt wasn't pity. Strictly speaking, she should not be capable of pity. But she felt
something, felt it poignantly.

"Kill me," the pathetic thing pleaded.

The bloodshot eyes were haunted. The half-
formed face was a mask of misery.

Erika began to tell him that her program forbade
her to kill either the Old Race or the New except in
self-defense or at the order of her maker. Then she
realized that her program did not anticipate this situation.

Karloff did not belong to the Old Race, but he
did not qualify as one of the New Race, either. He
was something other, singular.

None of the rules of conduct under which Erika
lived applied in this matter.

Looking over the sustaining machinery, ignorant
of its function, she said, "I don't want to cause you
pain."

"Pain is all I know," he murmured. "Peace is all I want."

She threw switches, pulled plugs. The purr of motors and the throb of pumps subsided into silence.

"I'm going," Karloff said, his voice thickening into a slur. His bloodshot eyes fell shut. "Going . . ."

On the floor, in the corner, the hand spasmed, spasmed.

The bodiless head's last words were so slurred and whispery as to be barely intelligible: *"You . . . must be . . . angel."*

She stood for a while, thinking about what he'd said, for the poets of the Old Race had often written that God works in mysterious ways His wonders to perform.

In time she realized that Victor must not find her here.

She studied the switches that she'd thrown, the plugs that she'd pulled. She reinserted one of the plugs. She repositioned the hand on the floor directly under the switches. She put the remaining plug in the hand, tightened the stiff fingers around it, held them until they remained in place without her sustained pressure.

In the pantry once more, she needed a minute to find the hidden switch. The shelves full of canned food slid into place, closing off the entrance to Victor's studio.

She returned to the painting by van Huysum in the drawing room. So beautiful.

To better thrill Victor sexually, she had been permitted shame. From shame had come humility. Now it seemed that from humility had perhaps come pity, and more than pity: mercy.

As she wondered about her potential, Erika's hope was reborn. *Her* feathered thing, perched in her heart if not her soul, was a phoenix, rising yet again from ashes.

CHAPTER 74

FROM THE SWIVELING BEACONS on the roofs of police cruisers and ambulances, unsynchronized flares of red and white and blue light painted a patriotic phantasmagoria across the face of the apartment building.

Some in pajamas and robes, others dressed and primped for the news cameras, the neighbors gathered on the sidewalk. They gossiped, laughed, drank beer from paper cups, drank beer from cans, ate cold pizza, ate potato chips from the bag, took snapshots of the police and of one another. They seemed to regard the eruption of sudden violence and the presence of a serial killer in their midst as reason for celebration.

At the open trunk of the department sedan, as Carson stowed the shotgun, Michael said, "How can he jump up and run away after a four-story face plant?"

"It's more than gumption."

"And how are we gonna write up this report without landing in a psych ward?"

Slamming the trunk lid, Carson said, "We lie."

A Subaru Outback angled to the curb behind them, and Kathleen Burke got out. "Can you believe—*Harker*?"

"He always seemed like such a sweetheart," Michael said.

"The moment I saw that suicide note on Roy Pribeaux's computer," Carson informed Kathy, "I didn't believe that he wrote it. Yesterday, ragging Michael and me, Harker used the same phrase that ends Pribeaux's note—'one level below Hell.'"

Michael confirmed: "Harker told us that to catch this guy, we were going to have to go to a weirder place—one level below Hell."

Surprised, Kathy said, "You mean you think he did it on purpose, he *wanted* you to tumble to him?"

"Maybe unconsciously," Carson said, "but yeah, he did. He threw the pretty boy off the roof after setting him up to take the rap for both Pribeaux's string of murders and those that Harker himself committed. But with those four words—'one level below Hell'—he lit a fuse to destroy himself."

"Deep inside, they pretty much always want to

be caught," Kathy agreed. "But I wouldn't expect Harker's psychology to . . ."

"To what?"

She shrugged. "To work that way. I don't know. I'm babbling. Man, all the time I'm profiling him, the bastard's on my doorstep."

"Don't beat yourself up," Carson advised. "None of us suspected Harker till he all but pointed the finger at himself."

"But maybe I *should* have," Kathy worried. "Remember the three nightclub murders six months ago?"

"Boogie City," Carson recalled.

"Sounds like a place people go to pick their noses," Michael said.

"Harker and Frye were on that case," Kathy said.

Michael shrugged. "Sure. Harker shot the perp. It was an iffy shoot, but he was cleared."

"After a fatal OIS," Kathy said, "he had six hours of mandatory counseling. He showed up at my office for two of the hours but then never came back."

"No offense, Dr. Burke," Michael said, "but lots of us think mandatory counseling sucks. Just because Harker bailed doesn't mean you should've figured he had severed heads in his refrigerator."

"Yeah, but I knew something was eating him, and I didn't push him hard enough to finish the sessions."

The previous night, Carson had passed on the

opportunity to tell Kathy the Spooky Time Theater story about monsters in New Orleans. Now there was no way to explain that she hadn't any reason to feel conscious-stricken, that Harker's psychology was *not even human*.

Trying to make as light of the situation as possible, Carson said to Michael, "Is she doomed to Hell, or what?"

"She reeks of brimstone."

Kathy managed a rueful smile. "Maybe sometimes I take myself too seriously." Her smile faltered. "But Harker and I seemed to have such... rapport."

A paramedic interrupted. "'Scuse me, detectives, but we've given Ms. Parker first aid, and she's ready for you now."

"She doesn't need to go to the hospital?" Carson asked.

"No. Minor injuries. And that's not a girl who traumatizes easy. She's Mary Poppins with attitude."

CHAPTER 75

JENNA PARKER, blithe spirit, lived in a collection of plush teddy bears, inspirational posters—EVERY DAY IS THE FIRST DAY OF YOUR LIFE, JUST SAY NO TO THE BLUES—and cute cookie jars.

The ceramic cookie jars were for the most part confined to the kitchen. There were a clown jar, a polar-bear jar, a brown-bear jar, a Mother Hubbard jar, a Mickey Mouse jar, a Wookie jar. Jars in the form of a puppy, a kitten, a raccoon, a rabbit, a gingerbread house.

Carson's favorite was a jar in the shape of a tall stack of cookies.

Apparently Jenna Parker didn't spend much time cooking, for the jar collection occupied half the counter space. Doors had been taken off some of the cabinets, so that the shelves could serve as display space for more cookie jars.

"Don't you dare say anything," Carson muttered to Michael as they entered the kitchen and were confronted by the aggressively cheerful ceramic figures.

Pretending wide-eyed innocence, he said, "About what?"

Jenna sat on a stool, wearing a pink jogging suit with a small appliqué of a running turtle on the left breast. She was nibbling a cookie.

For a woman who had such a short time ago been naked, strapped to an autopsy table, and about to be dissected alive, Jenna seemed remarkably cheerful. "Hi, guys. Want a cookie?"

"No thanks," Carson said, and Michael managed to decline, as well, without shtick.

Holding up one bandaged thumb like a child proudly displaying a boo-boo, Jenna said, "I mostly just tore off my thumbnail when I fell. Isn't that great?"

"Imagine how good you'd feel," Michael said, "if you'd broken a leg."

Well, he had repressed himself for the better part of a minute.

Jenna said, "I mean, considering I could've been sitting here with my heart cut out, what's a thumbnail?"

"A thumbnail is zip, zero, nada," said Michael.

"It's a feather on the scale," she said.

"Dust in the balance," he agreed.

"It's a shadow of nothing."

"De nada."

"Peu de chose," she said.

"Exactly what I would've said if I knew French." She grinned at him. "For a cop, you're fun."

"I majored in banter at the police academy."

"Isn't he fun?" Jenna asked Carson.

Rather than stuff one or both of them into a damn cookie jar, Carson said impatiently, "Miss Parker, how long have you been Jonathan Harker's neighbor?"

"I moved in about eleven months ago. From day one, he was a sweetie."

"A sweetie? Did you and he . . ."

"Oh, no. Johnny was a man, yeah, and you know what *they're* like, but we were just good buds." To Michael, she said, "That thing I just said about men—no offense."

"None taken."

"I like men," she said.

"I don't," he assured her.

"Anyway, I'll bet you're not like other men. Except where it counts."

"Peu de chose," he said.

"Oh, I'll bet it's not," Jenna said, and winked.

Carson said, "Define 'buds' for me."

"Once in a while Johnny would come over for dinner or I'd go across the hall to his place. He'd cook pasta. We'd talk about life, you know, and destiny, and modern dance."

Boggled, Carson said, "Modern dance? *Harker?*"

"I was a dancer before I finally got real and became a dental hygienist."

Michael said, "For a long time, I wanted to be an astronaut."

"That's very brave," Jenna said with admiration.

Michael shrugged and looked humble.

Carson said, "Miss Parker, were you conscious any time after he chloroformed you?"

"On and off, yeah."

"Did he talk to you during this? Did he say *why?*"

"I think maybe he said having sex with me would be like having sex with a monkey."

Carson was nonplussed for a moment. Then she said, "You *think* he said it?"

"Well, with the chloroform and whatever he pumped into me through the IV, I was sort of in and out of it. And to be perfectly frank, I was going out to a party when he grabbed me, and I had a little bit of a pre-party buzz on. So maybe he said it or maybe I dreamed he said it."

"What else did you maybe dream he said?"

"He told me I was pretty, a fine example of my species, which was nice, but he said that he was one of the new race. Then this weird thing."

"I *wondered* when this would get weird," Michael said.

"Johnny said he wasn't allowed to reproduce but was reproducing anyway, dividing like an ameba."

Even as those words chilled Carson, they

invoked in her a sense of the absurd that made her feel as if she were a straight man in a burlesque revival. "What do you think he meant by that?"

"Well, then he pulled up his T-shirt, and his belly was like a scene from *Alien,* all this squirming inside, so I'm pretty sure all of that was just the drugs."

Carson and Michael exchanged a look. She would have liked to pursue this subject, but doing so would alert Jenna to the fact that she might have experienced what she thought she had only dreamed.

Jenna sighed. "He was a sweetie, but sometimes he could get so down, just totally bummed out."

"About what?" Carson asked.

Jenna nibbled her cookie, thinking. Then: "He felt something was missing in his life. I told him happiness is always an option, you just have to choose it. But sometimes he couldn't. I told him he had to find his bliss. I wonder . . ."

She frowned. The expression came and went from her face twice, as though she wore a frown so seldom that she didn't know how to hold on to one when she needed it.

Carson said, "What do you wonder?"

"I told him he had to find his bliss, so I sure hope his bliss didn't turn out to be chopping people to pieces."

CHAPTER 76

THROUGH THE CODED DOOR, out of Mercy, Randal Six finds himself in a six-foot-wide, eight-foot-high corridor with block-and-timber walls and a concrete floor. No rooms open from either side of this passageway.

Approximately a hundred and forty feet from him waits another door. Happily, there are no choices. He has come too far to retreat. He can only go forward.

The floor has been poured in three-foot-square blocks. By taking long strides—sometimes *bounding*—Randal is able to spell himself along these oversize boxes toward the farther end of the corridor.

At the second door, he finds a locking system identical to the first. He enters the code he used previously, and this barrier opens.

The corridor is actually a tunnel under the hospital grounds. It connects to the parking garage in the neighboring building.

Father owns this five-story structure, too, in which he houses the accounting and personnel-management departments of Biovision. He can be seen coming and going from there without raising questions.

Using the secretly constructed underground passageway between buildings, his visits to the Hands of Mercy, which he owns through a shell company, can be concealed.

This second door opens into a dark place. Randal finds a light switch and discovers a twelve-foot-square room with concrete walls.

The floor is concrete, as well, but it is a single pour, with no form lines. In other words, it is one big empty box.

Directly opposite the doorway at which he stands is another door no doubt opening to the parking garage.

The problem is that he can't cross twelve feet and reach that door in a single step. To spell himself to that exit, he will have to take several steps within the same empty box.

Every step is a letter. The rules of crosswords are simple and clear. One letter per box. You can't put multiple letters in one box.

That way lies chaos.

Just considering the possibility, Randal Six shudders with fear and disgust.

One block, one letter. No other method is able to bring order to the world.

The *threshold* in front of him shares an *h* with the *chamber* that waits before him. Once across the threshold, he must finish spelling the last five letters of the other word *a-m-b-e-r*.

He can reach the next door in five steps. That is no problem. But he only has one empty box.

Randal stands at the threshold of this new room. He stands. He stands at the threshold. He stands, thinks, puzzles, puzzles. . . . He begins to weep with frustration.

CHAPTER 77

WHEN BULLETS WEREN'T FLYING, Carson could take a more thoughtful look at Harker's apartment. Signs of a dysfunctional personality were at once evident.

Although every piece of furniture was a different style from the others, in clashing colors and uncomplementary patterns, this might mean nothing more than that Harker had no taste.

Although his living room had considerably more contents than did Allwine's—where there had been nothing but a black-vinyl chair—it was underfurnished to the point of starkness. Minimalism, of course, is a style preferred by many people who are perfectly sane.

The absence of any artwork whatsoever on the walls, the lack of bibelots and mementoes, the disinterest in beautifying the space in any way reminded her too much of how Allwine had lived.

At least one inspirational poster or cute cookie jar would have been welcome.

Instead, here came Dwight Frye out of the kitchen, looking as greasy as ever but, as never before, contrite. "If you're gonna rip me a new one, don't bother. I've already done it."

Michael said, "That's one of the most moving apologies I've ever heard."

"I knew him like a brother," Frye said, "but I didn't know him at all."

Carson said, "He had a passion for modern dance."

Frye looked baffled, and Michael said approvingly, "Carson, you might get the hang of this yet."

"For real he went out that kitchen window?" Frye asked.

"For real," Carson said.

"But the fall would've killed him."

"Didn't," Michael said.

"He didn't have a damn parachute, did he?"

Carson shrugged. "We're amazed, too."

"One of you fired two rounds from a twelve-gauge," Frye noted, indicating the pellet holes in the wall.

"That would be me," said Carson. "Totally justified. He shot at us first."

Frye was puzzled. "How could you not take him down at such close range?"

"Didn't entirely miss."

"I see some blood," Frye said, "but not a lot. Still and all, even gettin' winged by a twelve-gauge—that's got to sting. How could he just keep on keepin' on?"

"Moxie?" Michael suggested.

"I've drunk my share of Moxies, but I don't expect to laugh off a shotgun."

A CSI tech stepped out of the bedroom. "O'Connor, Maddison, you gotta see this. We just found where he *really* lived."

CHAPTER 78

FATHER PATRICK DUCHAINE, shepherd to the congregation at Our Lady of Sorrows, took the phone call in the rectory kitchen, where he was nervously eating sugar-fried pecans and wrestling with a moral dilemma.

After midnight, a call to a priest might mean that a parishioner had died or lay dying, that last rites were wanted, as well as words of comfort to the bereaved. In this case, Father Duchaine felt sure that the caller would be Victor, and he was not wrong.

"Have you done what I asked, Patrick?"

"Yes, sir. Of course. I've been all over the city since we had our little conference. But none of our people has seen one of us acting . . . strangely."

"Really? Can you assure me there isn't a renegade among the New Race? No . . . apostate?"

"No, sir, I can't absolutely assure you. But if there is one, he's given no outward sign of a psychological crisis."

"Oh, but he has," Victor said coolly.

"Sir?"

"If you'll turn on your radio or watch the first TV news in the morning, you'll get quite an earful about our Detective Harker of the Homicide Division."

Father Duchaine nervously licked his lips, which were sugary from the pecans. "I see. It was some policeman, was it? Do you . . . do you feel that I've failed you?"

"No, Patrick. He was clever."

"I was exhaustive . . . in my search."

"I'm sure you did everything that you possibly could."

Then why this call? Father Duchaine wanted to ask, but he dared not.

Instead, he waited a moment, and when his maker said nothing, he asked, "Is there anything more you need me to do?"

"Not at the moment," Victor said. "Perhaps later."

All the sugar had been licked from Father Duchaine's lips, and his mouth had gone dry, sour.

Searching for words that might repair his maker's damaged trust in him, he heard himself saying, "God be with you." When only silence answered him, he added, "That was a joke, sir."

Victor said, "Was it really? How amusing."

"Like in the church—when you said it to me."

"Yes, I remember. Good night, Patrick."

"Good night, sir."

The priest hung up. He plucked fried pecans from the dish on the kitchen counter, but his hand shook so badly that he dropped the nuts before he could convey them to his mouth. He stooped, retrieved them.

At the kitchen table with a water glass and a bottle of wine, Jonathan Harker said, "If *you* need sanctuary, Patrick, where will *you* turn?"

Instead of answering, Father Duchaine said, "I've disobeyed him. I've lied to him. How is that possible?"

"It may not *be* possible," said Harker. "At least not without terrible consequences."

"No. I think perhaps it's possible because . . . my programming is being rewritten."

"Oh? How can it be rewritten when you're not in a tank anymore or hooked up to a data feed?"

Father Duchaine looked toward the ceiling, toward Heaven.

"You can't be serious," Harker said, and took a long swallow of communion wine.

"Faith can change a person," Father Duchaine said.

"First of all, you're not a person. You're not

human. A real priest would call you a walking blasphemy."

This was true. Father Duchaine had no answer to the charge.

"Besides," Harker continued, "you don't really have any faith."

"Lately, I'm . . . wondering."

"I'm a murderer," Harker reminded him. "Killed two of them and one of us. Would God approve of your giving me sanctuary any more than Victor would?"

Harker had put into words a key element of Father Duchaine's moral dilemma. He had no answer. Instead of replying, he ate more sugar-fried pecans.

CHAPTER 79

IN THE BACK OF the bedroom closet, Harker had broken through the lath and plaster. He had reconfigured the studs and cats to allow easy passage to the space beyond.

Leading Carson, Michael, and Frye through the wall, the young tech said, "This building was at one time commercial on the ground floor, offices in the upper three, and it had an attic for tenant storage."

On the other side of the wall were rising steps — wood, worn, creaky.

As he led them upward, the tech said, "When they converted to apartments, they closed off the attic. Harker somehow found out it was here. He made it into his go-nuts room."

In the high redoubt, two bare bulbs hanging on cords from the ridge beam shed a dusty yellow light.

Three large gray moths swooped under and around the bulbs. Their shadows swelled, shrank, and swelled again across the finished floor, the finished walls, and the open-rafter ceiling.

A chair and a folding table that served as a desk were the only pieces of furniture. Books were stacked on the table, also here and there on the floor.

An enormous homemade light box covered two-thirds of the north wall and provided backlighting for dozens of X-ray images: various grinning skulls from various angles, chests, pelvises, spines, limbs. . . .

Scanning this macabre gallery, Michael said, "I thought when you went through the back of a wardrobe, you came out in the magical land of Narnia. Must've taken a wrong turn."

In the northwest corner stood a three-way mirror with a gilded frame. On the floor in front of the mirror lay a white bath mat.

Treading on fleeting phantoms of moths, serving as a screen for projections of their flight, Carson passed the mirror and crossed the room to a different display that covered the south wall from corner to corner, floor to ceiling.

Harker had stapled to the drywall a collage of religious images: Christ on the cross, Christ revealing His sacred heart, the Virgin Mary; Buddha; Ahura Mazda; from the Hindu faith, the goddesses Kali and Parvati and Chandi, the gods Vishnu and

Doma and Varuna; Quan Yin, the Queen of Heaven and goddess of compassion; Egyptian gods Anubis, Horus, Amen-Ra . . .

Bewildered, Frye asked, "What is all this?"

"He's crying out," Carson said.

"Crying out for what?"

"Meaning. Purpose. Hope."

"Why?" Frye wondered. "He *had* a job, and with benefits that don't get much better."

CHAPTER 80

RANDAL SIX STANDS motionless at the threshold of the next room for so long, so tensely, that his legs begin to ache.

The New Race does not easily fatigue. This is Randal Six's first experience with muscle cramps. They burn so intensely that at last he takes advantage of his ability to block pain at will.

He has no watch. He has never before needed one. He estimates that he has stood, riveted by his predicament, in this same spot for perhaps three hours.

Predicament is a woefully inadequate word. The correct one has fewer letters and stronger meaning: *plight*.

Although he has spared himself physical agony,

he cannot escape mental anguish. He despises himself for his inadequacies.

At least he has stopped weeping. Long ago.

Gradually his impatience with himself darkens into an intense anger at Arnie O'Connor. If not for Arnie, Randal Six would not be in this plight.

If ever he reaches the O'Connor boy, he *will* get the secret of happiness from him. Then he will make Arnie pay dearly for all this suffering.

Randal is also plagued by anxiety. Periodically his two hearts race, pounding with such terror that sweat pours from him and his vision becomes blood-dimmed.

He fears that Father will discover him missing and will set out in search of him. Or perhaps Father will finish his current work and leave for the night, whereupon he will find Randal standing here in autistic indecision.

He will be led back to the spinning rack and secured upon it in a cruciform. The rubber wedge, secured by chinstrap, will be inserted between his teeth.

Although he has never seen Father in a rage, he has heard others speak of the maker's wrath. There is no hiding from him and no mercy for the object of his fury.

When Randal thinks that he hears the sound of a door opening at the farther end of the hall, behind him, he closes his eyes and waits with dread.

Time passes.

Father does not appear.

Randal must have mistaken the sound or imagined it.

As he stands with his eyes still closed, however, and as his hearts seek a normal rhythm, a calming pattern arises in his mind's eye: arrangements of empty white boxes against a black background, intersecting in the beautiful virgin lines of an unworked crossword puzzle.

While he concentrates on this barren image for its soothing effect, a solution to his plight occurs to him. When there are not squares of vinyl tile or concrete or other material on the floor in front of him, he can draw them with his imagination.

Excited, he opens his eyes, studies the floor of the room beyond the threshold, and tries to paint upon it the five boxes that he must have to finish spelling *chamber* when he crosses *threshold*.

He fails. Though with eyes closed he had been able to see those boxes clearly in his mind, the concrete floor before him remains resistant to the imposition of imagined geometries.

Tears almost overtake him again before he realizes that he does not need to have his eyes open to traverse this room. Blind men walk with the help of canes and patient dogs. His imagination will be his white cane.

Eyes shut, he sees five boxes. He steps straight forward five times, spelling as he goes: *a-m-b-e-r.*

When the word is complete, he opens his eyes

and finds that he stands at the outer door. The electric door behind him has fallen shut. The portal before him has a simple latch that is always engaged from the farther side, always disengaged from this side.

He opens the door.

Triumph.

Beyond lies a parking garage, dimly lighted and deserted at this hour. Silent, still, smelling faintly of dampness and lime.

To exit this small room, Randal Six merely closes his eyes and imagines *threshold* printed in blocks from left to right, immediately in front of him. Conveniently, the word *garage* intersects at the letter *r.*

With his eyes closed, he determinedly takes three steps, *a-g-e,* into the enormous space beyond. The door falls shut behind him, now locked from this side.

There is no going back.

The daunting dimensions of the parking garage awe and for a moment nearly overwhelm him. No room of his experience in Mercy has prepared him for this immensity.

An inner quaking seems to knock bones against bones. He feels like a highly compressed pellet of matter at the instant before the universe's creation, and with the impending Big Bang, he will expand and explode outward in every direction, racing to fill an infinite void.

With more powerful reason than he has heretofore been able to apply to his condition, he convinces himself that the void will not pull him apart, will not scatter him to eternity. Gradually his panic subsides, fades entirely.

He closes his eyes to imagine blocks, and doggedly he spells his way forward. Between each word, Randal opens his eyes to scope the route ahead and to determine the length of the next word that he will need.

In this fashion, he eventually comes to an exit ramp and climbs to the street. The Louisiana night is warm, moist, droning with mosquitoes.

By the time he travels the better part of a block and turns right into an alleyway, the brush of dawn paints a faint gray light in the east.

Panic threatens him once more. In daylight, with everyone awake and on the move, the world will be a riot of sights, sounds. He is certain that he cannot tolerate so much sensory input.

Night is a better environment. Darkness is his friend.

He must find a place to hide until the day passes.

CHAPTER 81

EXHAUSTED, CARSON SAILED through sleep with no nightmares, only a simple continuous dream of being aboard a black boat under a black sky, knifing silently through black water.

She had not gotten to bed until well after dawn. She woke at 2:30, showered, and ate Hot Pockets while standing in Arnie's room, watching the boy at work on the castle.

At the foot of the bridge that crossed the moat, in front of the gate at the barbicon, at each of two entrances from the outer ward to the inner ward, and finally at the fortified entrance to the castle keep, Arnie had placed one of the shiny pennies that he had been given by Deucalion.

She supposed the pennies were, in Arnie's mind,

talismans that embodied the power of the disfig-
ured giant. Their mighty juju would prevent
entrance by any enemy.

Evidently Arnie trusted Deucalion.

So did Carson.

Considering the events of the past two days,
Deucalion's claim to be Frankenstein's monster
seemed no more impossible than other things that
she had witnessed. Besides, he possessed a quality
that she had never encountered before, a substan-
tialness that eluded easy description. His calm was
of an oceanic depth, his gaze so steady and so
forthright that she sometimes had to look away,
not because the occasional soft pulse of light in his
eyes disturbed her, but because he seemed to see
too deeply into her for comfort, through all her
defenses.

If Deucalion was the storied creation of Victor
Frankenstein, then during the past two centuries,
while the human doctor had become a monster,
the monster had become human—and perhaps
had become a man of unusual insight and caliber.

She needed a day off. A month. There were others working on the case now, seeking Harker. She
didn't need to push herself seven days out of seven.

Nevertheless, by prior arrangement, at 3:30 in
the afternoon, Carson was waiting at the curb in
front of her house.

At 3:33, Michael arrived in the plainwrap sedan.

Earlier in the day, Carson had experienced a moment of weakness. Michael had driven the car when they left Harker's apartment building.

Now, as she got in the passenger's seat, Michael said, "I drove all the way here and never exceeded a speed limit."

"That's why you're three minutes late."

"Three whole minutes? Well, I guess I just blew every chance we have to find Harker."

"The only thing we can't buy more of is time," she said.

"And dodo birds. We can't buy any of them. They're extinct. And dinosaurs."

"I called Deucalion at the Luxe. He's expecting us at four o'clock."

"I can't wait to enter this one in my interview log—'discussed case with Frankenstein monster. He says Igor was a creep, ate his own boogers.'"

She sighed. "I was sort of hoping that the concentration needed to drive would mean less patter."

"Just the opposite. Driving keeps me mentally fluid. It's cool being the wheel man."

"Don't get used to it."

When they arrived at the Luxe Theater, after four o'clock, the sky had grown as dark as an iron skillet.

Michael parked illegally at a red curb and hung a POLICE card on the rearview mirror. "Lives in a theater, huh? Is he buddies with the Phantom of the Opera?"

"You'll see," she said, and got out of the car.

Closing his door, looking at her across the roof, he said, "Do his palms grow hairy when the moon is full?"

"No. He shaves them just like you do."

CHAPTER 82

FOLLOWING A LONG NIGHT and longer day at Mercy, Victor ate what was either a late lunch or an early dinner of seafood gumbo with okra and rabbit étouffée at a Cajun restaurant in the Quarter. Although not as satisfyingly exotic as his Chinese meal the previous night, the food was good.

For the first time in nearly thirty hours, he went home.

Having enhanced his physiological systems to the extent that he needed little sleep and therefore could accomplish more in the lab, he sometimes wondered if he worked too much. Perhaps if he allowed himself more leisure, his mind would be clearer in the laboratory, and consequently he would do even better science.

Periodically over the decades, he had engaged in

this debate with himself. He always resolved it in favor of more work.

Like it or not, he had given himself to a great cause. He was the kind of man who would work selflessly in the pursuit of a world ruled by reason, a world free of greed and peopled by a race united by a single goal.

Arriving at his mansion in the Garden District, he chose work over leisure yet again. He went directly to his hidden studio behind the pantry.

Karloff had perished. The life-support machines were not in operation.

Stunned, he circled the central worktable, uncomprehending until he proceeded far enough to discover the hand on the floor. The thrown switches were directly above it. Furthermore, clutched in its fingers was a plug that it had pulled from a socket.

Although disappointed by this setback, Victor was amazed that Karloff had been able to shut himself down.

For one thing, the creature had been programmed to be incapable of self-destruction. On that issue there had been no wiggle room in the directives by which it had been governed.

More important, the hand could not have functioned separate from its own life-support system. The moment it had broken free of its feed and drain lines, it had lost the low-voltage current needed to fire its nerves and operate its musculature. At that point, it should have at once fallen still, limp, dead—and should have begun to decompose.

Only one explanation occurred to Victor. Apparently, Karloff's telekinetic power had been strong enough to animate the hand as if it were alive.

When controlling the hand at a distance, Karloff had shown the ability only to flex a thumb and to imitate an arpeggio by strumming an imaginary harp with those four fingers. Small, simple tasks.

To make the hand tear loose of its connections, to cause it to drop to the floor and then to climb three feet up the face of these machines to throw the life-support switches, to cause it to pull the plug, as well . . . That required far greater telekinetic power and more precise control than he had previously exhibited.

An incredible breakthrough.

Although Karloff was gone, another Karloff could be engineered. The setback would be temporary.

Excited, Victor sat at his desk and accessed the experiment file on his computer. He clicked the camera icon and called up the twenty-four-hour video record of events in the studio.

Scanning backward from the present, he was surprised when Erika suddenly appeared.

CHAPTER 83

AS WHEN SHE had been to the Luxe the previous evening, Carson found one of the front doors unlocked. This time, no one waited in the lobby.

A set of double doors stood open between the lobby and the theater.

Surveying the refreshment stand as they passed it, Michael said, "When you buy popcorn here, I wonder if you can ask for it *without* the cockroaches."

The theater itself proved to be large, with both a balcony and a mezzanine. Age, grime, and chipped plaster diminished the Art Deco glamour but did not defeat it altogether.

A fat man in white slacks, white shirt, and white Panama hat stood in front of the tattered red-velvet drapes that covered the giant screen.

He looked like Sidney Greenstreet just stepped out of *Casablanca*.

The Greenstreet type gazed toward the ceiling, transfixed by something not immediately evident to Carson.

Deucalion stood halfway down the center aisle, facing the screen. Head tipped back, he slowly scanned the ornate architecture overhead.

The strangeness of the moment was shattered with the silence when a sudden flapping of wings revealed a trapped bird swooping through the vaults above, from one roost in the cornice to another.

As Carson and Michael approached Deucalion, she heard him say, "Come to me, little one. No fear."

The bird flew again, swooped wildly, swooped... and alighted on Deucalion's extended arm. Seen close and still, it proved to be a dove.

With a laugh of delight, the fat man came forward from the screen. "I'll be damned. We ever get a lion in here, you're my man."

Gently stroking the bird, Deucalion turned as Carson and Michael approached him.

Carson said, "I thought only St. Francis and Dr. Doolittle talked to animals."

"Just a little trick."

"You seem to be full of tricks, little and big," she said.

The fat man proved to have a sweet voice. "The poor thing's been trapped here a couple days, living off stale popcorn. Couldn't get it to go for the exit doors when I opened them."

Deucalion cupped the bird in o̲ne immense hand, and it appeared to be without fear, almost in a trance.

With both pudgy hands, the man in white accept-ed the dove from Deucalion and moved away, toward the front of the theater. "I'll set it free."

"This is my partner, Detective Maddison," Carson told Deucalion. "Michael Maddison."

They nodded to each other, and Michael—pre-tending not to be impressed by the size and appear-ance of Deucalion—said, "I've gotta be straight with you. I'll be the first to admit we're in weird woods on this one, but I still don't buy the Transylvania thing."

"That's movies. In real life," Deucalion said, "it was Austria."

"We need your help," Carson told him. "As it turns out, there were two killers."

"Yes. It's on the news."

"Yeah. Well, only one of them seems to have been . . . the kind that you warned me about."

"And he's a detective," Deucalion said.

"Right. He's still loose. But we've found his . . . playroom. If he's really one of Victor's people, you'll be able to read his place better than we can."

Michael shook his head. "Carson, he's not a psy-chologist. He's not a profiler."

In a matter-of-fact tone, arresting precisely

because of its lack of drama, Deucalion said, "I understand murderers. I am one."

Those words and an accompanying throb of light through the giant's eyes left Michael briefly speechless.

"In my early days," Deucalion said, "I was a different beast. Uncivilized. Full of rage. I murdered a few men...and a woman. The woman was my maker's wife. On their wedding day."

Obviously sensing the same convincing gravitas in Deucalion that had impressed Carson, Michael searched for words and found these: "I know that story, too."

"But *I* lived it," said Deucalion. He turned to Carson. "I don't choose to go out in daylight."

"We'll take you. It's an unmarked car. Inconspicuous."

"I know the place. I saw it on the news. I'd rather meet you there."

"When?" she asked.

"Go now," he said. "I'll be there when you are."

"Not the way she drives," said Michael.

"I'll be there."

Toward the front of the theater, the fat man shouldered open an emergency-exit door to the waning afternoon. He released the dove, and it flew to freedom in the somber pre-storm light.

CHAPTER 84

VICTOR FOUND ERIKA in the library. She nestled in an armchair, legs tucked under her, reading a novel.

In retrospect, he should have forbidden her to spend so much time with poetry and fiction. Emily Dickinson, indeed.

The authors of such work imagined that they addressed not merely the mind but the heart, even the soul. By their very nature, fiction and poetry encouraged an emotional response.

He should have insisted that Erika devote most of her reading time to science. Mathematics. Economic theory. Psychology. History.

Some history books might be dangerous, as well. In general, however, nonfiction would educate her with little risk of instilling in her a corrupting sentimentality.

Too late.

Infected with pity, she was no longer useful to him. She fancied that she had a conscience and the capacity for caring.

Pleased with herself for the discovery of these tender feelings, she had betrayed her master. She would betray him again.

Worse, drunk with book-learned compassion, she might in her ignorant fulsomeness dare to pity *him* for one reason or another. He would not tolerate her foolish sympathy.

Wise men had long warned that books corrupted. Here was the unassailable proof.

As he approached, she looked up from the novel, the poisonous damn novel, and smiled.

He struck her so hard that he broke her nose. Blood flew, and he thrilled at the sight of it.

She endured three blows. She would have endured as many as he wished to rain on her.

Victor was not sufficiently satisfied merely to strike her. He tore the book out of her hands, threw it across the room, seized her by her thick bronze hair, dragged her from the chair, and threw her onto the floor.

Denied the choice of turning off the pain, she suffered. He knew precisely how to maximize that suffering. He kicked, kicked.

Although he had enhanced his body, Victor was not the physical equal of one of the New Race. In time he exhausted himself and stood sweat-soaked, gasping for breath.

Every injury she sustained, of course, would heal without scar. Already, her lacerations were healing, her broken bones knitting together.

If he wished to let her live, she would be as good as new in just a day or two. She would smile for him again. She would serve him as before.

That was not his wish.

Pulling a straightbacked chair away from a reading desk, he said, "Get up. Sit here."

She was a mess, but she managed to get to her knees and then to the chair. She sat with her head bowed for a moment. Then she raised it and straightened her back.

His people were amazing. Tough. Resilient. In their way, proud.

Leaving her in the chair, he went to the library bar and poured cognac from a decanter into a snifter.

He wanted to be calmer when he killed her. In his current state of agitation, he would not be able fully to enjoy the moment.

At a window, with his back to her, he sipped the cognac and watched the contusive sky as its bruises grew darker, darker. Rain would come with nightfall, if not before.

They said that God created the world in six days and rested on the seventh. They were lying.

First, there was no God. Only brutal nature.

Second, Victor knew from hard experience that the creation of a new world was a frustrating, often a tedious, and a time-consuming endeavor.

Eventually, calm and prepared, he returned to Erika. She sat in the chair as he had left her.

Taking off his sport jacket and draping it over the back of an armchair, he said, "This can be a perfect city. One day...a perfect world. Ordinary flawed humanity—they resist perfection. One day they will be . . . replaced. All of them."

She sat in silence, head raised, but not looking at him, gazing instead at the books on the shelves.

He removed his necktie.

"A world stripped clean of fumbling humanity, Erika. I wish you could be here with us to see it."

When creating a wife for himself, he modified—in just a few ways—the standard physiology that he gave to other members of the New Race.

For one thing, strangling one of them would have been extremely difficult. Even if the subject had been obedient and docile, the task might have taken a long time, might even have proved *too* difficult.

Every Erika, on the other hand, had a neck structure—windpipe, carotid arteries—that made her as vulnerable to a garrote as was any member of the Old Race. He could have terminated her in other ways, but he wished the moment to be intimate; strangulation satisfied that desire.

Standing behind her chair, he bent to kiss her neck.

"This is very difficult for me, Erika."

When she did not reply, he stood straight and gripped the necktie in both hands. Silk. Quite elegant. And strong.

"I'm a creator and a destroyer, but I prefer to create."

He looped the tie around her neck.

"My greatest weakness is my compassion," he said, "and I must purge myself of it if I'm to make a better world based on rationality and reason."

Savoring the moment, Victor was surprised to hear her say, "I forgive you for this."

Her unprecedented audacity so stunned him that his breath caught in his throat.

When he spoke, the words came in a rush: "*Forgive me?* I am not of a station to need forgiveness, and you are not of a position to have the power to grant it. Does the man who eats the steak need the forgiveness of the steer from which it was carved? You foolish bitch. And *less* than a bitch because no whelp would ever have come from your loins if you had lived a thousand years."

Quietly, calmly, almost tenderly, she said, "But I will never forgive you for having made me."

Her audacity had grown to effrontery, to impudence so shocking that it robbed him of all the pleasure that he expected from this strangulation.

To Victor, creation and destruction were equally

satisfying expressions of *power*. Power alone motivated him: the power to defy nature and to bend it to his will, the power to control others, the power to shape the destiny of both the Old Race and the New, the power to overcome his own weaker impulses.

He strangled her now, cut off the blood supply to her brain, crushed her windpipe, strangled her, strangled her, but with such fury, in such a blind rage, that by the time he finished, he was not a man of power but merely a grunting beast fully in the thrall of nature, out of control, lost to reason and rationality.

In her dying, Erika had not only denied him but defeated him, humiliated him, as he had not been in more than two centuries.

Choking with wrath, he pulled books off the shelves, threw them to the floor, scores of books, hundreds, tore them and ground them under his heels. Tore them and ground them. Threw them and tore them.

Later, he went to the master suite. He showered. Restless and energized, he had no interest in relaxation. He dressed to go out, though he did not know for where or what purpose.

From another decanter, he poured another cognac into another snifter.

On the intercom, he spoke with William, the butler, who was on duty in the staff room. "There's a dead thing in the library, William."

"Yes, sir."

"Contact my people in the sanitation department. I want that useless meat buried deep in the landfill, and right away."

At the window, he studied the lowering sky, which had grown so dark with thunderheads that an early dusk had come upon the city.

CHAPTER 85

AT HARKER'S APARTMENT BUILDING, Carson and Michael took the elevator to the fourth floor to avoid the stink of mildew in the public stairwell.

Homicide, CSI, and curious neighbors had long ago faded away. The building almost seemed deserted.

When they reached the fourth floor, they found Deucalion waiting in the hallway, outside Harker's apartment.

To Carson, Michael murmured, "I didn't see the Batmobile parked out front."

"You won't admit it," she said, "but you're convinced."

To her surprise, he said, "Almost."

Evidently having heard Michael's murmured

words, Deucalion said, "I used the Batcopter. It's on the roof."

By way of apology, Michael said, "Listen, that crack didn't mean anything. That's just me. If I see a joke, I go for it."

"Because you see so much in life that disturbs you, the cruelty, the hatred," Deucalion said. "You armor yourself with humor."

For the second time in an hour, Michael found himself without a comeback.

Carson had never imagined that such a day would dawn. Maybe this was one of the seven signs of the Apocalypse.

She slit the police seal on the door, used her Lockaid gun, and led them inside.

"Minimalism minimalized," said Deucalion as he moved into the sparsely furnished living room. "No books."

"He's got some books in the attic," Carson said.

"No mementoes," Deucalion continued, "no decorative items, no photographs, no art. He hasn't found a way to have a life. This is the cell of a monk . . . but one who has no faith."

Trying to get back in the saddle, Michael said, "Carson, he's an absolute whiz at this."

Deucalion looked toward the kitchen but didn't move in that direction. "He sometimes sits at the table in there, drinking. But whiskey doesn't provide him with the escape he needs. Only occasional oblivion."

Earlier, the standard premises search had turned up a case of bourbon in the kitchen.

Looking toward the bedroom, Deucalion said, "In there, you will most likely find pornography. Only a single item. One video."

"Exactly," she confirmed. "We found one."

When it turned up in the search, Michael had referred to the porn video by various titles— *Transvestitesylvania, The Thing with Two Things*—but now he said nothing, impressed to silence by Deucalion's insights.

"He found no thrill in images of copulation," Deucalion said. "Only an even more profound sense of being an outsider. Only greater alienation."

CHAPTER 86

FEARFUL OF THE day-bright world in all its dazzling busyness, Randal Six earlier took refuge in an alleyway Dumpster.

Fortunately, this enormous container is half filled with nothing more offensive than office trash, largely paper and cardboard. There is no restaurant or produce-market garbage, no organic stench and slime.

Throughout the day, until the storm clouds come, the sun beats down on Randal. This is the first sun of his life, bright and hot, frightening at first, but then less so.

He sits with his back to a corner, cushioned by paper refuse, his world reduced to manageable dimensions, and works one crossword puzzle after another in the book that he brought with him from his room in the Hands of Mercy.

Frequently traffic passes through the alleyway. And people on foot. Initially he pauses in his puzzle at each possibility of an encounter, but eventually he realizes that they are not likely to disturb him.

If a sanitation truck comes to empty the Dumpster, he is not sure how he will cope. This possibility didn't occur to him until he had already taken sanctuary in the container. His hope is that trash is not collected every day.

Having missed breakfast and then lunch, he grows hungry as the day progresses. Considering his accomplishments to this point, he can endure a little hunger.

At Mercy, Randal's untouched meals will alert the staff to his absence, though perhaps not for a while. Sometimes, when particularly deep in autistic detachment, he leaves a meal untouched for hours. He has been known to eat both breakfast and lunch an hour before dinner—then leave his dinner until near midnight.

Before departing Mercy, he closed his bathroom door. They may think that he is in there.

From time to time, people toss bags of trash and loose objects into the bin. The top of the big Dumpster is over their heads, so they cannot easily look in and see him.

Sometimes the trash strikes him, but it's never

a problem. When the people leave, Randal pushes the new stuff away and reestablishes his cozy nest.

Midafternoon, a man singing "King of the Road" approaches along the alley. He can't carry a tune.

Judging by the sound, he's pushing some kind of cart. The wheels clatter on the cracked pavement.

Between lines of the song, the cart-pusher grumbles incoherent chains of four-letter words, then resumes singing.

When this man stops at the Dumpster, Randal Six puts aside his puzzle book and pen. Instinct tells him that there may be trouble.

Two grimy hands appear at the rim of the bin. The singer takes a grip, grunts and curses as he clambers up the side of the Dumpster.

Balanced on the edge of the big container, half in and half out, the man spots Randal. His eyes widen.

The guy is perhaps in his thirties, bearded, in need of a bath. His teeth are crooked and yellow when he reveals them to say "This here's *my* territory, asshole."

Randal reaches up, grabs the man by his shirt-sleeves, pulls him into the Dumpster, and breaks his neck. He rolls the dead body to the farther end of the container and covers it with bags of trash.

In his corner once more, he picks up the puzzle book. He turns to his page and finishes spelling *derangement*.

The dead man's cart stands near the Dumpster.

Eventually someone might notice it and wonder about its owner.

Randal will have to deal with the problem if and when it arises. Meanwhile, crosswords.

Time passes. Clouds darken the sky. Although still warm, the day grows cooler.

Randal Six is not happy, but he is content, at ease. Later, he will be happy for the first time.

In his mind's eye is the city map, his route to happiness, the O'Connor house at the end of the journey, his guiding star.

CHAPTER 87

BECAUSE OF THEIR fine-tuned metabolism, members of the New Race did not easily become drunk. Their capacity for drink was great, and when they did become inebriated, they sobered more quickly than did those of the Old Race.

Throughout the day, Father Duchaine and Harker opened bottle after bottle of communion wine. This use of the church's inventory troubled the priest both because it was in effect a misappropriation of funds and because the wine, once blessed, would have become the sacred blood of Christ.

Being a soulless creature made by man but charged with religious duty, Father Duchaine had over the months and years grown ever more torn between what he was and what he wished to be.

Regardless of the moral issue of using this particular wine for purposes other than worship, the alcoholic content of the brew was less than they might have wished. Late in the afternoon, they began to spike it with Father Duchaine's supply of vodka.

Sitting in armchairs in the rectory study, the priest and the detective tried for the tenth—or perhaps the twentieth—time to pull the most troubling thorns from each other's psyches.

"Father will find me soon," Harker predicted. "He'll stop me."

"And me," the priest said morosely.

"But I don't feel guilty about what I've done."

"Thou shalt not kill."

"Even if there is a God, His commandments can't apply to us," said Harker. "We're not His children."

"Our maker has also forbidden us to murder ... except on his instructions."

"But our maker isn't God. He's more like ... the plantation owner. Murder isn't a sin ... just disobedience."

"It's still a crime," said Father Duchaine, troubled by Harker's self-justifications, even though the plantation-owner analogy had a measure of truth in it.

Sitting on the edge of his armchair, leaning forward, tumbler of vodka-spiked wine clasped in both hands, Harker said, "Do you believe in evil?"

"People do terrible things," the priest said. "I

mean, real people, the Old Race. For children of God, they do terrible, terrible things."

"But evil," Harker pressed. "Evil pure and purposeful? Is evil a real presence in the world?"

The priest drank from his glass, then said, "The church allows exorcisms. I've never performed one."

With the solemnity of both profound dread and too much booze, Harker said, "Is *he* evil?"

"Victor?" Father Duchaine felt that he was on dangerous ground. "He's a hard man, not easy to like. His jokes aren't funny."

Harker rose from his chair, went to a window, and studied the low, threatening sky that impressed an early dusk upon the day.

After a while, he said, "If he's evil . . . then what are we? I've been so . . . confused lately. But I don't feel evil. Not like Hitler or Lex Luthor. Just . . . incomplete."

Father Duchaine slid to the edge of his chair. "Do you think . . . by living the right way, we might in time develop the souls that Victor couldn't give us?"

Returning from the window, adding vodka to his glass, Harker said with serious demeanor, "Grow a soul? Like . . . gallstones? I've never thought about it."

"Have you seen *Pinocchio*?"

"I've never had patience for their movies."

"This marionette is made of wood," Father Duchaine said, "but he wants to be a real boy."

Harker nodded, downed half his drink, and said, "Like Winnie the Pooh wants to be a real bear."

"No. Pooh is delusional. He already thinks he's a real bear. He eats honey. He's afraid of bees."

"Does Pinocchio become a real boy?"

Father Duchaine said, "After a lot of struggle, yes."

"That's inspiring," Harker decided.

"It is. It really is."

Harker chewed his lower lip, thinking. Then: "Can you keep a secret?"

"Of course. I'm a priest."

"This is a little scary," Harker said.

"Everything in life's a little scary."

"That's so true."

"In fact, that was the theme of my homily last Sunday."

Harker put down his drink, stood before Duchaine. "But I'm more excited than scared. It started two days ago, and it's accelerating."

Expectantly, Patrick rose from his chair.

"Like Pinocchio," Harker said, "I'm changing."

"Changing . . . how?"

"Victor denied us the ability to reproduce. But I . . . I'm going to give birth to something."

With an expression that seemed to be as much pride as fear, Harker lifted his loose-fitting T-shirt.

A subcutaneous face was taking shape beneath the skin and the surface fat layers of Harker's abdomen. The thing was like a death mask but in motion: blind eyes rolling, mouth opening as though in a silent scream.

Recoiling in shock, Father Duchaine crossed himself before he realized what he had done.

The doorbell rang.

"Birth?" the priest said agitatedly. "What makes you think it's birth instead of biological chaos?"

Sudden sweat sheathed Harker's face. Sullen at this rejection, he pulled down his T-shirt. "I'm not afraid. Why should I be?" But clearly he was afraid. "I've murdered. Now I create—which makes me more human."

The doorbell rang again.

"A breakdown in cell structure, metastasis," Father Duchaine said. "A terrible design flaw."

"You're envious. That's what you are—envious in your chastity."

"You've got to go to him. Get his help. He'll know what to do."

"Oh, he'll know what to do, all right," Harker said. "There's a place waiting for me in the land-fill."

The doorbell rang a third time, more insistently than before.

"Wait here," said Father Duchaine. "I'll be back. We'll figure out what to do... something. Just wait."

He closed the door when he left the study. He crossed the parlor to the front hall.

When the priest opened the front door, he discovered Victor on the porch.

"Good evening, Patrick."

Striving to conceal his anxiety, Father Duchaine said, "Sir. Yes. Good evening."

"Just 'good evening'?"

"I'm sorry. What?" When Victor frowned, Duchaine understood. "Oh, yes. Of course. Come in, sir. Please come in."

CHAPTER 88

MOTH SHADOWS BEAT an ever-changing tattoo across the faces of Christ, Buddha, Amen-Ra.

In the attic above Jonathan Harker's apartment, Carson, Michael, and Deucalion gathered at the wall-to-wall collage of gods, on which Harker must have spent scores of hours.

"It seems to express such yearning," Carson said. "You can feel his anguish."

"Don't be too moved by it," Deucalion advised. "He would embrace any philosophy that filled the void in him."

He peeled away an image of Christ in the Garden of Gethsemane, then one of Buddha, revealing different forms and faces beneath, their nature at first mysterious.

"God was only his most recent obsession," Deucalion explained.

As other pictures were peeled away, Carson saw an underlying collage of Nazi images and symbols: swastikas, Hitler, goose-stepping soldiers.

"Under all these faces of traditional gods is another god that failed him," Deucalion said. "A god of violent social change and racial purity. There are so many of those."

Perhaps at last fully convinced of Deucalion's nature, Michael said, "How did you know there was a second layer?"

"Not just a second," Deucalion said. "Also a third."

When Hitler and his ilk were torn off the wall, there was revealed an even eerier collage: images of Satan, demons, satanic symbols.

Deucalion said, "The unique despair of a creature without a soul eventually leads to desperation, and desperation fosters obsession. In Harker's case, this is only the surface of it."

Peeling away a horned-and-fanged demonic face, Carson said, "You mean . . . more layers under this?"

"The wall feels spongy, padded," Michael said.

Deucalion nodded. "It's been papered over twenty times or more. You might find gods and goddesses again. When new hopes fail, old hopes return in the endless cycle of desperation."

Instead, Carson found Sigmund Freud in the

fourth layer. Then other pictures of equally solemn men.

"Freud, Jung, Skinner, Watson," Deucalion said, identifying each newly revealed face. "Rorschach. Psychiatrists, psychologists. The most useless gods of all."

CHAPTER 89

FATHER DUCHAINE RETREATED from the threshold as Victor stepped through the front door into the rectory foyer.

The master of the New Race looked around with interest. "Cozy. Quite nice. A vow of poverty doesn't preclude certain comforts." He touched one finger to Father Duchaine's Roman collar. "Do you take your vows seriously, Patrick?"

"Of course not, sir. How could I? I've never actually gone to the seminary. I've never taken vows. You brought me to life with a manufactured past."

In what might have been a warning tone, Victor said, "That's worth remembering."

With a sense of entitlement, Victor proceeded along the hall, deeper into the house, without invitation.

Following his master into the parlor, the priest asked, "To what do I owe the honor of this visit, sir?"

Surveying the room, Victor said, "The authorities haven't found Detective Harker yet. We're all at risk until I reacquire him."

"Would you like me to mobilize our people to search for him?"

"Do you really think that would do any good, Patrick? I'm not so sure."

As Victor moved across the living room toward the door of the study, Father Duchaine said, "Can I get you coffee, sir? Brandy?"

"Is that what I smell on your breath, Patrick? Brandy?"

"No. No, sir. It's . . . it's vodka."

"There's only one thing I want now, Patrick. A tour of your lovely home."

Victor crossed to the study door, opened it.

Holding his breath, Father Duchaine followed his maker across that threshold—and found that Harker had gone.

Circling the room, Victor said, "I programmed you with a fine education in theology. Better than anything you could have gotten from any university or seminary."

He paused to look at the bottle of wine and bottle of vodka that stood side by side on the coffee table. Only one glass stood on the table.

With alarm, Father Duchaine noticed that a wet

ring marked the table where Harker's glass had stood.

Victor said, "With your fine education, Patrick, perhaps you can tell me—does *any* religion teach that God can be deceived?"

"Deceived? No. Of course not."

The second ring could have been left by Father Duchaine's glass. He might have moved it to where it stood now, leaving the ring. He hoped that Victor would consider that possibility.

As Victor continued around the study, he said, "I'm curious. You've had some years of experience with your parishioners. Do you think they lie to their god?"

Feeling as though he were walking a tightrope, the priest said, "No. No, they mean to keep the promises they make to Him. But they're weak."

"Because they're human. Human beings are weak, those of the Old Race. Which is one reason why my people will eventually destroy them, replace them."

Although Harker had slipped out of the study, he must have taken refuge somewhere.

In the living room once more, when Victor didn't return to the front hall but went instead toward the adjoining dining room, Father Duchaine followed nervously.

The dining room proved to be deserted.

Victor pushed through the swinging door into the kitchen, and Father Duchaine followed like a dog afraid that its hard master would find a cause for punishment.

Harker had gone. In the kitchen, the door to the back porch stood open. The draft entering from the storm-dark twilight smelled faintly of the rain to come.

"You shouldn't leave your doors open," Victor warned. "So many of God's people have a criminal bent. They would burglarize even a priest's home."

"Just before you rang the bell," Father Duchaine said, amazed to hear himself lying so boldly, "I stepped outside for a breath of fresh air."

"Fresh air is of no special value to those of you I've made. You're designed to thrive without exercise, on any diet, in fresh air and in foul." He rapped his knuckles on Father Duchaine's chest. "You are an exquisitely efficient organic machine."

"I'm grateful, sir, for all that I am."

From the kitchen to the hall, from the hall to the foyer, Victor said, "Patrick, do you understand why it's important that my people infiltrate organized religion as well as every other aspect of human society?"

The answer came to the priest not from thoughtful consideration but from programming: "Many years from now, when the time comes to liquidate those of the Old Race who remain, there must be nowhere they can turn for support or sanctuary."

"Not to the government," Victor agreed,

"because we will *be* the government. Not to the police or the military ... or to the church."

Again as if by rote, Father Duchaine said, "We must avoid a destructive civil war."

"Exactly. Instead of civil war ... a very civil extermination." He opened the front door. "Patrick, if you ever felt in any way ... incomplete ... you would come to me, I assume."

Warily, the priest said, "Incomplete? What do you mean?"

"Adrift. Confused about the meaning of your existence. Without purpose."

"Oh, no, sir. I know my purpose, and I'm dedicated to it."

Victor met Father Duchaine's eyes for a long moment before he said, "Good. That's good. Because there's a special risk for those of you who serve in the clergy. Religion can be seductive."

"Seductive? I don't see how. It's such nonsense. Irrational."

"All of that and worse," Victor agreed. "And if there were an afterlife and a god, he would hate you for what you are. He would snuff you out and cast you into Hell." He stepped onto the porch. "Good night, Patrick."

"Good night, sir."

After Father Duchaine closed the door, he stood in the foyer until his legs became so weak that he had to sit.

He went to the stairs, sat on a riser. He clutched

one hand with the other to quell the tremors in them.

Gradually his hands changed position until he found them clasped in prayer.

He realized that he had not locked the door. Before his maker could open it and catch him in this betrayal, he made fists of his hands and beat them against his thighs.

CHAPTER 90

STANDING AT THE folding table that served as Harker's desk in the go-nuts room, Deucalion sorted through the stacks of books.

"Anatomy. Cellular biology. Molecular biology. Morphology. This one's psychotherapy. But all the rest . . . human biology."

"And why did he build this?" Carson asked, indicating the light box on the north wall, where X-rays of skulls, spines, rib cages, and limbs were displayed.

Deucalion said, "He feels that something's missing in him. He's long been trying to understand what it is."

"So he studies pictures in anatomy books, and compares other people's X-rays to his own. . . ."

"When he learned nothing from that," Michael

said, "he started opening real people and looking inside them."

"Except for Allwine, Harker chose people who seemed whole to him, who seemed to have what he lacked."

Michael said, "In the statement Jenna gave, she says Harker told her he wanted to see what she had inside that made her happier than he was."

"You mean, leaving out Pribeaux's victims, Harker's weren't just selected at random?" Carson asked. "They were people he knew?"

"People he knew," Deucalion confirmed. "People he felt were happy, complete, self-assured."

"The bartender. The dry cleaner," Michael said.

"Harker most likely had drinks from time to time in that bar," Deucalion said. "You'll probably find the dry cleaner's name in his checkbook. He knew those men, just like he knew Jenna Parker."

"And Alice's looking glass?" Michael asked, pointing to the three-way mirror in the corner of the attic.

"He stood there in the nude," Deucalion said. "Studying his body for some...difference, deficiency...something that would reveal why he feels incomplete. But that would have been before he started to look...inside."

Carson returned to the books on the table, opening them one by one to pages that Harker had marked with Post-its, hoping to learn more from what, specifically, had interested him.

"What will he do now?" Michael asked.

"What he's been doing," Deucalion said.

"But he's on the run, in hiding. He doesn't have time to plan one of his . . . dissections."

As Carson picked up the book on psychotherapy, Deucalion said, "He's more desperate than ever. And when the desperation increases, so does the obsession."

One of the bookmarks was not a Post-it. Carson discovered an appointment card for Harker's third session with Kathleen Burke, the appointment that he didn't keep.

She turned and looked at the mural of stapled images.

Where they had peeled at the collage, the fourth layer had been revealed below the demons and devils. Freud, Jung. Psychiatrists . . .

In memory, Carson heard Kathy as they had stood talking with her the previous night in front of this very building: *But Harker and I seemed to have such . . . rapport.*

Reading her as he always could, Michael said, "Something?"

"It's Kathy. She's next."

"What'd you find?"

She showed him the appointment card.

He took it from her, turned with it to Deucalion, but Deucalion was gone.

CHAPTER 91

A FRACTION OF THE DAY remains, but filtered through the soot-dark clouds, the light is thin, gray, and weaves itself with shadows to obscure more than illuminate.

For hours, the supermarket shopping cart—piled with garbage bags full of salvaged tin cans, glass bottles, and other trash—has stood where the vagrant left it. No one has remarked upon it.

Randal Six, fresh from the Dumpster, means to push the cart to a less conspicuous place. Perhaps this will delay the discovery of the dead man in the bin.

He curls both hands around the handle of the cart, closes his eyes, imagines ten crossword squares on the pavement in front of him, and begins to spell *shopaholic.* He never finishes the word, for an amazing thing happens.

As the shopping cart rolls forward, the wheels rattle across the uneven pavement; nevertheless, the motion is remarkably, satisfyingly smooth. So smooth and continuous is this motion that Randal finds he can't easily think of his progress as taking place letter by letter, one square at a time.

Although this development spooks him, the relentless movement of the wheels *through* squares, rather than from one square to another in orderly fashion, doesn't bring him to a halt. He has... momentum.

When he arrives at the second *o* in *shopaholic,* he stops spelling because he is not any longer sure which of the ten imagined squares he is in. Astonishingly, though he stops spelling, he keeps moving.

He opens his eyes, assuming that when he no longer visualizes the crossword boxes in his mind's eye, he will come to a sudden stop. He keeps moving.

At first he feels as if the cart is the motive force, pulling him along the alleyway. Although it lacks a motor, it must be driven by some kind of magic.

This is frightening because it implies a lack of control. He is at the mercy of the shopping cart. He must go where it takes him.

At the end of a block, the cart could turn left or right. But it continues forward, across a side street, into the next length of the alleyway. Randal remains on the route that he mapped to the O'Connor house. He keeps moving.

As the wheels revolve, revolve, he realizes that the cart is not *pulling* him, after all. He is *pushing* the cart.

He experiments. When he attempts to increase speed, the cart proceeds faster. When he chooses a less hurried pace, the cart slows.

Although happiness is not within his grasp, he experiences an unprecedented gratification, perhaps even satisfaction. As he rolls, rolls, rolls along, he has a taste, the barest taste, of what freedom might be like.

Full night has fallen, but even in darkness, even in alleyways, the world beyond Mercy is filled with more sights, more sounds, more smells than he can process without spinning into panic. Therefore, he looks neither to the left nor the right, focuses on the cart before him, on the sound of its wheels.

He keeps moving.

The shopping cart is like a crossword-puzzle box on wheels, and in it is not merely a collection of aluminum cans and glass bottles but also his hope for happiness, his hatred for Arnie O'Connor.

He keeps moving.

CHAPTER 92

IN THE BUNGALOW of the seashell gate with the unicorn motif, behind the windows flanked by midnight-blue shutters decorated with star shapes and crescent moons, Kathy Burke sat at her kitchen table reading a novel about adventure in a kingdom ruled by wizardry and witchery, eating almond cookies and drinking coffee.

From the corner of her eye, she saw movement and looked up to discover Jonathan Harker standing in the doorway between the kitchen and the dark hall.

His face, usually red from the sun or from anger, was whiter than pale. Disheveled, sweating, he looked malarial.

Although his eyes were wild and haunted, although his nervous hands plucked continually at his stretched and saturated T-shirt, he spoke in a meek and ingratiating manner weirdly out of sync with his aggressive entrance and his appearance: "Good evening, Kathleen. How're you? Busy, I'm sure. Always busy."

Taking her lead from his tone, Kathy calmly put a bookmark in her novel, slid it aside. "It didn't have to be this way, Jonathan."

"Maybe it did. Maybe there was never any hope for me."

"It's partly my fault that you are where you are. If you'd stayed in counseling—"

He took a step into the room. "No. I've hidden so much from you. I didn't want you to know... what I am."

"I've been a lousy therapist," she said by way of ingratiation.

"You're a good woman, Kathy. A very fine person."

The weirdness of this exchange—her self-efface-ment, Harker's flattery—in light of his recent crimes, was impossible to sustain, and Kathy thought furi-ously about where the encounter might lead and how best to manage it.

Fate intruded when the phone rang.

They both looked at it.

"I'd prefer you didn't answer that," said Harker.

She remained seated and did not challenge him. "If I'd insisted that you keep your appointments, I might have recognized signs that you were... head-ing for trouble."

A third ring of the phone.

He nodded. His smile was tortured. "You would have. You're so insightful, so understanding. That's why I was afraid to talk with you anymore."

"Will you sit down, Jonathan?" she asked, indicating the chair across the table from her.

A fifth ring.

"I'm so tired," he acknowledged, but he made no move toward the chair. "Do I disgust you . . . what I've done?"

Choosing her words carefully, she said, "No. I feel . . . a kind of grief, I guess."

After the seventh or eighth ring, the phone fell silent.

"Grief," she continued, "because I so much liked the man you were . . . the Jonathan I knew."

"There's no going back, is there?"

"I won't lie to you," she said.

Harker moved tentatively, almost shyly toward Kathleen. "You're so complete. I know if only I could look inside you, I'd find what I'm missing."

Defensively, she rose from her chair. "You know that makes no sense, Jonathan."

"But what else can I do but . . . keep looking?"

"I only want what's best for you. Do you believe that?"

"I guess . . . Yes, I do."

She took a deep breath, took a risk: "Then will you let me call someone, make arrangements to turn you in?"

For an anguished moment, Harker looked around the kitchen as if he were trapped. He might have snapped then, but his tension subsided into anxiety.

Sensing that she was winning him over to surrender, Kathy said, "Let me call someone. Let me do the right thing."

He considered her offer for a moment. "No. No, that wouldn't be a good thing."

He looked across the kitchen, intrigued by something.

When Kathy followed the direction of his gaze, she saw the knife rack filled with gleaming blades.

LEAVING HARKER'S APARTMENT, Michael hadn't made any attempt to get behind the wheel. He tossed the keys to Carson.

He rode shotgun—literally, holding the weapon between his knees, the muzzle toward the ceiling.

By habit, as they rocketed through the night, he said, "Stop trying for the land-speed record. The dispatcher will have someone there ahead of us, anyway."

Accelerating, Carson came back at him: "Did you say something, Michael? 'Yes, Carson, I said, *Faster, faster.*' Yeah, that's what I thought you said, Michael."

"You do a lousy imitation of me," he complained. "You're not nearly funny enough."

❂

WITH ONE HAND on his abdomen, as if suffering a stomachache, Harker prowled the kitchen, moving toward the knife rack and then away, but then toward it once more. "Something's happening," he said worriedly. "Maybe it's not going to be like I thought it would."

"What's wrong?" Kathy asked warily.

"Maybe it's not going to be good. Not good at all. Something's coming."

Abruptly his face wrenched with pain. He let out a strangled cry and clasped both hands to his abdomen.

"Jonathan?"

"I'm *splitting*."

Kathy heard tires squeal and brakes bark as a fast car pulled to a stop in her driveway.

Looking toward the sound, terror trumping his pain, Harker said, *"Father?"*

❂

INSTEAD OF THE WALK-in unicorn gate, Carson favored the driveway and slid to a stop so close to the garage door that even a wizard couldn't have charmed himself thin enough to fit between the building and the sedan's bumper.

She pulled her piece from her paddle holster as she exited the car, and Michael chambered a shell in the shotgun as he came around the back of the car to join her.

The front door of the house flew open, and Kathy Burke ran onto the porch, down the steps.

"Thank God," Carson said.

"Harker went out the back," Kathy said.

Even as she spoke, Carson heard running footsteps and turned, seeking the sound.

Harker had come along the farther side of the garage. He was off the lawn, into the street, before Carson could draw down on him.

By now he was in too public an area—houses across the street—to allow her to take a shot. The risk of collateral damage was too high.

Michael ran, Carson ran, Harker ahead of them, down the middle of the residential street.

In spite of the doughnuts and the grab-it dinners eaten on their feet, in spite of the ass-fattening time spent at desks filling out the nine yards of paperwork that had become the bane of modern police work, Carson and Michael were fast, movie-cop fast, wolf-on-a-rabbit fast.

Harker, being inhuman, being some freak brewed up in a lab by Victor Frankenstein, was faster. Along Kathy's block to the corner and left into another street, along another block and right at the next corner, he opened up his lead.

Lightning tore the sky, magnolia shadows jumped across the pavement, and a blast of thunder rocked the city so hard that Carson thought she could feel it rumbling in the ground, but the rain did not fall at once, held off.

They traded the neighborhood of bungalows for low-rise office and apartment buildings.

Harker ran like a marathon man on meth, moving away, away—and then mid-block he made the mistake of veering into an alleyway that proved to dead-end in a wall.

He came to the eight-foot-high brick barrier, flung himself at it, scrambled up like a monkey on a stick, but abruptly screamed as if torn by horrendous pain. He fell off the wall, rolled, sprang at once to his feet.

Carson shouted at him to freeze, as if there were a hope in hell that he would, but she had to go through the motions.

He went at the wall again, leaped, grabbed the top, too fast for her to sight on him, and clambered over.

"Get out in front of him!" she shouted to Michael, and he raced back the way they had come, looking for a different route into the street beyond the wall.

She holstered her pistol, dragged a half-filled garbage can to the end of the alley, climbed onto it, gripped the top of the wall with both hands, levered up, got a leg over.

Although she was sure that Harker would have escaped, Carson discovered that he had fallen again. He was lying faceup in the street, wriggling like a snake with a broken back.

If their kind could turn off pain in a crisis, as

Deucalion claimed, either Harker had forgotten that option or something was so wrong with him that he had no control of it.

As she came off the wall, he got to his feet again, staggering toward an intersection.

They were near the waterfront. Ship-chandlers' offices, ship brokerages, mostly warehouses. No traffic at this hour, businesses dark, streets silent.

At the intersection, Michael appeared in the street ahead.

Trapped between Carson and Michael, Harker turned toward the alleyway on the left, which led toward the waterfront, but it was fenced to twelve feet, with a wide padlocked gate, so he veered toward the front of a warehouse.

When Michael closed on him with the shotgun, Carson held back, giving him a clear approach.

Harker built speed toward the man-door at the front of the warehouse, as if he didn't see it.

Following the usual protocol, Michael shouted for Harker to stop, to drop, to put his hands behind his head.

When Harker hit the door, it held, and he screamed, but he didn't bounce off and go down as he ought to have done. He seemed to *stick* to it.

The crash of impact was followed at once by Harker's cry of rage and the shriek of tortured metal.

Michael shouted again, five steps from point-blank position.

The warehouse door sagged. Hinges snapped with reports as loud as gunshots. The door went down, and Harker disappeared inside just as Michael halted and brought the 12-gauge into firing position.

Carson joined him at the entrance. "He's going to try to get out the back."

Once Harker was on the waterfront—the docks, the boats, the cargo esplanade—there were a thousand ways for him to disappear.

Offering Michael her pistol, grip first, she said, "You two-gun him at the back when he comes out. Gimme the shotgun, and I'll move him through to you."

This made sense because Michael was taller than she, stronger, and therefore could scale the twelve-foot alleyway fence faster than she could.

He took her pistol, gave her the shotgun. "Watch your ass. I'd hate for anything to happen to it."

The mantle of the black sky cracked. Volcanic blaze of light, volcanic boom. At last the pent-up rain fell in a volume to inspire ark builders.

CHAPTER 93

TO THE RIGHT of the broken door, Carson found switches. Light revealed a reception area. Gray-tile floor, pale-blue walls. A few chairs. Low railings to the left and right, desks beyond.

Directly ahead was a service counter. At the left end, a gate stood open.

Harker might have been crouched against the farther side of the counter, waiting for her, but she doubted she would find him there. His priority wasn't to waste her, just to get away.

She cleared the gate fast, swiveling the 12-gauge to cover the area behind the counter. No Harker.

A door stood ajar behind the clerical pen. She pushed it open with the shotgun barrel.

Enough light came from behind her to reveal a short hallway. No Harker. Deserted.

She stepped inside, flicked on the hall light. She listened but heard only the thunder and the insistent crash of rain on the roof.

To each side stood a door. Signs identified them as men's and women's lavatories.

Harker wouldn't have stopped to take a pee, wash his hands, or admire himself in a mirror.

Assuring herself that he would have no desire to get behind her and take her by surprise, that he only wanted to escape, Carson went past the lavatories toward another door at the end of the hall.

She glanced back twice. No Harker.

The end door featured a traffic-check window through which she saw darkness beyond.

Conscious that she was a backlit target as long as she lingered on the threshold, Carson cleared it fast and low, scanning left and right in the flush of light that accompanied her. No Harker.

The door fell shut, leaving her in darkness. She backed up against the wall, felt the switches pressing into her back, slid aside, held the 12-gauge with one hand, snapped on the lights.

Suspended from the thirty-foot ceiling, a series of lights in cone-shaped shades revealed a large warehouse with goods stacked on pallets to a height of twenty feet. A maze.

She turned right across the open ends of the aisles, looking into each. No Harker. No Harker. No Harker. Harker.

Thirty feet from the mouth of the aisle, moving away from her, Harker hobbled as if in pain, bent forward, cradling his torso with both arms.

Thinking of the people he'd sliced open, thinking of the makeshift autopsy table in his bedroom, where he had been prepared to dissect Jenna Parker, Carson went after him with no intention of cutting him any slack. Closing to within twenty feet before shouting his name, she brought up the shotgun, finger on the trigger rather than on the guard.

If he dropped like he should, she'd cover him, use her cell phone to get Michael, get backup.

Harker turned to face her. His wet hair hung over his face. The shape of his body seemed . . . *wrong.*

The son of a bitch didn't drop. From him came the eeriest sound that she had ever heard: part a cry of agony, part excited laughter, part an expression of brute rage.

She fired.

The pellets hit him in a tight group, where his cradling arms crossed his abdomen. Blood sprayed.

So fast that it seemed as if he were not a real figure but one in a time-lapse film, Harker clambered up a wall of crates, out of the aisle.

Carson chambered another round, tracked him as if he were a clay disk in a skeet shoot, and blew a chunk off the top crate, missing him as he vanished over the palisade.

SAYING A PRAYER for the family jewels, Michael jammed Carson's pistol into his waistband, scaled the fence at the mouth of the alleyway, wincing as an ax of lightning chopped the night, figuring it would whack the steel chain-link and electrocute him.

He got over the fence, into the alley, unfried, and ran through drenching rain and the rolling echoes of thunder to the rear of the warehouse.

A concrete ramp led up to the loading dock at the back. A big roll-up door and a man-door served that deep platform. Harker would come out of the smaller door.

He drew Carson's pistol but left his own holstered. He was not literally going to two-gun the fugitive, one pistol in each hand. For the best possible placement of shots, he needed a two-hand grip on the weapon.

If as advertised Harker proved to be as hard to bring down as a charging rhino, Michael might empty a magazine trying to pop both his hearts. If after that Harker was still on the move, there would not be time to eject a magazine and slap in a fresh one. He'd drop Carson's piece, draw his own, and hope for the kill with the *next* ten rounds.

Embracing this strategy, Michael realized that although the Frankenstein story seemed like a can of Spam, he had gone for it as eagerly as if it had been filet mignon.

Inside, the 12-gauge boomed. Almost at once, it boomed again.

Thrusting one hand into his jacket pocket, he felt spare shotgun shells. He'd forgotten to give them to Carson. She had one round in the breach, three in the magazine. Now only two left.

The 12-gauge boomed again.

She was down to one round, with no backup handgun.

Waiting for Harker on the loading dock wasn't a workable plan any longer.

Michael tried the man-door. It was locked, of course, but worse, it was steel plate, resistant to forced entry, with three deadbolts.

Movement startled him. He reeled back and discovered Deucalion at his side—tall, tattooed, totemic in the lightning.

"Where the hell—"

"I understand locks," Deucalion interrupted.

Instead of applying the finesse his words implied, the huge man grabbed the door handle, wrenched it so hard that all three of the lock assemblies pulled out of the steel frame with a *pop-crack-shriek* of tortured metal, and threw the torqued door onto the loading dock.

"What the *hell*," Michael asked, "was that?"

"Criminal trespass," Deucalion said, and disappeared into the warehouse.

CHAPTER 94

WHEN MICHAEL FOLLOWED Deucalion into the warehouse, the giant wasn't there. Whatever he might be, the guy gave new meaning to the word *elusive*.

Calling out to Carson would alert Harker. Besides, the storm was louder in here than outside, almost deafening: Rain roared against the corrugated metal roof.

Crates of various sizes, barrels, and cubes of shrink-wrapped merchandise formed a labyrinth of daunting size. Michael hesitated only briefly, then went searching for the minotaur.

He found hundreds of hermetically sealed fifty-gallon drums of vitamin capsules in bulk, crated machine parts, Japanese audio-video gear, cartons of sporting equipment—and one deserted aisle after another.

Frustration built until he thought maybe he would shoot up a few boxes that claimed to contain Kung Fu Elmo dolls, just to relieve the tension. If they had been Barney the Dinosaur dolls, he would more likely have acted on the impulse.

From overhead, louder than the rain, came the sound of someone running along the top of the stacked goods. The crates and barrels along the right side of the aisle shuddered and creaked and knocked together.

When Michael looked up, he saw something that was Harker but not Harker, a hunched and twisted and grotesque form, vaguely human but with a misshapen trunk and too many limbs, coming toward him along the top of the palisade. Maybe the speed with which it moved and the play of shadow and light fooled the eye. Maybe it was not monstrous at all. Maybe it was just old pain-in-the-ass Jonathan, and maybe Michael was in such a state of paranoid agitation that he was mostly *imagining* all the demonic details.

Pistol in a two-hand grip, he tried to track Harker, but the fugitive moved too fast, so Michael figured the first shot he would get would be when Harker leaped toward him and was airborne. At the penultimate moment, however, Harker changed directions and sprang off the right-hand stacks, across the ten-foot-wide aisle, landing atop the left-hand palisade.

Gazing up, in spite of the extreme angle, Michael got a better look at his adversary. He could no longer cling to the hope that he had imagined Harker's grotesque transformation. He couldn't swear to the precise details of what he glimpsed, but Johnny definitely was not in acceptable condition to be invited to dinner with genteel company. Harker was Hyde out of Jekyll, Quasimodo crossed with the Phantom of the Opera, minus the black cape, minus the slouch hat, but with a dash of H. P. Lovecraft.

Landing atop the merchandise to the left of Michael, Harker crouched low, on all fours, maybe on all sixes, and with what sounded like *two* voices quarreling with each other in wordless shrieks, he scrabbled away, back in the direction from which he had come.

Because he didn't suffer from any doubts about his manhood, because he knew that valor was often the better part of courage, Michael considered leaving the warehouse, going back to the station, and writing a letter of resignation. Instead, he went after Harker. He soon lost track of him.

LISTENING BEYOND the storm, breathing air that had been breathed by the quarry, Deucalion moved slowly, patiently, between two high ramparts of palleted goods. He wasn't searching so much as waiting.

As he expected, Harker came to him.

Here and there, narrow gaps in each wall of crates gave a view of the next aisle. As Deucalion came to one of these look-throughs, a pale and glistening face regarded him from eight feet away in the parallel passageway.

"Brother?" Harker asked.

Meeting those tortured eyes, Deucalion said, "No."

"Then what are you?"

"His first."

"From two hundred years?" Harker asked.

"And a world away."

"Are you as human as me?"

"Come to the end of the aisle with me," Deucalion said. "I can help you."

"Are you as human as me? Do you murder and create?"

With the alacrity of a cat, Deucalion scaled the palisade, from floor to crest, in perhaps two seconds, three at most, crossed to the next aisle, looked down, leaped down. He had not been quick enough. Harker was gone.

CARSON FOUND A SET of open spiral stairs in a corner. Rapid footsteps rang off metal risers high above. A creaking noise preceded a sudden loud rush of rain. A door slammed shut, closing out the immediate sound of the downpour.

With one shot left and ready in the breach, she climbed.

The steps led to a door. When she opened it, rain lashed her.

Beyond lay the roof.

She flipped a wall switch. Outside, above the door, a bulb brightened in a wire cage.

After adjusting the latch so the door wouldn't automatically lock behind her, she went out into the storm.

The broad roof was flat, but she could not see easily to every parapet. In addition to the gray screens of rain, vent stacks and several shedlike structures—perhaps housing the heating-cooling equipment and electrical panels—obstructed her view.

The switch by the door had activated a few other lamps in wire cages, but the deluge drowned most of the light.

Cautiously, she moved forward.

SOAKED, CHILLED even though the rain was warm, certain that the phrase "like a drowned rat" would for the rest of his life bring him to tears, Michael moved among the vent stacks. Warily, he circled one of the sheds, making a wide arc at each corner.

He had followed someone—something—onto the roof and knew that he was not alone here.

Whatever their purpose might be, the cluster

of small structures looked like cottages for roof Hobbits. After circling the first, he tried the door. Locked. The second was locked, too. And the third.

As he moved toward the fourth structure, he heard what might have been the rasp of hinges on the door he had just tried—and then from a distance Carson shouting his name, a warning.

IN EACH BLAZE of lightning, the shatters of rain glittered like torrents of beveled crystals in a colossal chandelier, but instead of brightening the roof, these pyrotechnics added to the murk and confusion.

Rounding a collection of bundled vent pipes, Carson glimpsed a figure in this darkling crystal glimmer. She saw him more clearly when the lightning passed, realized that he was Michael, twenty feet away, and then she spotted another figure come out of one of the sheds. "Michael! Behind you!"

Even as Michael turned, Harker—it had to be Harker—seized him and with inhuman strength lifted him off his feet, held him overhead, and rushed with him toward the parapet.

Carson dropped to one knee, aimed low to spare Michael, and fired the shotgun.

Hit in the knees, staggered, Harker hurled Michael toward the edge of the building.

Michael slammed into the low parapet, started

to slide over, nearly fell, but hung on and regained the roof.

Although Harker should have been down, shrieking in agony, his knees no more supportive than gelatin, he remained on his feet. He came for Carson.

Rising from a position of genuflection, Carson realized she had fired the last round. She held on to the weapon for its psychological effect, if any, and backed away as Harker approached.

In the light of the rain-veiled roof lamps, in a quantum series of lightning flashes of escalating brightness, Harker appeared to be carrying a child against his chest, though his arms were free.

When the pale thing clinging to Harker turned its head to look at her, Carson saw that it was not a child. Dwarfish, but with none of a dwarf's fairy-tale appeal, deformed to the point of malignancy, slit-mouthed and wicked-eyed, this was surely a phantasm, a trick of light and lightning, of rain and gloom, mind and murk conspiring to deceive.

Yet the monstrosity did not vanish when she tried to blink it away. And as Harker drew nearer, even as Carson backed away from him, she thought the detective's face looked strangely blank, his eyes glazed, and she had the unnerving feeling that the thing clinging to him was in *control* of him.

When Carson backed into a stack of vent pipes, her feet skidded on the wet roof. She almost fell.

Harker surged toward her, like a lion bounding toward faltering prey. The shriek of triumph seemed to come not from him but from the thing fastened to—surging out of?—his chest.

Suddenly Deucalion appeared and seized both the detective and the hag that rode him. The giant lifted them as effortlessly and as high as Harker had lifted Michael, and threw them from the roof.

Carson hurried to the parapet. Harker lay face-down in the alley, more than forty feet below. He lay still, as if dead, but she had seen him survive another killing fall the previous night.

CHAPTER 95

A SET OF SWITCHBACK fire stairs zigzagged down the side of the warehouse. Carson paused at the top only long enough to take three spare shotgun shells from Michael and load them in the 12-gauge.

The iron stairs were slippery in the rain. When she grabbed the railing, it felt slick under her hand.

Michael followed close behind her, too close, the open stairs trembling and clanking under them. "You see that *thing*?"

"Yeah."

"That face?"

"Yeah."

"It was coming out of him."

"What?"

"Out of him!"

She said nothing. Didn't know *what* to say. Just kept racing down, turning flight to flight.

"The thing *touched* me," Michael said, revulsion thick in his voice.

"All right."

"It's *not* all right."

"You hurt?"

"If it's not dead—"

"It's dead," she hoped.

"—kill it."

When they reached the alleyway, Harker remained where he had fallen, but he no longer lay facedown. He had turned to the sky.

His mouth sagged open. His eyes were wide, unblinking; rain pooled in them.

From hips to shoulders, the substance of him was...gone. His chest and abdomen had collapsed. Rags of skin and torn T-shirt hung on shattered fragments of his rib cage.

"It came *out* of him," Michael declared.

A scrape and clank drew their attention to a point farther along the alleyway, toward the front of the warehouse.

Through the blear of rain, in the scintillation of lightning, Carson saw a pale trollish figure crouched beside an open manhole from which it had dragged the cover.

At a distance of thirty feet, in the murk of the tropical storm, she could see few details of the thing. Yet she *knew* that it was staring at her.

She raised the shotgun, but the pallid creature dropped into the manhole, out of sight.

Michael said, "What the hell *was* that?"

"I don't know. Maybe . . . maybe I don't want to know."

❧

CSI, ME PERSONNEL, a dozen jakes, and the usual obnoxious gaggle of media types had come, and the storm had gone.

The buildings dripped, the puddled street glistened, but nothing looked clean, nothing smelled clean, either, and Carson suspected that nothing would ever quite *feel* clean again.

Jack Rogers had shown up to oversee the handling and transport of Jonathan Harker's remains. He was determined not to lose evidence this time.

At the back of the plainwrap sedan, stowing the shotgun, Carson said, "Where's Deucalion?"

Michael said, "Probably had a dinner date with Dracula."

"After what you've seen, you aren't still resisting this?"

"Let's just say that I'm continuing to process the data."

She slapped him affectionately—but hard enough—alongside the head. "Better get an upgraded logic unit."

Her cell phone rang. When she answered it, she heard Vicky Chou in a panic.

CHAPTER 96

FINISHED, PROGRAMMED, having received a down-loaded education in language and other basics, Erika Five lay in the sealed glass tank, awaiting animation.

Victor stood over her, smiling. She was a lovely creature.

Although four Erikas had failed him, he had high hopes for the fifth. Even after two hundred years, he was learning new techniques, better design solutions.

He keyed commands into the computer that was associated with this tank—number 32—and watched as the milky solution in which Erika lay was cycled out of the container to be replaced with a clear cleansing solution. Within a few minutes, this second bath drained, leaving her dry and pink.

The numerous electrodes, nutrient lines, drains, and service tubes connected to her automatically withdrew. At this decoupling, she bled from a few veins, but only for a moment; in members of the New Race, such small wounds healed in seconds.

The curved glass lid opened on pneumatic hinges as a triggering shock started Erika breathing on her own.

Victor sat on a stool beside the tank, leaned forward, his face close to hers.

Her luxurious eyelashes fluttered. She opened her eyes. Her gaze was first wild and fearful. This was not unusual.

When the moment was right and Victor knew she had passed from birth shock to engagement, he said, "Do you know what you are?"

"Yes."

"Do you know why you are?"

"Yes."

"Do you know who I am?"

For the first time, she met his eyes. "Yes." Then she lowered her gaze with a kind of reverence.

"Are you ready to serve?"

"Yes."

"I'm going to enjoy using you."

She glanced at him again, and then humbly away.

"Arise," he said.

The tank revolved a quarter of a turn, allowing her to swing her legs out easily, to stand.

"I have given you a life," he said. "Remember that. I have given you a life, and I will choose what you do with it."

CHAPTER 97

ON THE DARK and rain-soaked lawn, a supermarket shopping cart full of aluminum cans and glass bottles stood alongside the house, near the back porch.

Carson, followed by Michael, glanced at the cart, puzzled, as she hurried past it to the porch steps.

Vicky Chou, in a robe and slippers, waited in the kitchen. She held a meat fork as if she intended to use it as a weapon.

"The doors were locked. I know they were," she said.

"It's all right, Vic. Like I told you on the phone, I know him. He's all right."

"Big, tattooed, *really* big," Vicky told Michael. "I don't know how he got in the house."

"He probably lifted the roof off," Michael said. "Came down through the attic."

Deucalion stood in Arnie's room, watching the boy work on the castle. He looked up as Carson and Michael came through the door.

Arnie spoke to himself, "Fortify. Fortify. Fortify and defend."

"Your brother," Deucalion said, "sees deeply into the true nature of reality."

Mystified by this statement, Carson said, "He's autistic."

"Autistic . . . because he sees too much, too much yet not enough to understand what he sees. He mistakes complexity for chaos. Chaos scares him. He struggles to bring order to his world."

Michael said, "Yeah. After everything I've seen tonight, I'm struggling, too."

To Deucalion, Carson said, "Two hundred years . . . you and this Victor Frankenstein . . . So why now? Why here?"

"On the night I came alive . . . perhaps I was given the task of destroying Victor when the moment arrived."

"Given by whom?"

"By whoever created the natural order that Victor challenges with such anger and such ego."

Deucalion took a penny from the stack on the table, which he had given earlier to Arnie. He flipped it, snatched it from midair, clutched it in his fist, opened his hand. The penny was gone.

"I have free will," Deucalion said. "I could walk away from my destiny. But I won't."

He flipped the penny again.

Carson watched him, transfixed.

Again he snatched it, opened his hand. No penny.

Michael said, "Harker and these . . . these other things Victor has made—they're demonic. But what about you? Do you have . . ."

When Michael hesitated, Carson finished his question: "Man-made and yet . . . do you have a soul? That lightning . . . did it bring you one?"

Deucalion closed his hand, opened it an instant later, and the two missing pennies were on his palm. "All I know is . . . I suffer."

Arnie had stopped working on the castle. He rose from his chair, mesmerized by the two pennies on Deucalion's palm.

"I suffer guilt, remorse, contrition. I see mysteries everywhere in the weave of life . . . and I believe."

He put the pennies in Arnie's open hand.

"Victor was a man," Deucalion continued, "but made a monster of himself. I was a monster . . . but feel so human now."

Arnie closed his fist around the coins and at once opened it.

Carson's breath caught. The pennies were gone from Arnie's hand.

"Two hundred years," Deucalion said, "I've lived as an outsider in your world. I've learned to treasure flawed humanity for its optimism in spite of its flaws, for its hope in the face of ceaseless struggle."

Arnie closed his empty hand.

"Victor would murder all mankind," Deucalion said, "and populate the world with his machines of blood and bone."

Arnie stared at his clenched fist—and smiled.

"If you do not help me resist," Deucalion said, "he is arrogant enough to succeed."

Again Arnie opened his hand. The pennies had reappeared.

"Those who fight him," Deucalion said, "will find themselves in the struggle of their lives. . . ."

From Arnie's hand, Deucalion retrieved one of the two pennies.

"Leave it to blind fate?" he asked Michael. His gaze moved to Carson. "Heads, you fight beside me . . . tails, I fight alone."

He flipped the penny, caught it, held out his fist.

Before he could reveal the penny, Carson put her hand on his, to keep his fist closed. She looked at Michael.

He sighed. "Well, I never did want to be a safety engineer," he acknowledged, and placed his hand atop hers.

To Deucalion, Carson said, "Screw fate. We fight."

DARK, DRY, QUIET, the crawl space under the house provides Randal Six with an ideal environment. The spiders do not bother him.

The journey from Mercy has been a triumph, but it has frayed his nerves and rubbed his courage raw. The storm had almost undone him. The rain, the sky afire with lightning and shadows leaping on the earth, the crashes of thunder, the trees shuddering in the wind, the gutters overflowing with dirty water awhirl with litter...Too much data. Too much input. Several times he almost shut down, almost fell to the ground and curled into a ball like a pill bug.

He needs time now to recover, to regain his confidence.

He closes his eyes in the dark, breathes slowly and deeply. The sweet smell of star jasmine threads to him through the crisscrossed lattice that screens the crawl space.

From directly overhead come three muffled voices in earnest conversation.

In the room above him is happiness. He can feel it, radiant. He has arrived at the source. The secret is within his grasp. This child of Mercy, in the spidery dark, smiles.

DEAN KOONTZ is the author of many #1 *New York Times* bestsellers. He lives in Southern California with his wife, Gerda, their golden retriever, Anna, and the enduring spirit of their golden, Trixie.

Correspondence for the author should be addressed to:

Dean Koontz
P.O. Box 9529
Newport Beach, California 92658

NEW YORK TIMES BESTSELLER
DEAN KOONTZ
"A genuine work of pop art . . . squarely in the column of must-reads." —The Denver Post
your heart belongs to me
A NOVEL

WATCH FOR

YOUR HEART BELONGS TO ME

by

DEAN KOONTZ

#1 *New York Times* Bestselling Author

ON SALE IN PAPERBACK
NOVEMBER 2009

FOR ONE MAN,
THEY ARE THE FIVE MOST
TERRIFYING WORDS OF ALL. . . .

DEAN KOONTZ

BREATHLESS

A Novel